Lilian Jackson Braun composed her first poem at the age of two. She began writing her *Cat Who . . .* detective series when one of her own Siamese cats mysteriously fell to its death from her apartment block. Since then twenty *Cat Who . . .* novels have been published, all featuring the very talented Koko and Yum Yum, Siamese cats with a bent for detection. She is currently working on the next novel in this internationally bestselling series.

Lilian Jackson Braun and her husband, Earl, live with their two cats, Koko III and Pitti Sing, in the mountains of North Carolina.

The Cat Who . . . series by Lilian Jackson Braun:

1. The Cat Who Could Read Backwards
2. The Cat Who Ate Danish Modern
3. The Cat Who Turned On and Off
4. The Cat Who Saw Red
5. The Cat Who Played Brahms
6. The Cat Who Played Post Office
7. The Cat Who Knew Shakespeare
8. The Cat Who Sniffed Glue
9. The Cat Who Went Underground
10. The Cat Who Talked to Ghosts
11. The Cat Who Lived High
12. The Cat Who Knew a Cardinal
13. The Cat Who Moved a Mountain
14. The Cat Who Wasn't There
15. The Cat Who Went Into the Closet
16. The Cat Who Came to Breakfast
17. The Cat Who Blew the Whistle
18. The Cat Who Said Cheese
19. The Cat Who Tailed a Thief

The Cat Who Sang For The Birds

Lilian Jackson Braun

HEADLINE

First published in Great Britain in 1998
by HEADLINE BOOK PUBLISHING

First published in paperback in Great Britain in 1998
by HEADLINE BOOK PUBLISHING

10 9 8 7 6 5 4 3 2 1

ISBN 0 7472 5392 7

Printed and bound in Great Britain by
Clays Ltd, St Ives plc

HEADLINE BOOK PUBLISHING
A division of Hodder Headline PLC
338 Euston Road
London NW1 3BH

Dedicated to Earl Bettinger,
the husband who . . .

One

Following an unseasonable thaw and disastrous flooding, spring came early to Moose County, 400 miles north of everywhere. In Pickax City, the county seat, flowerboxes on Main Street were blooming in April, birds were singing in Park Circle, mosquitoes were hatching in the bogs, and strangers were beginning to appear in the campgrounds and on the streets of downtown.

One afternoon in late May, a brown van pulled into a parking lot alongside a small green sedan, and a man wearing a black jersey slipped out of the driver's seat. He glanced furtively to the left and right, and, leaving the motor running, he opened the tailgate. Then he unlocked the trunk of the sedan and quickly transferred something from his vehicle to the other, after which he lost no time in driving away.

An out-of-towner, witnessing the surreptitious maneuver, might have described him as a Caucasian male, middle-aged, about six feet two, with slightly graying hair and an enormous pepper-and-salt moustache. On the other hand, any resident of

Pickax (population 3,000) would have recognized him immediately. He was James Mackintosh Qwilleran, columnist for the *Moose County Something* and – by a fluke of fate – the richest man in northeast central United States. He had reason to be furtive about the parking-lot caper. In Pickax, everyone knew everyone's business and discussed it freely on the phone, on street corners, and in the coffee shops. Individuals would say:

'It's nice that Polly Duncan got herself such a rich boyfriend. She's been a widow for a heck of a long time.'

'That green sedan she drives – he gave it to her for a birthday present. Wonder what she gave him.'

'He does her grocery shopping at Toodle's Market while she's at work, and puts the stuff in her car.'

'Makes you wonder why they don't get married. Then she could quit her job at the library.'

The sidewalk gossips knew it all. They knew that Qwilleran had been an important crime reporter Down Below, as they called the mega-cities south of the Forty-Ninth Parallel. They knew that something sinister had wrecked his career. They would say:

'Then he come up here, by golly, and fell kerplunk into all them millions! Talk about luck!'

'More like billions, if you ask me, but he deserves it. Nice fella. Friendly. Nothin' highfalutin about Mr Q!'

'You can say that again! Pumps his own gas. Lives in a barn with two cats.'

'And danged if he don't give most of his dough away!'

The truth was that Qwilleran was bored with high finance, and he had established the Klingenschoen Foundation to distribute his wealth for the betterment of the community. This generosity, plus his genial personality, had made him a local hero. For his part, he was contented with small-town life and his relationship with the director of the library. Still, his brooding gaze carried a burden of sadness that made the good folk of Moose County ask each other questions.

One Thursday in May he went to the newspaper office to hand in copy for his column, 'Straight from the Qwill Pen.' Then he stopped at the used book store and browsed for a while, buying a 1939 copy of Nathanael West's book, *The Day of the Locust*. At Toodle's Market he asked Grandma Toodle to help him select fruit and vegetables for Polly. These he transferred to her car on the library parking lot, hoping to avoid notice by the ubiquitous busybodies.

That touchy business completed, he was driving home when he heard sirens and saw flashing lights heading south on Main Street. With a journalist's instinct he followed the emergency vans, at the same time calling the city desk on the car phone.

'Thanks, Qwill,' the city editor said, 'but we were tipped off earlier, and Roger's already on his way there.'

The speeding vehicles, including Roger's gray van, turned into the street leading to the high school. By the time Qwilleran arrived on the scene, the reporter was snapping newsphotos of a gruesome accident in front of the school.

Scattered about were the remains of two wrecked cars, victims covered with blood, broken glass everywhere. One passenger appeared to be trapped inside the worst wreck. Horrified students crowded the school lawn, restrained by a yellow cordon of police tape. Ambulance crews were in action. A drunk driver was hustled to a patrol car. Stretcher bearers rushed one serious case to a medical helicopter that had landed on the school parking lot. Meanwhile, groans and cries rose from the shocked onlookers as they recognized their bloodied classmates. Finally the rescue squad's metal cutters sliced through the car body to reach the trapped victim, who was taken away in a body bag.

At that point the principal's voice on the public address system ordered all students to return to the building at once and report to the auditorium.

Qwilleran, watching the rescue with mounting wonder, stroked his moustache in perplexity and beckoned to the reporter, who had started packing his photo gear.

Roger looked up. 'Hey! I like that black shirt, Qwill. Where'd you get it?'

'Never mind the shirt! What goes on here?'

'You don't know?' The reporter glanced around before saying in a confidential tone, 'Mock accident. To discourage underage drinking. Tomorrow night's the Spring Fling.'

'Do you think it will work?'

'It should give them a jolt. Students got a sudden order to leave the building immediately because of contamination in the ventilating system. I got a little queasy myself when I saw all the blood . . . and I knew it was fake!'

Qwilleran huffed into his moustache. 'To tell the truth, Roger, it would have fooled me if your deskman hadn't said the paper was tipped off *earlier*. What did he mean by that?'

'We got a release on the story about an hour ago. The whole thing was a fantastic job of planning and secrecy.'

'Got time for a cup of coffee at Lois's?'

'Sure. There's another assignment at two-thirty, but it's only a kids' art show. I can be late.' Roger headed for his van. 'Meet you there.'

Lois's Luncheonette, just off Main Street, was a shabby eatery that had been feeding downtown workers and shoppers for thirty years. Lois Inchpot – the loud, bossy, hard-working proprietor – served large portions of moderately priced comfort food to loyal customers who considered her a civic treasure. The restaurant was empty when the two newsmen arrived.

'What'll you guys have?' Lois yelled through the kitchen pass-through. 'The lunch specials are off! And we're low on soup!'

'Just coffee,' Qwilleran called to her, 'unless you have any apple pie left.'

'One piece, is all. Flip a coin.'

Roger said, 'You take it, Qwill. I'd just as soon have lemon.'

He was a pale young man with a neatly trimmed beard, stark black against his unusually white complexion. A former history teacher, he had switched to journalism when the *Moose County Something* was launched. He was married to the daughter of the second wife of the publisher. Nepotism in Moose County was not only ethically acceptable but enthusiastically practiced.

'So!' Qwilleran began. 'How come I didn't know about this melodrama at the school?' More than anything else he disliked being uninformed and taken by surprise. 'Who dreamed it up, anyway?'

'Probably the insurance companies. What's so amazing, they were able to keep it under wraps in spite of all the different organizations and personnel involved.'

'And in spite of our three thousand nosey Nellies and congenital gossips,' Qwilleran added. 'All of Pickax knows I've started doing Polly's grocery shopping, even though I slink around like a footpad.'

'That's the price you pay for living in a crime-free, unpolluted paradise,' the younger man said. 'What did you think of the kids who did the playacting? They're all students who've been affected in some way by drunk drivers. What did you think of their bloody makeup? It was done by paramedics from EMS.'

'They all did a convincing job, and I'll bet they actually enjoyed it, but will their efforts accomplish anything?'

'I hope so. Everyone's being asked to sign a pledge not to drink at school parties.'

Lois interrupted with two plates of pie in one hand, two mugs of coffee in the other, and forks and spoons in the apron pocket. 'If you guys spill anythin', clean it up!' she ordered with swaggering authority. 'I just finished settin' up for supper, and my help don't come on till four-thirty.'

'Yes, ma'am,' Qwilleran said with a show of meekness. To Roger he put the usual question: 'Anything new at the paper?'

'Well, there was some vandalism last week that would have made a sensational story, but—'

'So much for your crime-free paradise,' Qwilleran interrupted.

'Yeah . . . well . . . At the editorial meeting this morning there was the usual go-round. I know you newsguys from Down Below are hipped on the public's right to know, but we have different ideas up here. If we reported the vandalism in any depth, we'd be (a) boosting the perpetrator's ego, and (b) encouraging copycats, and (c) starting a witch-hunt.'

'So you decided in favor of censorship,' Qwilleran said to tease him.

'We call it small-town responsibility!' A flush came to Roger's pale face. He was a native of Moose County, and Junior Goodwinter, the young managing editor, was a fourth-generation native. Arch Riker, the publisher, was a transplant from Down Below, reluctant to abandon his journalistic integrity. Qwilleran had lived in the north country long enough to appreciate both sides of the argument.

'What's this about a witch-hunt?' he asked.

'Well, in every small town there's an element that's itching to be another Salem. Last night somebody spray-painted the front of an old farmhouse with the word *witch* in big yellow letters, two feet high. An old woman lives there alone. She's in her nineties and kind of odd, but this neck of the woods is full of oddballs.'

Qwilleran felt a tremor on his upper lip and tamped his moustache with his knuckles. 'Which farmhouse?'

'The old Coggin place on Trevelyan Road, right in back of your property.'

'I know the house, but I've never met the occupant. Is she a dowser, by any chance?'

'Not that I'm aware.'

Qwilleran said, 'My column in Tuesday's paper was about dowsing, you know, sometimes called water-witching. It's controversial Down Below. How do you feel about it?'

'Most people around here wouldn't start to drill a well without hiring a dowser to pick the spot,' Roger said. 'It sounds crazy – using a forked stick to locate underground water – but they say it works, so I don't knock it. Qwill, how do you keep coming up with ideas for the "Qwill Pen"? I would've run dry a long time ago.'

'It's not easy. Fortunately I had a tenth-grade teacher who taught me how to write a thousand words about anything – or nothing. Talk about witches! That woman bewitched us with her big, round, watery eyes! Behind her back we called her Mrs Fish-eye, but she knew her craft, and she knew how to teach! Every time I sit down at the typewriter to pound out another column, I mutter a thank-you to Mrs Fish-eye.'

'I wish I could've had that kind of impact on kids in my history classes,' said the ex-teacher.

'Maybe you did. Maybe your students never told you. I never told Mrs Fish-eye how I appreciated her, and now it's too late. I don't even remember her real name, and I doubt whether she's still alive. She was old when I was in tenth grade.'

'You thought she was old. She was probably thirty.'

'True. Very true,' Qwilleran said, staring into his coffee mug.

'Say, Qwill, I've been meaning to ask: What's that skinny bike I see you riding on Sandpit Road?'

'A British Thanet, circa 1950. A collector's item. It was advertised in a bike magazine.'

'It looks brand new.'

'It's called a Silverlight. I can pick it up with my little finger. I believe Thanet was influenced by aircraft design.'

'It's sure a slick piece of work,' Roger said.

'More coffee?' Lois yelled from the kitchen. She knew Qwilleran never said no to coffee. 'Made a fresh pot just for you,' she said as she poured. 'Don't know why.'

'I don't know why either,' he said to her. 'I'm an undeserving wretch, and you're a good soul with a kind heart and a sweet disposition.'

'Bosh!' she said, smiling as she waddled back to the kitchen.

'How's your family, Roger?' Qwilleran regretted he could never remember the names and ages of his friends' offspring, or even how many there were and which sex.

'They're fine. They're all excited about Little League soccer. I'm coaching the team, believe it or not – the Pickax Pygmies . . . How are your cats?' Roger was mortally afraid of cats, and it was an act of courage even to inquire about their health.

'Those fussy bluebloods are glad to be back in the barn after spending the winter in a condo; it cramped their royal style. I've just built a gazebo behind the barn so they can enjoy the fresh air and commune with the wildlife.'

'Speaking of barns, Qwill, I've got a great favor to ask.' Roger looked at him hopefully. 'I'm the only reporter working weekends this month, and there's a breaking story Saturday afternoon, but . . . that's when I'm duty-bound to drive a vanload of kids to the big game with the Lockmaster Lilliputians. I need someone to cover for me.'

'What's the assignment?' Experience had made Qwilleran wary of substituting. 'What's the barn connection?'

'Well, it's not exactly as exciting as a three-alarm fire. It's in the metal storage barn at the Goodwinter Farmhouse Museum. It's a dedication. An open house for the general public.'

'Hmff,' Qwilleran murmured. He remembered arriving in Moose County as a city-bred greenhorn from Down Below. Roger had been the first native to cross his path. Patiently and without ridicule, Roger had explained that the threatening footsteps thudding across the roof after dark were those of a raccoon and not a burglar. The hair-raising screams in the middle of the night were not those of a woman being abducted but a wild rabbit being seized by an owl. 'Well, I suppose I could handle it,' he said to the anxious young reporter. 'Spot news for Monday, I suppose.'

'Deadline Monday noon. Take pictures. Probably front page . . . Gee, thanks, Qwill! I really appreciate it!' Roger looked at his watch. 'I've gotta jump on my horse.'

'You take off. I'll get the tab.' The offer was not all magnanimity; at the cash register it was possible to scrounge some turkey or pot roast for the Siamese.

'Do your spoiled brats eat codfish?' Lois inquired as she banged the keys on the old-fashioned machine. 'Tomorrow's special – fish 'n' chips.'

'Thank you. I'll consult them.' He knew very well that Koko and Yum Yum turned up their well-bred noses at anything less than top-grade red sockeye salmon.

Returning home, Qwilleran drove around the Park Circle, where Main Street divided into one-way northbound and southbound lanes. On the perimeter of the traffic circle were two venerable churches, the stately courthouse, and a public library that resembled a Greek temple. Yet the most imposing structure was a fieldstone cube that sparkled in the sunlight. Originally the Klingenschoen mansion, it was now a small theater for plays and concerts, its gardens paved for parking. The four-stall carriage house was still there, and the apartment above was occupied by a woman who took special orders for meatloaf, macaroni and cheese, and other freezables for a bachelor's larder.

At the rear of the parking lot Qwilleran's brown van passed through an ornamental iron gateway into an ancient grove of evergreens so dense that all was dark and silent even in midday. Suddenly the drive opened into a clearing where a huge structure, more than a hundred years old, loomed like an enchanted castle. This was Qwilleran's barn, octagonal and four stories high.

The first story was the original fieldstone foundation, with walls so thick that small windows cut in the stone looked like crossbow ports in a medieval fort. Above the foundation the walls were shingled with weathered wood, and the octagonal roof was centered with a cupola. New windows cut in the walls had odd shapes dictated by the massive interior timbers bracing the structure.

Then there were the doors. In its heyday, this had been a drive-through barn, with doors large enough for a farm wagon and a team of horses. Now the two large openings were filled with glass panels and doors of human scale. A formal double door faced east, leading from the foyer; a single door on the west connected the barnyard with the kitchen.

The interior was even more spectacular. As renovated by an architect from Down Below, it featured a continuous ramp that spiraled up to the roof, connecting balconies on three levels. In the central open space, which soared a good forty feet, stood a huge white fireplace cube with white cylindrical stacks rising to the roof. The cube divided the main floor into lounge area, library, dining room, and foyer.

Though not especially designed to be cat-friendly, that was what the barn proved to be. The cube, a good eight feet high, was a safe perch just beyond human reach. The ramp was made-to-order for a fifty-yard dash; before each meal, eight thundering paws spiraled to the top and down again. Odd-shaped windows admitted triangles and rhomboids of sunlight that tantalized the cats by moving throughout the day.

Arriving home, Qwilleran parked his van in the barnyard and checked the antique sea chest that stood at the back door and served for package deliveries. It was empty. He stood with his hand on the doorknob as he had a moment's qualms about his housemates. Were they all right? Had they wrecked the interior in a fit of catly exuberance? Would they meet him with a yowling welcome and waving tails?

When he entered the kitchen, the premises were hushed, with no visible signs of life.

'Koko! Yum Yum!' he shouted – three times with increasing concern – before starting a search. Circling the main floor counterclockwise, he stopped short when he reached the foyer. 'You rascals!' he said with relief and rebuke. 'You gave me a scare!'

The two elegant Siamese were standing on their hind legs, gazing out the low-silled windows that flanked the front door. They were watching a congregation of seven black crows just outside the glass. They had never seen such birds at such close range. Briefly, they turned glassy eyes toward the person who had called their names, but they were still under the spell of these creatures who strutted in unison like a drill team – all seven to the north, then right-about-face and all seven to the south.

'I've brought you guys a treat,' Qwilleran said.

Reluctantly they moved away from their posts and followed him to the kitchen, walking stiffly on long slender brown legs. When they reached the sunlight streaming through the west windows, their fawn fur glistened with iridescence, and their dark brown masks framed brilliant blue eyes.

Suddenly black noses twitched, brown ears pricked forward, and whiplike brown tails waved in approval. Turkey! It was diced and served on separate plates.

Then Qwilleran produced a white canvas tote bag with the logo of the Pickax Public Library and announced, 'All aboard!' He lowered it to the floor and spread the handles. Koko was the first to jump in, settling down in the bottom and making himself as compact as possible. Yum Yum followed, landing on top of him. After some good-natured shifting and squirming, they settled in, and other items were tucked in around them. It was the easiest, quickest, safest way to transport two indoor cats, some reading matter, and a coffee thermos to the gazebo. It was only a few yards from the barn – a free-standing octagonal structure, screened on all eight sides.

It had been the landscaper's idea to introduce a bird garden to the scrubby barnyard.

'We don't have many birds around here,' Qwilleran had told him, questioning the proposal.

'Start an avian garden, and they will come!' the enthusiastic young man assured him. 'The cats will flip their whiskers! What they like best is the movement of the birds – the flitting, swooping, hopping, and tail-twitching.'

So Qwilleran gave the okay, and Kevin Doone brought in selected trees and shrubs, some tall grasses, three birdfeeders, and two birdbaths, one on a pedestal and the other at ground level. The birds came. The Siamese were ecstatic.

Qwilleran reported the success of the gazebo to Polly Duncan when they talked on the phone in the early evening. She thanked him for the groceries and complimented him on his choice of produce.

'Mrs Toodle gets all the credit,' he said. 'I don't know a zucchini from a cucumber.'

'What did you have for dinner, dear?' Polly asked, always concerned about his casual eating habits.

'I thawed some macaroni and cheese.'

'You should have a salad.'

'I leave the salads to you and the rabbits.' His tone became stern. 'Did you take your twenty-minute walk today, Polly?'

'I didn't have time, but my bird club meets at the clubhouse tonight, and I'll go early and use the treadmill in the gym.'

Her voice was soft and low, and she had a gentle laugh that he found both soothing and stimulating. He liked to keep her talking. 'Any excitement at the library today?' he asked. 'Any anti-computer demonstrations? Any riots?'

Under Polly's direction, the library had recently been automated, thanks to a Klingenschoen grant, but many subscribers disliked the electronic catalogue. They preferred to make inquiries at the desk and be escorted to the card catalogue by a friendly clerk, who probably attended their church and might even be engaged to marry the son of someone they knew. That was Pickax style. The barcode scanner and the mouse were alien and suspect.

On the phone, Polly said to Qwilleran, 'We need to schedule some hands-on workshops for subscribers, especially the older ones.'

'What did you do with the old card catalogue?' he asked.

'It's in the basement. I suppose we'll—'

'Don't throw it out,' he interrupted. 'Come the revolution, you can move it back upstairs. Someday the pencil-pushers will rise up and overthrow the computerheads, and sanity will return.'

'Oh, Qwill,' she laughed. 'You're on your soapbox again! What did you do today when you weren't pushing a pencil?' She knew he drafted his twice-weekly column in longhand, while sitting in a lounge chair with his feet propped on an ottoman.

'I picked up an old copy of *The Day of the Locust*, in mint condition. If you're in the mood for scathing comedy, we might read a portion aloud this weekend. Where would you like to have dinner Saturday night?'

'How about Onoosh's? I'm hungry for Mediterranean.' Changing her tone, she said, 'I heard something bizarre today. You know the old Coggin farmhouse on Trevelyan Road? Someone painted the front of it with the word *witch*.'

'Yes, I know. The editor thought it wise to keep it out of the paper. How did you find out?' he asked, as if he didn't know. The library was – and always had been – the central intelligence agency of the community.

'My assistant's daughter belongs to the Handy Helpers, and they were called in to obliterate the graffiti. The sheriff spotted it on his early morning patrol and alerted them. The paint was gone, I believe, before Mrs Coggin knew it was there.'

Qwilleran had once written a column about the enthusiastic band of volunteers recruited through all the churches. Some had technical skills; others were simply young people with energy and strong backs. When household emergencies confronted the poor, the aged, or the infirm, the crisis squad was geared to respond on the double.

'Have you ever met Mrs Coggin?' Polly asked.

'No, but I've caught a glimpse of her in her backyard. Not many signs of life around there, except for chickens and dogs.'

'She's in her nineties, but smart and spunky, they say. I suppose she's considered eccentric, but the nature of the vandalism was scurrilous!'

As Qwilleran listened, he was stroking his moustache slowly, a gesture meaning his suspicions were being alerted. There might be more to the accusatory epithet than met the eye. His career in journalism had taught him one thing: there's always a story behind the story.

Polly said, 'But I must stop babbling and go to the clubhouse, although I find walking on that treadmill a colossal bore.'

'It's good for you,' he reminded her.

'And salads are good for you, dear! À bientôt.'

'À bientôt!'

Qwilleran cradled the receiver slowly and fondly. No one else had ever been concerned about his diet; for that matter, had he ever been concerned about anyone's cardiovascular system?

In front of him was a wall of bookshelves covering the

fireplace cube and filled with pre-owned volumes from Eddington Smith's dusty bookshop. The sight of their mellow spines, like the sound of Polly's mellow voice, always pleased him. He agreed with Francis Bacon: *Old friends to trust, old wood to burn, old authors to read.*

The titles were arranged in categories, and Koko liked to nestle in snug spaces between Biography and Drama or between History and Fiction. Occasionally he raised his nose to sniff the fish glue used in old bindings. Sometimes he pushed a book off the shelf. It would land on the floor with a *thlunk*, and he would peer over the edge of the shelf to view his accomplishment. That was Qwilleran's cue to pick it up and read a few pages aloud, savoring familiar words and thoughts, while the Siamese enjoyed hearing a familiar voice. He had a full, rich voice for reading aloud.

Strangely, the titles the cat dislodged often had prophetic significance, or so it seemed; it could be coincidence. Yet . . . several hours before the vandals branded the old woman a witch, Koko had shoved *The Crucible*, an Arthur Miller play, off the shelf. Why would he choose that particular moment to draw attention to a work about the Salem witchcraft trials? Koko never did anything without a motive, and the incident gave Qwilleran an urge to visit Mrs Coggin.

Two

As a journalist, Qwilleran was interested in newsworthy characters; as one who had never known his grandparents, he was drawn to octogenarians and nonagenarians. That was reason enough to visit Mrs Coggin. Another incentive was Koko's cavalier treatment of *The Crucible*.

While Qwilleran was feeding the Siamese the next morning, he began to wonder how the aged eccentric would react to a casual visit from a stranger. There was no listing for her in the telephone directory. Just 'dropping in' or 'stopping by' was customary in the north country but not in Qwilleran's book. He still had some city blood in his veins.

Nevertheless, he rationalized. On the roadside across from her house there was a newspaper sleeve as well as a rural mailbox . . . All residents over ninety received a free subscription to the *Moose County Something* . . . If she read it, she should recognize his moustache. It appeared at the head of his column every Tuesday and Friday and was better known in Moose

County than George Washington's wig on the one dollar bill . . . A token of neighborliness, such as muffins from the Scottish bakery, might be in order.

'How does that sound, Koko?' he asked the cat, who was concentrating on his breakfast.

'Yargle,' came the reply as Koko tried to swallow and comment at the same time.

In mid-morning, Qwilleran set out from the barn carrying a baker's box tied with red plaid ribbon. He said goodbye to the cats, told them where he was going, and estimated when he would return. The more you talk to cats, he believed, the smarter they become. Koko was disturbingly smart. Qwilleran called him a fine fellow and had a great deal of respect for him. Yum Yum was a dainty little female with winning ways and a fondness for laps, the contents of wastebaskets, and small shiny objects she could hide under the rug.

He gave them some parting instructions. 'Don't answer the phone. Don't pull the plug on the refrigerator. Don't open the door to poll-takers.'

They looked at him blankly.

From the barn a narrow lane led east to the county highway, a matter of a few tenths of a mile. It wound through the bird garden, then a meadow that had once been a blighted apple orchard, then an age-old grove of evergreens and hardwoods. At the end, fronting on Trevelyan Road, was the two-acre plot where Polly had been building a house until health problems forced her to abandon the project. Fortunately, the Klingenschoen Foundation took it off her hands and gave it to the local art community as a center for exhibitions and related activities.

The new Art Center had a residential air, being sided with the stained cedar popular in the north country. As Qwilleran walked past, he found everything shipshape for the official opening – except the driveway and parking lot. These paved areas were crisscrossed with brown mud tracked in from the highway. Trevelyan Road was used chiefly by farmers, and mud from the fields was transferred to the pavement by truck tires and tractor treads, thence to the Art Center premises. Officers of the Arts Council had drawn the condition to the attention of county officials, but what could be done? In farming country, mud happens! Yet, the new manager of the Art Center had written an irate letter to the newspaper, a move that brought angry replies from the agricultural sector.

Across the road from the handsome new building was a dilapidated farmhouse surrounded by a hundred acres of well-tilled farmland. The house was sadly neglected and would have appeared abandoned but for the chickens pecking around the wheels of a rusty truck in the front yard. As Qwilleran approached, five elderly mongrels limped and waddled from behind the house.

'Good dogs! Good dogs!' he said as he headed for the front stoop. They followed him with benign curiosity, too tired or too old to bark.

Nevertheless, the front door was flung open, and a scrawny woman in strange clothing screeched, 'Who be you?'

Qwilleran raised the bakery box and replied in a pleasant voice, 'A messenger from the *Moose County Something*, bringing a present to one of our favorite readers!'

'Laws a'mighty!' she exclaimed. 'I declare it be the moustache from the paper! Come on in and have a sup. There be a pot o' coffee b'ilin' on the stove.' She spoke in a local patois common among old-timers in the area. Polly was doing research on Old Moose as an almost forgotten dialect. Qwilleran was glad he had brought his tape recorder.

The entrance hall was totally dark. Groping blindly in her wake he found himself in a large, dusty, cluttered kitchen. Besides a pot-bellied stove, pots and pans and a dry sink with hand pump, there were such furnishings as a narrow cot, a chest of drawers, and a large, old-fashioned Morris chair with torn upholstery. This was where she lived!

She cleared rolled-up newspapers and assorted litter from a wooden table and a scarred wooden chair. 'Sit ye down!' she invited as she poured coffee from an enameled tin pot into thick china mugs with chipped handles. It had been boiling on a kerosene heater. The cast-iron stove, not needed in this weather, was piled high with rolled-up newspapers.

Qwilleran said, 'I hope you like these muffins, Mrs Coggin. They're carrot and raisin.'

She bit into one with good teeth, large but discolored. 'So they be! Ain't had nothin' so fancy since Bert passed on. That were twenty year ago. Livin' alone, a body gets to livin' mighty plain. He were seventy-eight, Bert were, when he passed on. I be ninety-three.'

'You don't look it,' Qwilleran said. 'There's something youthful about you.' She was indeed spirited and agile.

'Yep. Can read the paper 'thout glasses. Never had no store-bought teeth. Live off the land and work hard, that be the ticket.'

Yet her face was furrowed and leathery, and her scant white hair was untamed. This wild aspect, plus her screeching voice and odd attire, could easily give rise to gossip. In spite of the mild weather and glowing kerosene heater, she was wearing a long heavy skirt over farmer's workpants, topped with layers of men's shirts and sweaters. She clomped around the raw wood floor in sixteen-eyelet field boots, somewhat too large.

'How long were you married, Mrs Coggin?'

'Sixty year. This be Bert's chair.' She flopped down in the Morris chair and propped her boots on a wooden crate. 'And these be Bert's boots.'

'Have you had this land all that time?'

'One acre, we started with. Worked it together. Di'n't have a horse. I pulled the plow. I were young, then. I be ninety-three now. Do my own chores. Grow my own turnips and kale. Drive my own truck.'

'But how do you cultivate all this acreage, Mrs Coggin?'

'Some young lads been tillin' it since Bert passed on. Hunnerd acres, all-a-ways back to the river. With them big machines, it ain't like it were. Good lads, they be. Paid me rent, they did, for twenty year, 'thout missin' a month.'

'I think I know them – the McBee brothers.'

'Don't rent the land no more. Sold the whole caboodle! No more taxes to pay, an' I can live here 'thout payin' rent. This new feller loves the soil, he does, like Bert did. He's gonna plant food crops – taters an' beans, not just hay and field corn.'

'Sounds like a good deal. Have you always lived in this area, Mrs Coggin?'

'Nope. Growed up in Little Hope.'

'Then you probably know Homer Tibbitt.' The retired high school principal was now official county historian.

'Yep. Lived on the next farm. Set my cap for that boy, I did, but he up and went away to school, so I married Bert. He were a good farmer and a good man. Give me three boys, he did. All moved away now. No tellin' where they be. Passed on, mebbe.'

'You probably have great-grandchildren.'

She shrugged. 'Don't know where they be.'

Qwilleran glanced at the hand pump in the kitchen sink. He

counted four oil lamps. 'I don't see any electric lights.'

'Don't need none.'

'Do you have a telephone?'

'Nope. Waste o' money . . . Want more coffee?'

He declined politely. Though notorious for his powerhouse coffee, Qwilleran was floored by the thick brew that had been boiling on the kerosene heater all morning. 'What do you think of your new neighbors across the street?' he asked.

'A plague on 'em! They be writin' letters to the paper 'bout mud! It be good honest farm dirt, an' we be trackin' it for seventy year! Let 'em take their fancy stuff and go somewhere else. They come in here with all them cars, pollutin' the air and botherin' my hens! Artists, they say they be! Likely drawin' pitchers of folks 'thout clothes on!'

Qwilleran said, 'I'm hoping we'll all be able to live together in peace.'

'Well, I ain't gonna write no letters to the paper. Me, I mind my own business. I be ninety-three.'

'Your dogs are very friendly.'

'Pore ol' things! Nobody wants 'em. They come around, starvin' and shiverin'. I give 'em a blanket in the shed and somethin' t'eat.'

'Do they have names?'

'I call 'em Blackie, Spot, Dolly, Mabel, and Li'l Yaller. Yessir! When I pass on, I be leavin' my money to take care o' pore ol' dogs. All I want – I want a tombstone next to Bert's, an' the words I want on it be: "Maude Coggin. Worked Hard. Loved Animals. Mound Her Own Business."'

With assorted reactions Qwilleran walked away from the Coggin farm. He hoped there was no feud brewing between the art community and the farmers . . . He knew Polly would appreciate the bucolic philosophy and Old Moose vernacular, which he had taped surreptitiously . . . He wondered if he should send a case of dog food to the Coggin Shelter for Pore Ol' Dogs.

It was too early for the newspaper delivery, but he stopped at his mailbox on the side of the road. There were few letters. Business correspondence went to a post office box and was handled by a secretarial service; fan mail went to the newspaper office.

In the Art Center parking lot the large number of cars prompted him to go in and investigate. He found a light interior with walls and vinyl floors in the pale neutral compatible with art. Volunteers were setting up the opening exhibit in two galleries. There was also a room with chairs and tables for classes and sliding glass doors opening to a patio. Down a hall were studios with north light, an office for the manager, and stairs leading to a future gallery on the lower level.

Most of the helpers were middle-aged women in blue denim smocks with the Art Center logo. There was one man on a stepladder, however, adjusting the track lights under the supervision of a businesslike young woman. 'Higher, higher,' she said, waving her arms. 'Now a little to the left.'

Catching a glimpse of Qwilleran, she rushed to his side, and her expression changed from stern to hospitable. 'You're Mr Q, aren't you?' she said. 'I'm Beverly Forfar, the manager.' Even while being pleasant she looked formidable, owing to the severe haircut that fitted her head like a helmet. Straight dark hair covered ears and eyebrows. She waved an arm around the interior. 'We have you to thank for all this, Mr Q.'

'Don't thank me. Thank those eggheads at the K Fund,' he

said. 'Do you think you'll be ready in time for the Sunday opening?'

'Absolutely! Even if the entire crew has to work around the clock!'

'Answer one question, Ms Forfar. How do galleries hang and rehang exhibits without leaving holes in the wall?'

'It's very simple. Our walls are plywood covered with carpet. The nails go into the plywood, and the carpet weave conceals the holes.'

'Well! . . . learn something every day! Don't let me keep you from your work. I'm only snooping.'

'Will you be covering the opening for the paper?'

'No, Roger MacGillivray is assigned, but I'll be here with friends. I hope you're having refreshments,' he added playfully.

'Oh, definitely!' Taking him seriously, she enumerated the two kinds of punch and seven kinds of sweets, before returning to the exhibit space.

The man on the stepladder – no one Qwilleran knew – was waiting patiently with the bemused attitude of a volunteer. He had a distinguished appearance, with a shock of white hair that was hard to overlook and gold-rimmed glasses that gave his eyes a friendly look.

'Now – the other bank of lights,' Ms Forfar instructed him, pointing and gesturing. 'Bring them all down . . . First one to the left . . . Others straight ahead . . . No, that one slightly to the right and higher, higher! . . . Not so high! Slightly to the left!'

The white-haired helper turned to look at her, caught Qwilleran's eye, smiled and shrugged, and Qwilleran composed an original Chinese proverb: *Man on ladder, directed by woman below – not good.*

Still, he decided, the manager was an attractive woman in

her way: buxom, but slim-hipped. No blue denim smock for her! She was wearing a bright yellow jumpsuit.

As he ambled toward the studios, he heard a loud male voice saying irritably, 'What did they hope to accomplish? They made fools of my kids! And my daughter has a weak heart; she could've had an attack!'

'What was it all about?' another man said quietly without any real show of interest.

Qwilleran maneuvered an oblique sightline into the studio and glimpsed an artist working at an easel while his subject sat in a chair on a raised platform. The subject, who had trouble sitting still, was Chester Ramsbottom, a county commissioner and owner of a restaurant, a chesty man with thinning hair and an air of authority.

'I'll tell you what it was all about!' he said belligerently. 'It was a stupid boondoggle! All fake! And the taxpayers will hafta foot the bill! They never consulted me about any of this, and I'd like to know why! They duped the kids into watching this fake accident, and they fell for it! It was an insult to their intelligence and, by God! I'm gonna investigate!'

'*Aw, shut your big yap, knucklehead!*' came a raucous voice from the next studio.

'Who said that?' the commissioner blurted, half rising from his chair.

'*Whoops, dearie!*' came the voice, followed by a wolf whistle. '*Ha ha ha ha ha!*'

Qwilleran moved quietly to the adjoining studio and saw a young woman at a drawing board, covering her face with her hands to stifle her giggles. In a large cage was a parrot-green bird with a touch of red on his tail. He was blinking and rocking on his perch.

'Pretty Polly!' Qwilleran said to him. 'Pretty Polly!'

'*Bug off, knucklehead!*' came the impolite reply.

The artist jumped up and threw a blanket over the cage. 'I'm sorry! You're Mr Q, aren't you? He doesn't like to be called Polly. His name is Jasper.'

'Is he yours?' The question was asked in disbelief. She was a diminutive young woman, rather like a twelve-year-old, and there was an innocence in her large brown eyes.

'My boyfriend gave him to me, and my mom won't let me have pets at home, so I'm keeping him here until I can get an apartment.'

Qwilleran glanced around the room. All the studios had narrow ledges on the sidewalls for displaying art, framed or unframed. Here the ledges were filled with butterfly paintings. On a side table he noted a butterfly guidebook, a ceramic vase covered with butterflies in low relief, and a bowl of peanuts.

'So you're the Butterfly Girl!' he said. 'Do you object to being called that?'

'No, I really like it,' she said. 'Do you like butterflies?'

'Actually, I've never paid much attention to them,' he said, 'but my cats like to see them flitting around. We don't have any like these in my backyard.'

The paintings on display were about the size of an average book, each with a brilliant butterfly flat-out and another of the same species with wings folded back, resting on a twig or sipping nectar from a flower. The artist explained. 'People prefer exotics, like the Paris Peacock and the Red Lacewing. The black-and-white one is a Tailed Emperor, and if you look closely you can see smidgens of blue, brown, orange, and maroon in the wings.'

'Hmmm,' he said, for want of a more intelligent response.

'A lot of people make collections, specializing in Blues or Swallowtails or Hairstreaks. They commission me to paint certain ones. It's a lot of fun.'

'I imagine so,' he said. 'Well, well . . . That's a beautiful vase.'

'Do you like it?' the Butterfly Girl said with eyes gleaming. 'That's my inspiration! My grandmother sent it from California . . . Do you mind if I uncover Jasper? The man next door has gone, I think.' She moved gracefully to the cage with a dancer's posture, and Qwilleran noted that her hair was piled tightly in a ballerina's topknot.

As soon as the cage was uncovered, Jasper squawked, '*Gimme a peanut! Monkey gimme a peanut!*'

'Who trained this bird?' Qwilleran asked.

'I don't know. My boyfriend bought him at a bird show Down Below.'

'He has a murderous beak. I wouldn't want to meet him in a dark alley.'

'He's an Amazon hookbill. They're supposed to be very intelligent.'

'He may have a high IQ, but his vocabulary needs to be cleaned up.'

'*Same to you, knucklehead!*'

Shaking his head in amused disbelief, Qwilleran said goodbye to the Butterfly Girl and returned to the portrait studio, where the artist now sat alone. He had a bifurcated beard that gave him a comic look and twinkling eyes that suggested he had no objection to painting fools. Qwilleran wondered how Ramsbottom would be depicted – as an arrogant county boss or a genial purveyor of barbecue sandwiches?

'You must be Paul Skumble,' he said. 'I'm Jim Qwilleran.

We've never met, but I commissioned you to do a double portrait for a wedding gift last winter.'

'I remember well. That was a sad case. Sorry it didn't work out. It would have been a challenge.'

'Are you relocating in Moose County?'

'No, my home and studio are still in Lockmaster, but I have several commissions up here, and I'm renting this studio on a temporary basis.'

'I'd like to have a portrait of a friend of mine, a librarian. I'd like her to be seated, holding a book. Would you be interested?'

'I think so. I'm very good at books. Some people say I paint books better than I paint faces.' His face crinkled with humor. He had a face that crinkled easily. Polly would like him.

'Will you be here on Sunday? I'd like you two to meet.'

'Is she willing to sit for a portrait? I don't copy photographs. Painting from life has a rich tonality that can't be faked.'

'She'll sit. Trust me,' Qwilleran said.

'Some people don't like to spend the time—'

'Leave it to me!'

As Qwilleran was leaving the building he beckoned Beverly Forfar away from her duties. 'How many visitors do you expect on Sunday?'

'We've provided refreshments for three hundred. I just hope we don't run out of punch. The open house is scheduled for one to five o'clock. Wouldn't it be awful if they all came at once?'

'Where will they park after the lot is filled?'

'On both sides of Trevelyan Road. We have permission, and the sheriff will monitor the situation.' She assumed a grim expression accentuated by the severity of her long straight bangs. 'Mr Q, can anything be done about that eyesore across the road?'

'The farmhouse? If I were an artist, I'd consider it picturesque,' he answered evasively.

'It might be if it didn't have that junk truck in the front yard, and those ratty dogs and chickens. They're always running out on the highway. They could cause accidents. I thought dogs were supposed to be tied up.'

'Only within the city limits,' Qwilleran said. 'This building is in Pickax, but the farmhouse is in the township, and there's no rural ordinance.'

'And how about the mud, Mr Q? It gets tracked into our parking lot and then into the building.'

'Unfortunately, Ms Forfar, this is farming country, and it's spring. In the growing season, it won't be such a problem.'

'Well, something should be done about it before it ruins our floors!' she said vehemently.

On the perimeter of the Art Center, at the beginning of the lane to Qwilleran's barn, a new sign read: PRIVATE DRIVE. It had been installed just in time; otherwise, three hundred visitors to the open house would tramp up the lane to look at the fabulous structure. The public had always been curious about the barn. Six months before, it had been the scene of a charity cheese-tasting party, with guests paying three hundred dollars apiece to attend the black-tie event. They were still talking about it – not so much because of the architecture or the twenty-two cheeses but because Koko, in his inimitable way, had stolen the show.

Concerning the new sign, Polly had questioned whether it would be enough to discourage sightseers.

'If not, we'll add "Beware of vicious animals,"' Qwilleran had told her. 'And if that doesn't work, we'll have to resort to a moat and drawbridge. It's not that I'm being asocial; I simply don't want strangers peering in the windows at the cats and getting idcas.'

Three

Qwilleran, never an early riser by choice, now found himself routed out of bed at dawn when the birds convened for their morning singsong and the Siamese wanted to join them. Koko and Yum Yum would station themselves outside his bedroom door, the one yowling in an operatic baritone and the other uttering soprano shrieks until he got up and transported them to the gazebo. Yum Yum simply wanted to bat insects on the screens, but Koko was fascinated by the chorus of trills, chirrups, whistles, warbles, and twitters. The cacophony reminded Qwilleran of the Pickax high school band tuning up for *Pomp and Circumstance.*

Still, he would take coffee and doughnuts to the gazebo and marvel at the clarion sounds coming from feathered creatures half the size of his thumb. He used the time, also, for doodling ideas for the 'Qwill Pen' column on a legal pad. He was working on a tribute to his tenth-grade teacher whose training in English composition had made his career possible. With a pencil he jotted notes:

Dear Mrs Fish-eye, wherever you are . . .
Great debt of gratitude long overdue . . .
Your influence, precepts, and criticism . . .
Something uncanny in your penetrating gaze . . .
The arduous assignments that we all hated . . .
And so on.

When he discussed the idea with Polly, she encouraged him, saying, 'Remember the letter I received from a museum curator in New York? He thanked me for helping him with student assignments twenty years before, and for stimulating his appetite for research. I was thrilled!'

The highlights of Qwilleran's life were his weekends with Polly Duncan, starting with Saturday night dinner. She was a charming woman of his own age, attractive in a classic way and endowed with the qualities he admired: intellect, a gentle voice, a musical laugh, and literary interests that matched his own. Never before had he met anyone who knew, or cared, that it was Chesterfield who said: *Let blockheads read what blockheads wrote.*

Polly lived in a condominium in Indian Village, a residential complex beautifully situated on the Ittibittiwassee River. When he picked her up on that Saturday evening in late May, her warm greeting was seconded by friendly nudges from Brutus, a dignified Siamese. Brutus had been Qwilleran's enemy before having a name change. His disposition had been further improved by the advent of a little companion – same breed, opposite sex.

'Where's Catta?' Qwilleran asked.

A tiny kitten, all ears and feet, struggled out from behind a chest of drawers. 'Be good kitties,' Polly said, stroking the husky male and hugging the featherweight female.

'Hail and farewell, good Brutus and gentle Catta!' Qwilleran declaimed with exaggerated respect.

On this evening they were having dinner at Onoosh's Mediterranean Café. Driving downtown in the brown van, they discussed the cost of feeding wildbirds . . . and the mud problem at the Art Center . . . and local efforts to eradicate illiteracy. Abruptly, as they reached the abandoned Buckshot mine, they were silent. They had passed it hundreds or even thousands of times, yet they always turned to look at the hushed scene posted as dangerous: the high chain-link fence, the evidence of a recent cave-in, and the ghostly shafthouse towering above the barren earth.

It was one of ten such monuments to Moose County's affluent past – the delirious days before the economic collapse. Now nothing was left of the ten mines but legends and towers of weathered wood.

Polly said, 'I wrote a sonnet to a shafthouse once, when I first moved here. I remember the first four lines, that's all:

> O silver temple to forgotten greed!
> How primitive, how stark, how deathly silent now,
> Where once a monster with a Golden Bough
> Upon the blood of shackled men did feed!'

Qwilleran exclaimed, 'Not bad! Not bad! Worthy of Milton!'

'Well, not quite,' she laughed, 'but you have to admit there's something poetic about the old wrecks. It's not surprising that one of our local artists chose to specialize in painting shafthouses. People love Duff Campbell's work.'

'Today,' he said, 'I met the young woman who specializes in painting butterflies. She's taken a studio at the Art Center.'

'I know her,' Polly said. 'Her parents have the drug store. She has a sweet personality and nice manners. Too bad she's not prettier. Her chin is too pointed for the width of her brow.'

'She has fine eyes, though, and moves like a dancer.'

'Yes, she attended boarding school in Lockmaster, where they stress ballet and equestrian arts. Whenever you see a straight spine and sleek head in Moose County, you're looking at a product of the Lockmaster Academy . . . Was there any other excitement at the Art Center today? I suppose they were preparing frantically for the grand opening.'

'Your favorite county commissioner was having his portrait painted in one of the studios.'

'Oh, no! Not Chester Ramsbottom!' Polly groaned. 'Do you realize he automatically opposes any measure designed to benefit libraries, education, and the arts? Your paper called him a knee-jerk bottom-liner – not the terminology I would have used, but true! Will you explain to me why the voters keep reelecting him?'

'He serves the best barbecue in the county, they say, and the conscience of the Moose County voter is in his belly.'

'I suppose he'll hang the portrait in his restaurant,' she said, 'and contrive some devious way to bill the taxpayers for it.'

Qwilleran said, 'I've heard that every customer celebrating a birthday in Chet's Bar gets a cream pie in the face – free!'

'Disgusting!' she muttered.

Onoosh's Café in Stables Row was the first ethnic restaurant to open in Pickax and environs. The mood was set by the scent of rare spices, the twang of exotic music in the background, the soft light from hanging lanterns shaded with beaded fringe, and the flicker of candles reflected in hammered brass tables. This, plus the Mediterranean menu, was heady fare for Pickax tastes, but the café was attracting a steadily growing clientele.

The servers, costumed in pantaloons and embroidered vests, were students from Moose County Community College, and the bartender was a sandy-haired, freckle-faced son of the American heartland, but Onoosh was authentic. She could be glimpsed through the kitchen pass-through: olive-skinned, dark-haired, sultry-eyed, and wearing a chef's floppy white hat.

As Qwilleran and Polly started dipping hummus with morsels of pita, she asked, 'Did you cover the museum reception for Roger this afternoon? How was it?'

'In a word, boring,' he said. 'The volunteers have spent three years cataloguing the collection, and they deserve credit, but all we saw was a storage barn filled with boxes, crates, cabinets, and plastic-shrouded furniture. For five dollars, tax-deductible, you can get a printout of the inventory. For another five you can get your grandmother's rusty eggbeater out of the vault and take a picture of it. The invited guests took one look at the situation and headed for the refreshment table.'

Polly said, 'The new manager seems to be a good organizer but lacking in imagination.'

'The museum has too much computer and not enough Iris Cobb. Even the cookies were boring. There's no way, Polly, that I can cover this non-event with any journalistic integrity.'

'You'll think of a way,' she said cheerfully. 'Just put your tongue in your cheek.'

After the appetizer came the tabbouleh, the only kind of salad that Qwilleran considered worth chewing.

'You could learn to make tabbouleh,' Polly said encouragingly. 'It's no more difficult than feeding the cats.'

He grunted in defense – why did everyone want him to learn to cook? He changed the subject. 'Have I told you how much I'm enjoying *Mark Twain A to Z*?' She had given the book to him for his birthday.

'I knew you would, dear. I've always thought you were brothers under the moustache.'

'Be that as it may, I've instructed Eddington Smith to start searching for old copies of anything by Mark Twain. There are about eighty titles published in his lifetime or posthumously.'

'He had a soft spot for cats,' she reminded him.

'I know that. He's the one who said: *If man could be crossed with the cat, it would improve man, but it would deteriorate the cat*.'

'Speaking of cats, Qwill, are Koko and Yum Yum enjoying the bird garden?'

'Why shouldn't they? They don't have to do any of the work! I'm constantly filling the feeders and birdbaths. Those devils eat more than I do, and their bathwater disappears faster than I can drink a cup of coffee!'

'Oh, Qwill! How you exaggerate!'

'They give rowdy splash parties; I've seen them! And one greedy bird sits in a tree and whines "Feed me! Feed me!" by the hour.'

'That's a male phoebe, introducing himself. I should start a birdlist for you. There must be at least two dozen species around the barn. Do you know you have a pileated woodpecker?'

'It doesn't sound good. What is it?'

'A large bird with a red tuft on his head like the pileus in ancient times. That was a pointed cap, you know. His call is very distinctive and is often followed by rapid drumming on a tree trunk.'

'I've heard the noisy clown,' Qwilleran said. 'His call sounds like an automatic weapon, and his drumming, as you call it, is like a jackhammer.'

'What lofty subject are you addressing in Tuesday's column?' she asked.

'Pencils! I've just discovered a source for the fat yellow pencils with thick soft leads that were standard equipment on my first newspaper job. I've ordered a gross. More and more I draft my copy longhand while sitting with my feet up.'

'Don't I remember old movies in which reporters loafed around the office with their hats on and their feet on the desk?'

'They weren't loafing, Polly! They were thinking. Words and ideas flow more easily in that position. It has something to do with blood flow.'

His discourse was interrupted by the arrival of the entrées. He was having a lamb shank with baked chick peas; she was having vegetarian stuffed grape leaves. 'Polly,' he said, 'I'd like to ask you a great favor. It would mean a lot to me.'

'What is it?' she asked warily.

'Would you sit for your portrait? I'd like to have it painted by Paul Skumble of Lockmaster.'

'Oh, dear!' she said in dismay. 'Wouldn't you rather have a good studio photo by John Bushland – retouched?'

'No. Oil paint has a rich tonality that can't be matched by any other medium. And since John Singer Sargent isn't available, I'd like to commission Skumble.'

'Well, I hear he's very good.' She was beginning to be more flattered than flustered. 'Where would the portrait hang?'

'In my suite on the balcony, across from the foot of the bed, where I'd see it first thing every morning.'

'Well! Wc'll have to think about that, won't we?'

'You can meet Skumble at the open house tomorrow. I think you'll find him congenial.'

Four

Before attending the grand opening of the Art Center, four friends met for Sunday brunch at Qwilleran's barn. He and Arch Riker had been fellow journalists Down Below. More than that, they had been classmates since kindergarten. When the *Moose County Something* was about to be launched, Riker moved north to realize his dream and become publisher and editor-in-chief of a small-town broadsheet. Besides reveling in his career change, he was enjoying marriage to a local woman of quite some status in the community.

Mildred Hanstable Riker had taught fine and domestic arts in Moose County schools for thirty years before becoming food writer for the *Something*. She was a warm-hearted humanitarian, a great cook, and a paragon of pleasing plumpness. Riker himself had a paunchy figure, and his ruddy face radiated mid-life contentment. Polly Duncan completed the foursome.

Brunch preliminaries were held in the gazebo, where the screened panels on all eight sides gave the impression of being pleasantly lost in the woods. The foursome pulled chairs into a semicircle overlooking the bird garden: the Siamese sat complacently at their feet, watching the crows, mourning doves, and blue jays.

Bloody Marys were served, with or without vodka, and Arch proposed a toast: 'May the roof never fall in, and may friends never fall out!' Then he asked Qwilleran in all seriousness, 'When are you going to put in your lawn?'

'You've gotta be kidding! I don't want to hear, or smell, any power mowers on my property! In that wide open space beyond the bird garden Kevin Doone is putting in a meadow of native grasses, wildflowers, and forbs. He's made a study of natural landscaping.'

'What are forbs?'

'To tell the truth, I'm not sure. Some kind of plant. My dictionary is vague about forbs, but I trust Kevin.'

Mildred said, 'He's very good. He's landscape consultant for Indian Village. Otherwise, the developers would have the whole complex looking like a golf course.'

Arch said, 'For someone who grew up on the sidewalks of Chicago, Qwill, you've become a sudden lover of nature.'

'Only if I don't have to water it, fertilize it, weed it, spray it, or prune it.'

There was a startling interruption as a crow chased a squirrel, the one flapping its wings threateningly and the other running for its life. Qwilleran explained the social situation: 'Small birds throw seeds out of the feeder; large birds pick them up off the ground, but the squirrels try to muscle in. The politics and economics of a bird garden are more complicated than I care to contemplate. Let's talk about something simple, like the newspaper business.'

'Okay,' Arch said. 'You saw the announcement of the adult spelling bee to benefit the literacy program. We're underwriting it, and I'm happy to say the business community is very supportive.'

'Whose idea was it?'

'Hixie suggested it, although it's been done in cities Down Below – quite successfully, I understand.'

Qwilleran thought, Here we go again!

Hixie Rice, the newspaper's promotion director, had a long history of brilliant ideas that ended in disaster, through no fault of her own. Her most recent debacle had been the Moose County Ice Festival that melted into oblivion in February. Failure never daunted her; she bounced back with yet another worthwhile idea.

Arch said, 'We lost our shirt on the Ice Festival, but an adult spelling bee should be foolproof. Business firms and other organizations pay a fee to enter a team and compete for a trophy, and the public pays an admission fee to applaud their favorite spellers. The audience has fun, and the sponsors get favorable publicity. I don't see how anything can go wrong . . . You're looking dubious, Qwill.'

'Not at all! I'm in favour of promoting literacy. The more people who can read, the greater our circulation and the more ads we sell and the more fan mail I get.'

'Oh, Qwill! I hope you're joking and not just being cynical,' Polly protested.

'I was recently shocked,' he said, 'to learn that a well-known businessman in Pickax can neither read nor write. He's gone to great lengths to conceal the fact.'

'Who? Who?' they clamored.

'That's privileged information.'

A beeper sounded, and the two women jumped up. 'Time to start the frittata,' Polly said. 'We'll ring the dinnerbell when we're ready.' They returned to the barn, laughing and chattering.

The men sat back in their chairs and gazed into the woods, at peace with the world. Neither of them spoke. They had been friends long enough to make silences comforting.

After a while Arch said, 'When are we going to fly Down Below for a weekend ballgame?'

'Exactly what was on my mind! We should check the schedules.'

'Do you think the girls will want to go along?'

'They enjoyed it last year – the shopping, that is, and the show Saturday night,' Qwilleran recalled. 'Let's sound them out.'

'I noticed a new baseball book on your coffee table. Don't tell me you broke down and bought a book that's less than fifty years old!'

'I didn't buy it. Polly brought it from the library. My record remains clean . . . Meanwhile, though, I picked up three interesting World War Two books from Eddington's dustbin: *The Pacific War*, *Fire Over London*, and *The Last 100 Days*. They came from an estate on Purple Point.'

At that point Koko attracted their attention by raising himself into a long-legged stretch with back humped and tail stiff. Then he lowered his front half and stretched his forelegs against the floor, after which he stretched one hind leg. Finally he confronted the men. 'Yow!' he said with a volume and clarity that reverberated through the woods.

'What's bugging him?' Arch asked.

'He knows the dinnerbell is about to ring.'

In a few seconds it rang.

'See? What did I tell you?' Qwilleran said with a touch of pride.

'Can you beat that!'

Koko was already standing over the canvas tote bag, and with a little assistance from Qwilleran both cats hopped into it, wriggling into place, and the four of them returned to the barn.

The dinnerbell that had summoned them was standing on the console table in the foyer – a cast brass handbell with a coiled serpent for a handle.

'Dutch Baroque,' said Arch, who had learned about antiques from his first wife, Down Below. 'Where'd you get it?'

'Amanda's studio. She said it came from Stockholm.'

'Could be. There was a lot of sea trade between Holland and Sweden at one time . . . and that Jacobean table is new! Where'd that come from?' He was looking at a small oval table with an oval stretcher and five sturdy turned legs.

'Exbridge & Cobb,' Qwilleran said. 'From Iris Cobb's personal collection.'

'It's an English tavern table, seventeenth century,' Arch said. 'Top worn thin by two centuries of scouring by conscientious barmaids. Bun feet worn off from dragging across a damp stone floor.'

'How about some soft background music to go with that?' Qwilleran suggested.

'I'm serious! It's the real thing! You can leave me this table when you die.'

'What makes you think you'll outlive me, you dirty dog?'

'Because Mildred makes him eat salads,' Polly said.

Brunch was served in the dining area, which was seldom used; guests were always taken out to dinner. It began with fruit soup, a concoction of pear and raspberry. Then came mushroom frittata and a warm salad of asparagus and yellow peppers. If Qwilleran had not later found two small yellow cartons in the trash container, he would never have guessed the eggs in the frittata were cholesterol-free. I might have known, he thought.

When they were having coffee in the lounge area, Mildred said, 'This is a great day for the art lovers of Moose County.' She had been one of the founders of the Arts Council and was now chairperson of the new Art Center.

'Are they one big happy family?' Qwilleran asked. 'Or do you have cliques and politics?'

'Just between us,' she confided, 'there is a certain amount of friction. I suppose we're a microcosm of the whole community, with the normal amount of jealousy, snobbery, and competitiveness – although outwardly we get along. Among the artists themselves, the differences are in matters of style and taste. Most of them do representational art, and in a group show the abstractionists don't want their work hung on the same wall with the butterflies and shafthouses.'

'How many of your members are active artists?'

'About twenty percent. Thirty percent, I'd say, are true art lovers. That leaves fifty percent who join because it's tax-deductible, or whatever.'

Polly said, 'A rumor has been circulating at the library that you're exhibiting nude drawings in the show today.'

Mildred rolled her eyes in exasperation. 'We never include nudes in a public exhibition because some people get upset over what they call "naked bodies." We show figure drawings only at receptions for members.'

'That explains the fifty-percent fringe membership,' Arch said dryly.

His wife squinted at him briefly and then went on. 'Some of our artists do very fine life studies, and the one who calls herself simply "Daphne" has won statewide prizes. She'll be teaching our class in figure drawing – with a live model, of course. She has a wonderful understanding of anatomy: cats, dogs, and horses, as well as humans.'

Arch looked at his watch. 'Let's go to the party before they run out of punch. I don't suppose it's spiked.'

'You suppose right,' Mildred said.

The two couples walked leisurely down the lane to the Art Center and heard the buzz of celebration even before they emerged from the woods: traffic noise, excited voices, children's cries. Qwilleran glanced across the road to see if Maude Coggin might be sitting on her porch, rocking and scowling at the intruders, but there was no activity. Dogs and chickens were no doubt locked up out of harm's way.

The paving around the new building was a gridiron of muddy tiretracks, and a volunteer on the entrance porch was exhorting visitors to wipe their feet thoroughly or take off their shoes. Several pairs were lined up at the door, prompting Arch to ask his wife, 'Do you see any cordovan alligator loafers in my size?'

In the lobby two works donated by local artists were being raffled off to benefit the Arts Council: Duff Campbell's watercolor, *Buckshot Shafthouse by Moonlight*, and W. C. Wyckoff's intaglio, *The Whiteness of White*. The latter was a large square of heavy white paper with a three-dimensional snowflake design pressed into the surface. Recessed under glass and framed in chrome, it looked quite elegant, everyone said, although they bought chances on the watercolor. Qwilleran bought five chances on the intaglio, having a fellow feeling for the neglected artist, whoever he or she might be.

'Aren't you afraid you'll win it?' Arch mumbled to him.

For anonymity, Qwilleran signed the raffle stubs with his unlisted phone number and an alias.

The manager, Beverly Forfar, looking snappy in a short-skirted suit and high heels, was much in evidence – greeting guests, directing traffic, and watching the white vinyl floor for possible mud. She flashed special smiles at important visitors; otherwise, she was strictly managerial.

In the galleries there was more talking than viewing of art: 'Somebody did a nice job of track-lighting here . . . What do you think they have in the punch? . . . My cousin has just bought her fourth shafthouse . . . How do you like the manager's haircut?'

Guests were dressed as if they had just come from church, or from hiking. There were civic leaders, students in MCCC shirts, oldsters with walking aids, families with small children, and a few strangers, whose identities were being wildly guessed. They were dealers from Down Below, looking for new talent. They were spies from the Lockmaster Art Center, looking for ideas to copy. They were undercover detectives, looking for offensive art or photography.

Qwilleran's party scattered: Arch to investigate the refreshment table, Mildred to confer with the manager, Polly to meet Paul Skumble. As soon as artist and librarian met, an immediate rapport was evident, and Qwilleran left them alone, wandering off to visit Jasper.

The Butterfly Girl's studio was crammed with visitors, chanting silly phrases at the parrot and then screaming when he replied, '*C'mon, baby, gimme a tickle! . . . Anybody wanna go to bed? . . . I'm a go-o-od boy!*' He bounced up and down on his perch and ruffled his feathers.

The artist herself stood in a far corner near the window, oblivious to the commotion. She was talking to a good-looking young man with unruly red hair, gazing at him amorously with the lustrous brown eyes that were her best feature. Then, catching sight of Qwilleran, she dragged her companion over to meet 'Mr Q.'

'This is my boyfriend, Jake Westrup,' she said. 'He's the one who gave me Jasper.'

'Yeah. I always wanted a parrot,' the fellow said, 'but when I got Jasper home I found out my roommate's allergic to feathers, and my boss wouldn't let me have a bird because we handle food, and it's against the law . . . Well, I gotta go to work now. Nice to meetcha, Mr Q . . . S'long, Monkey. See ya t'night.' He tweaked her chin.

Qwilleran, never having tweaked a woman's chin in his life, was offended by the man's impudence, but the Butterfly Girl seemed not to mind. He said to her, 'I don't believe I know your name.'

'Phoebe. Phoebe Sloan. My father has the drug store downtown.'

'Yes, of course. I know Sloan's very well. Phoebe is a beautiful name. It comes from the Greek word for *bright*.'

'My boyfriend doesn't like it,' she said apologetically. 'He calls me—'

Before she could finish, Beverly Forfar stormed into the studio. 'You'll have to throw the blanket over his cage, Phoebe! He's causing too much annoyance.'

'*Big Mama, come to baby!*' Jasper squawked.

Qwilleran made a discreet exit and went to see the collage demonstration. The woman who would be teaching a class in the art was doing a self-portrait with bits of torn newspaper. Also exhibited on ledges around the studio were landscapes created with fragments of cloth, snippets of wallpaper, theater tickets, shirt labels, and computer printouts. 'You don't have to be able to draw or paint,' she said. 'The bits and pieces are your paint. The process makes you think a little.'

Qwilleran moved on to the next demonstration. A calligrapher, who would teach a class in 'beautiful writing,' was using special pens to form the thick-and-thin letters of modified Old English script. He said, 'The practice of scribing began in ancient Rome and became an art in the Middle Ages. Sign up for the class, folks, and thumb your nose at computers!' For a donation to the Art Center, he would scribe any saying to order, at a dollar a word, suitable for framing. Qwilleran ordered three dollars' worth of Shakespeare, which looked quite profound in modified Old English: *Words, words, words!*

He caught up with Mildred in a studio that displayed charcoal drawings of animals. With a few fluid strokes the artist had captured the tranquillity of a well-fed cat, the alertness of a hunting dog, the sheer power of a galloping horse.

'Come and see these wonderful figure studies, Qwill,' said Mildred. 'Daphne is going to teach our class in life drawing. The human body is one of the greatest challenges in art.' Unframed drawings, large and small and covered in shrink-wrap, were filed on end in an open bin. Male and female figures were depicted with honesty and elegance – twisting, stooping, relaxing, reaching, running, leaping.

Qwilleran complimented the artist. 'You say so much with so few lines! What's the secret?'

'Anatomy,' said Daphne. 'You have to know how the human body is constructed, how the basic masses are connected, how the bones and muscles function. You have to use your brain more than your eye. That's what I teach.'

Arch was getting impatient. Art was not his area of interest. After signaling the women, he and Qwilleran waited for them on the porch.

'See anything you like?' Arch asked.

'A totem pole about two feet high. I like wood carvings. It would look good on the table in the foyer.'

'And it would be handy to have around in case you have to protect yourself.'

'I told them to put a "Sold" sticker on it. They won't let it go until the exhibition ends.'

'What do you think of Beverly Forfar?' Arch asked. 'I don't believe that name.'

'Or that hair! It looks like a patent-leather helmet.'

'She's a big woman. Top-heavy.'

'But with good legs. Neat ankles,' Qwilleran observed.

'High heels do a lot for a woman's ankles. Fran Brodie's another.'

'On a scale from one to ten, I'd give Fran a ten and Ms Forfar a seven.'

'What happened to Fran?' Arch asked. 'She hasn't been to chamber of commerce meetings lately.'

'She's on vacation. Before that, she was in Chicago, ordering furniture for the hotel do-over.'

'I hope it won't be anything fussy.'

'She told me it would be Gustav Stickley, whatever that is,' Qwilleran said, 'but you can rest assured that everything Fran does is first class.'

'Here come the girls.'

As the four of them walked back to the barn, Qwilleran asked Mildred about the Jasper incident.

'It got a little rowdy because the crowd was taunting him,' she explained. 'Under normal circumstances there's no reason why he can't stay until Phoebe finds an apartment. Beverly doesn't like him, that's the trouble. She's uptight about many things.'

'Where did you find her? How did she get the job?'

'She's a native. I had her in art classes when she was a teen. She went Down Below, married, worked in art galleries, and returned to Pickax after her divorce.'

'Well, here's the reason I'm inquiring, Mildred. If it wouldn't upset Beverly, I'd like to take Koko to meet Jasper – on a leash, of course.'

'Why not? We ought to give you a key and let you check the building when you pick up your mail. That is, if you don't mind.'

He agreed, and she gave him the key from her keyring.

Polly said, 'Jasper has obviously associated with the wrong companions. We had an Amazon at the bird club at one meeting, and he was a perfect gentleman, with a vocabulary of almost a hundred words. When he heard a bell ring, he'd tell his owner to answer the phone. She was a breeder. He called her "honeybunch" and kissed her ear. He could even sing *God Bless America*.'

Qwilleran said, 'I think I'll stick with cats . . . How were the refreshments, Arch? I never got near the table.'

'With my wife chairing the committee, you know they were good! There were some scruffy individuals stuffing cookies into their mouths and pockets, though. I wondered if they were artists or art patrons.'

Then Qwilleran wanted to know about the Butterfly Girl's

paintings. Were they art or commercial illustration?

Mildred said, 'You might call them decorative art – not original concepts, but hand-painted – and certainly popular.'

'How about the guy who paints shafthouses?' Arch asked. 'He asks a good price, but it can't take long to knock one out; there's no detail.'

'They're impressionist,' his wife said. 'You can't count the boards and the knotholes, but you can feel the light and the weather and the mood. Watercolor is a fluid medium, and you have to work fast, but it takes skill and assurance and artistry.'

Qwilleran said, 'If I could be any artist who ever lived, I'd be Winslow Homer.'

'I'd be Mary Cassatt,' Polly said.

Mildred nodded. 'Her work had simplicity and charm.'

'Am I entitled to make a choice?' Arch asked. 'I'd be Charles Schulz.'

The Rikers were driving Polly home, since all three of them lived in Indian Village. Qwilleran said to her, 'Phone me when you have time. I want to know what you arranged with Paul Skumble.'

'I will. I will!' she said. She seemed particularly radiant.

Five

Half an hour after Polly left Qwilleran's barn with the Rikers, she phoned him, and her first words were, 'I'm thrilled about having my portrait painted, Qwill! Thank you so much.'

'Let me remind you,' he said, 'that I had to twist your arm before you'd agree. Apparently you approve of Skumble's work.'

'Yes, and I like him, although I don't care for the goatish beard. But he's friendly and has a wry sense of humor. The question arose: whether to paint at the Art Center, which has a rather clinical atmosphere, or at my condo. He'd rather work in my own environment.'

'I didn't know he made house calls.'

'Well, in fact, he's coming out tomorrow evening to check the situation.'

'I see,' Qwilleran said, stroking his moustache. 'How many sittings will he require?'

'It's hard to say, until he starts the actual work. He does a preliminary sketch in charcoal and then the underpainting in grisaille, in the classic tradition. Tomorrow night he'll look at my wardrobe, and we'll decide what I should wear.'

'How about your new dress?' he said with a show of enthusiasm. He had helped her choose it at Aurora's Boutique.

'That would be nice, but . . . you see, it's fuchsia, and Paul was thinking of something blue to accentuate my eye color.'

'I hope you can wear your opals.'

'I'd love to – you know I would – but he says that pearls bring a certain luminosity to a woman's portrait.'

'Good! I'm all in favor of luminosity,' he said dryly.

'I'll call you again tomorrow evening, dear, as soon as Paul has left . . . Isn't this exciting?'

When the conversation ended, Qwilleran patted his moustache nervously, and Koko, who had been sitting on the telephone desk listening to every word, put in an ambiguous 'Yow!'

'Well, old boy, what do you think of that bucket of fish?' Qwilleran asked.

The cat rolled back on the base of his spine and scratched his ear with his hind leg.

Immediately the phone rang again, and the caller was a woman who sounded like Beverly Forfar. She asked to speak to Ronald Frobnitz.

'One moment, please,' he said, covering the mouthpiece while he experimented with a Frobnitzian voice. After a suitable interval he said with an adenoidal twang, 'Frobnitz speaking.'

'Mr Frobnitz, we have wonderful news for you! This is the Art Center calling, and you're the lucky winner of that magnificent intaglio by W. C. Wyckoff. Congratulations!'

'This is too good to be true,' he said nasally. 'I've never won anything in my life. Are you sure there isn't some mistake?'

'Oh, I assure you it's a fact! And you'll be happy to know it's valued at a thousand dollars. That's something you'll need to know for insurance purposes. Are you a local resident? I don't believe we've met.'

Her voice was ingratiating, and it was difficult to connect it with her forbidding row of bangs, but Qwilleran was not in the least confounded. A master of glib prevarication, he replied with less than a second's hesitation. 'I'm from San Francisco, visiting relatives here, and I just happened to attend your celebration. I recognized the intaglio as a superlative piece of work, never imagining I'd have the good fortune to own it.'

'How will you get it safely to San Francisco? Would you like us to crate it for you?'

'An excellent idea! You've been most kind, Ms . . . Ms . . .'

'Forfar. Beverly Forfar. I'm the manager.'

'You have a splendid facility for the appreciation of art, and I'm sure much of the credit goes to you personally.'

'Oh, thank you, Mr Frobnitz, but—'

'Now, let us see . . . my sister-in-law will have to pick it up and ship it to me, since I'm leaving first thing in the morning. When will it be ready? I don't want to rush you.'

'Just give us till Wednesday. It's been so nice talking to you, Mr Frobnitz!'

'My pleasure, Ms Forfar.'

Qwilleran hung up, chuckling. The conversation had reminded him of improvisation exercises in the college drama department, before he switched to journalism.

The Siamese were not amused, however. They had been listening to a person they knew, speaking in a voice they did not know.

'Sorry, you guys,' he said. He picked up Yum Yum and carried her around and around the main floor, speaking in soothing tones and massaging the scruff of her neck. Koko tagged along at his heels, twitching his ears this way and that.

The Frobnitz caper had done what such exercises were supposed to do – loosen one up – and Qwilleran went to his studio in a playful mood to write his coverage of the museum fiasco.

With that job finished, he phoned his neighbor in the Klingenschoen carriage house at the head of the lane. It was after eleven, but he knew she would be awake, reading spy fiction or baking cookies or talking to her grandson Down Below at late-night rates. Celia Robinson had found her way to Pickax through her acquaintance with the late Euphonia Gage, and she had found her way into local hearts through her volunteer work and cheerful disposition. Although Celia had the gray hair of age, she had the laughter of youth.

Besides supplying prepared dishes for Qwilleran's freezer, she occasionally fronted for him in matters that required his anonymity. She called him Chief; he called her Secret Agent 0013½. She laughed uproariously at his simplest quips; he found her absolutely trustworthy.

'Hope I'm not phoning too late,' he said in a chatty voice.

'You know me, Chief! I'm a night owl! I'm boiling potatoes for salad – just a little catering job I lined up for tomorrow night. I've been at Virginia's ever since church.'

'Her daughter is a Handy Helper, I believe.'

'Yes, a wonderful girl! Always dashing off to help some poor soul.'

'Did she say anything about removing graffiti from a farmhouse?'

'No. That's part of their motto: just help, don't talk about it.'

'A commendable policy.'

'Is there anything I can do for you, Chief?'

He changed his delivery from neighborly to official, speaking crisply and slowly. 'Your brother-in-law Ronald Frobnitz . . . left a message with me when he couldn't reach you . . . He's returning to San Francisco early tomorrow . . . and wishes you to pick up something and ship it to him.' He paused while she shifted gears from potatoes to intrigue.

Celia was quick to comprehend. 'Did he . . . did Ronald say what it is I'm supposed to pick up?'

'A work of art that he apparently won in a raffle at the Art Center today. It will be ready any time after Wednesday.'

'I wonder how big it is.'

'About thirty inches square and very flat. He wants you to keep it until he sends you an address label.'

'Glad to help, Chief. Do you know my brother-in-law very well?' Then she added, 'Just in case someone asks.'

'He has a wife and three beautiful children. He teaches psychology at some university in California. His hobby is racing cars . . . Did I hear a bell ring?'

'That's the potatoes!'

'Hang up! Talk to you later.'

Qwilleran had plans for Monday morning. He would walk downtown and have pancakes and sausage at Lois's Luncheonette, then go to the newspaper office and throw his copy on Junior Goodwinter's desk. If the young managing editor found it unfit to print, so be it! Let them run a couple of paragraphs of hype from the museum's publicity release!

When Monday came, however, the situation demanded change. Koko was restless. After hardly touching his breakfast, he kept jumping at the door handle of the broom closet. That was a place of incarceration for the Siamese when they misbehaved, but it also housed harnesses and leashes. Obviously Koko wanted an outing. Did he sense the presence of a parrot in the neighborhood, a few tenths of a mile away? Given his remarkable long-range instincts, it was not unthinkable.

The sight of buckles and straps sent Yum Yum flying up the ramp to the roof, but Koko pranced with excitement. For the hike down the lane, he was propped on Qwilleran's shoulder, and there was a firm hand on the leash. Though indifferent to flitting birds and scurrying squirrels, the cat tensed his body as they neared the Art Center and uttered guttural noises as they went through the private gate.

'Steady, old boy,' Qwilleran reassured him in a calm voice. 'It's only . . .' Then he saw the reason for Koko's alarm. Although there was no vehicle around, the door of the building was open – wide open – and Koko sensed trouble. *How did he know it should be closed?* Because Koko always knew when something was not as it should be: a faucet running, the oven left on, a light burning in daylight. His catly perception was uncanny.

Qwilleran quickened his step and tightened his grip on the leash. Entering cautiously, he saw muddy footprints on the light vinyl floor and allowed Koko to jump down. Without hesitation, the cat tugged the man toward the studio wing, sniffing the floor like a hound, until he came to a dark red splotch on the floor between the manager's office and the Butterfly Girl's studio.

'Someone killed him!' Qwilleran said aloud. 'Someone killed Jasper!'

'*Gimme a peanut!*' came the croaking reply.

Jasper's cage was uncovered, and he was rocking on his perch and blinking his large round eyes. His night blanket was on the floor, splashed with blood. The small table had been knocked over, scattering peanuts and the pieces of a smashed Oriental vase.

Someone, Qwilleran thought, had expected to steal the bird and had put a hand too close to the cage, only to have Jasper's powerful hookbill grab a finger. In confusion the intruder had fled from the building.

But Koko had seen enough of Jasper and the blood spots; he was tugging again at the leash, tugging toward the studio with animal sketches lined up around the walls. Ignoring the dogs and horses, he went directly to the open bin where shrink-wrapped drawings were stored. He stood on his hind legs and peered at the contents. Qwilleran had a look, too. Only the large figure studies were there. The small ones – there had been a dozen or more – were gone!

Now it was clear: it was the nudes they were after, not the bird. They had loaded the drawings in a sack and stopped on the way out to hear Jasper say something insulting or obscene.

Dragging Koko away from the scene and temporarily locking him in the restroom, Qwilleran called 911 from the manager's office across from the bloody field of action. He reported a break-in and possible burglary. Next he phoned the city desk at the *Something*. Finally he phoned the manager's home. Beverly Forfar lived on Pleasant Street and she arrived shortly after the sheriff's deputy.

'What's that noise?' were her first words as she walked in.

Koko was howling his protest, which was amplified by the tile walls of his prison.

Beverly inspected all the rooms, and Qwilleran drew her attention to the missing figure studies.

'Daphne might've taken them home,' she said. 'I'll call her.'

Roger MacGillivray was arriving with his camera, and Qwilleran gathered up the cat and made a stealthy exit via the side door. He wanted no photographs of Koko in the paper, no headlines about a feline bloodhound.

He was intensely protective of Koko's privacy. The cat's psychic aptitudes were known only to two other persons, both of them in law enforcement. Even Polly and Arch were ignorant of Koko's detective instincts; neither of them would take the notion seriously. Qwilleran himself was hard put for an explanation, except that normal cats had forty-eight whiskers, eyebrows included, and Koko had sixty.

When the news item appeared in that day's paper, it was said that the sheriff had responded to a call from 'a neighbor,' who had seen the front door open. Some 'works of art' were missing. The intruder had been 'pecked and chased away' by a pet parrot on the premises.

The item appeared on page three, because page one had already been made up. It featured Roger's glowing account of the Art Center opening and announced the names of the two raffle winners: Ronald Frobnitz and Thornton Haggis. (Hah! Qwilleran thought; the other guy used an alias, too.) Also on page one was his own tongue-in-cheek report on the dedication ceremony at the Farmhouse Museum:

> On Saturday afternoon at the Goodwinter Museum in North Middle Hummock a throng of 310 visitors drank 450 cups of tea and viewed a collection of 417 historic artifacts in the 1,800-square-foot steel barn, where 83 volunteers have spent a total of 2,110 hours cataloguing

and storing items donated by 291 residents of Moose County.

'This is the first and last time this storage facility is being shown to the public,' stated a museum spokesperson. 'As items are needed for changing exhibits in the farmhouse, the new system will tell us what we have available and exactly where it is stored.'

The computerized catalogue is made possible by public contributions and a matching grant from the Klingenschoen Foundation. Printouts of the inventory are available for a small donation to cover copying and handling. For a similar donation the donors of artifacts in storage may have access to them for photographing. All donations are tax-deductible.

At Qwilleran's request there was no by-line for the three paragraphs or the photos, which included shots of the museum manager, the steel barn, and visitors at the refreshment table. Accompanying the museum story was an anonymous poem of sorts in a decorative border:

NOSTALGIA

Twenty-four chairs with legs,
Ten chairs with one leg missing,
Gramophone with Caruso records,
Seven flags with 48 stars,
Doctor's folding operating table.
  And four white enamel bedpans.
Thirty-seven pieces of china, cracked,
Five handmade quilts, stained,

Two wooden washboards, mildewed,
Woman's hat with ostrich plumes, molted,
Nurse's uniform, circa 1910.
    And three bedpans in gray graniteware.
Two pearl-handled buttonhooks,
Box of 207 handwritten postcards,
Five school desks carved with initials,
Six-and-a-half pairs of high-buttoned shoes,
Hot-water bottle without a stopper.
    And two bedpans in blue spatterware.
Box of 145 photographs, unidentified,
Three straight razors,
Pair of men's gray suede spats,
Fur-lined sleighcoat, moth-eaten,
Set of surgical saws and scalpels.
    And one genuine Bennington bedpan.

Although Qwilleran avoided the newspaper office Monday afternoon, the chaos was reported to him. Readers calling with raves and rebukes jammed the phone lines, and the local telephone company curtailed service to the paper rather than jeopardize the entire county-wide system. The manager of the museum, a newcomer in Pickax, demanded the dismissal of the perpetrator of the outrage, unaware that the *Something* owed its existence to the Klingenschoen Foundation. An editorial meeting was called to consider the ruckus, but the executives and editors around the table gave a standing ovation to the coverage, and the meeting broke up in laughter.

In late afternoon, Qwilleran was sitting in the gazebo with the Siamese and a stack of magazines, when a sudden change in the cats' attitude attracted his attention. Their necks stretched and ears pointed forward as they stared down the lane toward the Art Center. A few minutes later, the crunch of footsteps on gravel sent Qwilleran out to see who was trespassing. The prowler who rounded the last bend in the lane was a chubby young boy.

Qwilleran was not fond of preteens. 'Looking for something?' he asked sharply, standing with his fists on his hips.

'Just moseying around,' the boy said amiably with an innocent expression on his rosy-cheeked face. He was one of Moose County's well-fed blond youths who grew up to be giants. 'What's that?' he asked.

'What's *what*?'

'The thing with screens all around.'

'It's a gazebo.'

'Oh . . . How do you spell it?' Qwilleran told him, and after the boy had studied the structure, he said, 'It's octagonal.'

'What did you say?'

'That means it has eight sides.'

Now Qwilleran was amused enough to relax his belligerence. 'What's your name?'

'Culvert.'

'Culvert? Is your father a highway engineer?'

'He's a farmer. We live on Base Line.'

'What's his name?'

'Rollo McBee.'

'I know him,' Qwilleran said. 'I know your uncle Boyd, too. I see them at the coffee shop. What are you doing up here?'

'My mom sent me. I took some soup and rice pudding to Mrs Coggin. She's a nonagenarian.'

At this Qwilleran was sufficiently impressed to invite the boy into the gazebo to meet the cats.

'I never saw any like these,' Culvert said.

'They're Siamese.'

'You've got the biggest moustache I ever saw. Does it feel weird?'

'Not anymore. The first twenty-five years are the hardest. How old are you?'

'Ten, in July.'

'You have a good vocabulary for your age.'

'I have my own dictionary.'

'Good for you! Are you going to be an etymologist when you grow up?'

The boy shook his head soberly. 'I'm going to be a photographer. I like to take pictures.'

'What kind of pictures?'

'People doing things. My dad milking cows. My mom baking bread. Mrs Coggin feeding the chickens . . . Well, I gotta go home to supper. Can I take a picture of the cats sometime?'

'You can give it a try.' Qwilleran chuckled. It would be ironic if the cats willingly posed for this kid after thwarting a professional photographer for the last few years.

Polly had promised to phone after Paul Skumble had left. It grew late, and Qwilleran was uneasy.

'I gave him a glass of wine and a simple supper,' she explained. 'He likes my house. We decided I'll wear my blue silk dress and pearls and sit in a high-backed Windsor in the library, with the leather-bound books from the Duncan family in the background – and a copy of *Hamlet* in my hand.'

'When will he start?'

'That's what we need to discuss, Qwill. He wants to work in daylight, and since I'm busy at the library all week, it will have to be done on a series of weekends. You know, dear, how I love our uninterrupted time together, but . . . what else can we do?'

Qwilleran thought, Why did I ever suggest this fandango? 'Don't worry,' he said, feigning indifference. 'There'll be plenty of other weekends.'

In what remained of the evening, Qwilleran read aloud to the Siamese, one of their favorite pastimes, especially before bedtime. It was Koko's responsibility to make the literary selection. They never read one title from cover to cover but sampled a chapter of this book or that. Qwilleran suspected they all sounded alike to his listeners, and he himself liked dipping into books he had read before. It was like running into an old friend on a street corner.

On this occasion Koko sensed new acquisitions from Eddington's bookshop. After serious sniffing of the three World War II titles, he dislodged *Fire Over London*, and Qwilleran caught it before it landed on the floor. As usual he stretched out in his lounge chair with his feet on the ottoman and Yum Yum on his lap, while Koko sat attentively on the wide arm of the chair. It was a toss-up whether the familiarity of this ritual was more comforting to the cats or the man.

After the reading session the Siamese had their usual nightly snack and then went up the ramp to their room on the third balcony. Their door was left open, since the addition of the bird garden, to accommodate their early-morning bird-watching through the foyer windows. The door to his suite was closed to prevent furry bodies from crawling under his blankets.

It was a clear night. The weather was calm. The stars were bright. Sometime during the small hours Qwilleran was jolted awake by a thumping against his door, followed by unearthly howling. He jumped out of bed and yanked open the door.

'Oh, my God!' he yelled, dashing to the phone.

The large windows on the east side of the barn framed a horrifying sight: a night sky turned brilliant orange! He punched 911. 'Building on fire – Trevelyan Road, quarter-mile north of Base Line – the new Art Center – surrounded by woods – forest fire a possibility.'

He pulled pants over his pajamas, whirled down the spiral staircase to the kitchen, grabbed the car keys and was gone.

Oh God! he groaned to himself as he drove recklessly down the lane. All those hopes! All that work! All that art! All that turpentine! . . . Some artist working late – and smoking, against regulations . . . Mildred will have a heart attack! he thought.

He could hear the frantic chorus of emergency vehicles: the wailing and honking of firefighting equipment; the sirens of police cars. As he drew closer, the scene became brighter: leaping red and yellow flames licking the black sky. The flames had not reached the grove of ancient trees . . . had not reached his new gate . . . had not reached the Art Center! It was the Coggin farmhouse on fire!

Six

Flames were leaping into the black sky, and the bulky figures of firefighters were silhouetted against the orange and red inferno. Powerful headlights glared, and blue lights flashed. Fire trucks, sheriff's cars, and the pickups of volunteers were angled in every direction. Another truck, a pumper from a nearby town, was approaching from the north.

Qwilleran had covered major fires for metropolitan newspapers Down Below but none as troubling as this simple farmhouse totally ablaze. Where was Maude Coggin? Had she managed to escape?

Water lines were trained on the flames, producing the hiss of steam and clouds of black smoke. With no wind, there was little danger of sparks igniting the Art Center; even so, a hose was showering the roof. Qwilleran spotted the fire chief in his white helmet; all others were anonymous in their black gear, yellow-striped for visibility. As soon as the flames were put down, some of those men went in with airpacks and came out with blackened faces and lowered heads.

The sheriff's yellow tape was stretched to define the danger zone, and Qwilleran moved around the perimeter, trying to see something – anything. The waiting ambulance was inside the tape, and officers from the Pickax police and sheriff's department only shrugged. 'Maybe no one was home,' one of them said encouragingly. The nightman from the *Something* knew nothing either; he was snapping routine shots that would look like any other firescene photos.

Qwilleran stayed until the house and outbuildings burned to the ground, leaving only mounds of charred rubble. Emergency vehicles started to back away. One firefighter lumbered up to him and said, 'We're pullin' back, Mr Q, but a couple of us'll stick around to watch for hotspots.'

His face was soot-covered, but Qwilleran recognized the voice. 'Are you Rollo? What about the woman who lived here?'

'Gone! . . . gone! Damn shame! Couldn't get in to make a rescue. Place went up like a matchbox. Burned up in her chair. Even if we coulda reached her, smoke got her first, most likely.'

Thinking of the recent vandalism, Qwilleran asked about the possibility of arson.

'The chief'll be investigatin'.'

The coroner's car arrived, and Qwilleran turned away, walking slowly to his van.

For the rest of the night he slept poorly, if at all, unable to shake off the mental image of Maude Coggin in her Morris chair, with her high-laced boots propped on a wooden crate, grinning girlishly and boasting about her age. She had been determined to live another ten years.

He visualized the headline: 'Woman, 93, dies in farm fire.' The morning news on WPKX would give the tragedy about twenty seconds, with another twenty seconds for the good news: the Art Center was saved. Beverly Forfar would be annoyed by the excessive mud on the highway and the shower of soot over everything. On the other hand, she would hardly grieve over the instantaneous disappearance of the 'eyesore,' with its rusty truck and bothersome livestock.

The Siamese sensed Qwilleran's troubled mood and refrained from pestering him until their hunger pangs exceeded their compassion. Then they raised their voices in protest, Yum Yum in her ear-piercing shriek and Koko with a different tune, in a minor key like the mournful bleating of a sheep: *aaaaaaaaa-aaaa-aaaaaa.* Qwilleran threw off his churned bedclothes and took the shortcut down to the kitchen, via the spiral staircase, where he fed the cats, activated the coffeemaker, and phoned the city room at the *Something.*

'Who covered the fire?' he asked.

'Dave shot a roll of film and got a noncommittal statement from the fire chief. They're investigating the cause of the fire, of course. It's not much of a story. Do you know anything, Qwill? It happened practically in your backyard.'

'I could supply some basic facts, but I wouldn't want . . .'

'Don't worry. We won't mention your name.' The entire staff observed what they called the Q Gag Rule.

'Okay, here goes,' Qwilleran began. 'The occupant of the house was Maude Coggin, ninety-three years old. Native of Little Hope. She and her late husband, Bert, started with one acre, back when they couldn't afford a horse. Maude had to be yoked to the plow – something she boasted about in later life. The farm grew to a hundred acres, which she rented out to other farmers after her husband's death. She kept the original farmhouse, which was without modern conveniences, but she liked the primitive life. Raised chickens. Kept a small garden. Grew turnips and kale.'

'Could we get a quote from someone who knew her?' the editor asked.

'You could quote a neighbor as saying that Mrs Coggin was proud of being able to look after herself. Her long life she owed to hard work. She was lively for her age and could read the *Moose County Something* without glasses. She was also a one-woman rescue league for decrepit old dogs that no one wanted . . . Does that wrap it up?'

'It wraps it up and ties it with ribbon. Thanks, Qwill.'

'No name, remember.'

'Right! No name. But . . . hold on! All Dave got last night was the usual fire film. Do you know of any pictures of her – or the house?'

'Mmmm . . . I might have a source. Let me work on it.' He was thinking about Culvert. If the boy's camera work equaled his vocabulary, it might work.

'And how about funeral arrangements, Qwill? Who'll have that information?'

'Good question. Let me work on that, too. I'll get back to you.'

Qwilleran replaced the receiver but sat motionless, thinking of the poor woman who 'mound' her own business – a virtual recluse even though she claimed to drive her own truck – where? To the bank? To church? To the store? She seemed to live well on fresh eggs, coffee, turnips and kale . . . and perhaps milk from the McBee cows and occasional rice pudding from the McBee kitchen. Who would handle the funeral arrangements? Would the epitaph on her tombstone be exactly the way she wanted it? Would she even have a tombstone? Who would handle her estate? Would her descendants know that she was gone – or care?

Qwilleran's impulse was to phone the McBee farm. He had a bantering acquaintance with Rollo at the coffee shop and a hand-waving acquaintance when their vehicles passed on the backroad. Both Rollo and his brother Boyd were volunteer firemen, however, and had been on duty most of the night. Rollo would be sleeping; Culvert would be at school; Mrs McBee did accounting for other farmers and might be making calls. Yet, surely they would have an answering machine. The Coggin story was on deadline. There was no time to waste. He took a chance. To his relief, a woman answered.

'Mrs McBee? This is your neighbor up the road, Jim Qwilleran. I'm sure Rollo is sleeping after his grueling night.'

'He's dead to the world! When he came home, he was so exhausted and so broken up, he just sat down and cried, and so did I! Culvert was so upset when he heard the news, I let him stay home from school. He always pretended Maude was his great-great-grandmother . . . Shall I tell Rollo to call you when he wakes up?'

'If you will. Meanwhile, the newspaper wants to know about funeral arrangements. Mrs Coggin has been part of Moose County history for almost a century, and the *Something* wants to give her proper recognition. What can I tell them about a funeral for her?'

'Well, she wasn't a church-goer, but I could ask our pastor to read a service, and he'd be only too willing.'

'Would you like me to contact the funeral home? The K Fund will handle expenses. The important thing is to give her a dignified and respectful farewell.'

'That would be very kind of you, Mr Q.'

'Also, when Culvert came to visit me the other day, he mentioned taking pictures of Mrs Coggin. Do you think they're suitable for publishing in the paper?'

'Well, I don't know. Would you like to see them?'

'I would, definitely, but we're on a tight deadline. If you'll have them ready, I'll drive past in ten minutes and pick them up.'

He took the fast route via Main Street and Base Line, and Culvert ran out to meet him with a photo developer's envelope. From there Qwilleran drove directly to the newspaper and threw the packet on the picture editor's desk. They looked at them together: Maude hanging washing on the line, peeling turnips, digging in the yard, picking tomatoes, feeding chickens, feeding the bedraggled dogs, and more.

'Better than I expected,' said the editor, choosing three and returning the rest. The ones he selected were Maude at the wheel of her truck (a close-up), Maude hanging laundry (action), and Maude feeding the dogs (a heart-breaker).

'Don't forget to give him a credit line,' Qwilleran said. 'He's only nine years old, and it'll be a thrill. His name is Culvert McBee. C-u-l-v-e-r-t.'

'Culvert? Are you sure?'

'Am I sure this is Moose County? And don't forget to pay for the shots, regular freelance fee.'

While in town, Qwilleran visited the Dingleberry Funeral Home and gave specific instructions. Their records showed the date and location of Bert Coggin's interment; a companion gravesite had been provided for his wife. They could even identify the stonecutter who inscribed the tombstone: H&H Monuments on Sandpit Road. Proudly the younger Dingleberry brothers pointed out that their archives went back five generations – to the days when furniture stores sold coffins and did undertaking on the side.

Next, Qwilleran called on his attorney, G. Allen Barter, who was accustomed to his client's breezy approach to matters of law. He said, 'Don't ask if she'd filed a will, Bart; she didn't even have running water. There could be heirs, but she didn't know where they are. There must be money in the bank, because she recently sold a hundred acres of prime farmland . . . It's your baby, Bart. Do whatever is necessary and bill the K Fund. If you need to ask questions, the families who knew her longest and most intimately are Rollo and Boyd McBee of Pickax Township. I'm just trying to expedite things.'

With those details off his mind, Qwilleran drove home by way of Trevelyan Road and the scene of the fire. Yellow tape still surrounded the site, which now looked sadly small for a house, shed, chicken coop, and outhouse. One could see where each of them had stood twelve hours before. The lone firefighter remaining on duty said, 'We're watching it because of the new building across the road. An easterly wind is coming up.'

The wind was blowing an odor of wet burnt rubbish across to the Art Center, and Qwilleran thought, Wait till Beverly comes to work and smells that stench! It was not yet noon, but there was a car on the parking lot, a magenta coupe, and a petite woman on the entrance porch was fumbling in a shoulder bag almost as big as herself. He recognized the Butterfly Girl. 'Having a problem?' he called out.

'I'm looking for my key,' she said. 'I guess it fell out of my keycase.'

'I have one.' He jumped out of the van.

'Isn't it ghastly, what happened across the road? We're so lucky it didn't reach us! Want to come in and say hello to Jasper?'

'Not today, thanks. Have you been here since the break-in Sunday night?'

'No, but Beverly phoned me and told me about my Chinese vase. I'm crushed! My grandmother gave it to me. I phoned her in California, and she said she's never seen another one like it. I think it was valuable.'

Qwilleran glanced at the devastation across the highway and said, 'Too bad.'

Driving toward the barn, he could picture the Siamese raising inquisitive noses and sniffing the acrid aftermath of the fire, all that distance away. Their olfactory sense was phenomenal. He could see Koko through the foyer window, doing his jumping-jack act. That meant the phone was ringing. Qwilleran hurried indoors.

A weary voice said, 'You called my house. This is Rollo. I slept in. That fire last night knocked me out – not just the work but the sadness, you know.'

'I understand. Believe me, I do. I talked to your wife, and we worked out funeral details.'

'Yeah, she told me. There's somethin' else I need to talk to you about, somewhere private.'

'Want to come over to the barn?' Qwilleran asked. 'The gate's not locked. We'll have a cup of coffee.'

Rollo McBee was a typical Moose County man of the soil. Fortyish, he was a rugged figure in work clothes, field boots, and a feed cap that he never removed. He looked like someone who rode a tractor, milked cows, built fences, reroofed the barn, repaired his own truck, left mud on the highway, and stayed up all night to fight a fire. Qwilleran had learned to admire the farmers for their wealth of specialized knowledge, skills, independence, perseverance, and ability to josh about bad weather and financial setbacks – also their willingness to help each other.

'Are you and Boyd twins?' he asked when Rollo arrived.

'Next best thing! Grew up together, sloppin' hogs and muckin' the cowbarn . . . Say! This is some place!' He gazed up at the balconies and catwalks. 'I remember this barn when it was a rat's nest. How come you fixed it up?'

'It was just standing here, empty, and breeding rodents, and I met a builder who needed a job. This is his idea.'

'I'll bet it's hard to heat.'

'You can say that again! . . . Let's sit at the snackbar. How about a sweet roll from the Scottish bakery?'

'You've got a lot of books,' Rollo said, looking with wonder at the shelves on the fireplace cube. 'My boy's that way – always readin'. Not interested in bein' a farmer. Maybe he's smart. The family farm's on the way out. Dawn says you borrowed some of his pictures.'

'Yes, and glad to get them. There'll be two or three in today's paper, front page. He'll get a credit line and freelance rate of payment – not bad for a nine-year-old.'

'Don't spoil him,' his father warned. 'Kids get spoiled when things come too easy.'

'I don't think you have anything to worry about, Rollo. He seems like a stable sort. And, by the way, the pictures they didn't use are on the desk over there. You can take them with you.'

Rollo turned to look at the desk, where Koko and Yum Yum were sitting on their briskets, listening. 'What are those? Cats?'

'Siamese . . . So, where do we stand, Rollo? Dingleberry is handling the funeral. Your wife said she'd line up the pastor. But we want to be sure it's well attended. There's nothing sadder than a funeral with only a handful of mourners.'

'No problem. Dawn can round up the Home Visitors Circle at the church. I can fire up members of the Farmers' Collective.'

'The estate will have to be handled by an attorney, so I alerted G. Allen Barter. The K Fund will cover expenses. You may hear from him if he needs more information, such as whether she had any heirs and where she did her banking.'

'That's what I wanted to talk to you about,' Rollo said. 'When Maude sold her land, she insisted on cash – I mean greenbacks. She didn't think checks were real money. When the deal was done, she showed me a boxful of money, and it sure didn't look like a hundred thousand. I asked if she'd counted it. She hadn't, so I counted one bundle of bills. You'd be surprised how many brand-new bills they can squeeze into one bundle. All hundreds, with Ben Franklin on 'em. He's the one said *Early to rise, makes a man healthy, wealthy and wise.* It don't work for farmers. It was all propaganda . . . So, anyway, I offered to drive Maude to the bank right away with that dough, and she said, "Not on yer life!" A lot of old people around here don't trust banks after what happened in the Depression and last year in Sawdust City. So I wanted to know how she'd keep the money safe. She said, "None o' yer business!" And that was that! No arguin' with Maude! Of course, I knew what she aimed to do with it.'

'Bury it?'

'What else? Old-timers bury their valuables ten paces north of the southeast corner of the barn. Then they die, and the stuff is never found. It's been goin' on since 1850. If Moose County ever has an earthquake, there'll be another Gold Rush up here.'

'You think she buried it in the barnyard?'

'I know one thing for sure: nobody hides anythin' in the house, where it could be hit by lightnin'. *Everybody knows that!* . . . See what I'm drivin' at?'

Qwilleran stroked his moustache. 'You're saying that . . . as soon as the paper hits the street with news of the fire . . .'

'All the treasure-hunters will be out there after dark with shovels and lanterns!'

'That's trespassing.'

'Okay, so the sheriff chases them away, but the new owners of the property will send a back-hoe to clear out the rubble; they'll be huntin' for the buried bucks! I'd hate like heck to see those robbers get their money back that way! Do you realize they paid her one-fourth of what the farm was worth? I felt like tellin' her she was robbed, but what good would it do? The idea of a hundred thousand knocked her silly! She'd never even seen a bill with Ben Franklin's picture!'

'They were going to let her live there rent-free,' Qwilleran added. 'Who bought the land?'

'A Lockmaster company called Northern Land Improvement. You can't trust anybody from Lockmaster. All sharpies! Right away they raised the tillage rent to Boyd and me. They also said they wanted to be paid by the quarter – in advance. We'd been payin' Maude once a month, and we'd paid for April, but they sent a bill for the whole second quarter. We'd already cultivated and bought seed, so we decided to go along with it for the rest of the year. There's other land we could rent, but Maude's tract was handy, right between Boyd's farm and mine.'

Qwilleran said, 'I've never heard of that company, but I have to admit I don't know Lockmaster well.'

'I phoned the number on the bill and talked to some fast-talkin' babe called Bernice but didn't get anywhere. She was very friendly – friendly like a snake . . . So now you see why I don't want those greedy buzzards to dig up the money they paid for the land.'

Suddenly Qwilleran thundered 'NO!' in the direction of the desk. The explosive shout sent the cats flying, while assorted desktop items landed on the floor. 'Sorry,' he said to his guest. 'Koko was licking Culvert's snapshots. There's something in the surface of photos that tastes good to cats.' He gathered up the clutter and examined the snapshots. A cat's saliva always left a rough spot. Only one picture was damaged – a shot of Maude in the barnyard, with her boot on the shoulder of a spade. She was digging a hole, and on the ground beside her was a two-pound coffee can.

It raised the hackles on Qwilleran's neck. He said, 'Here's a coincidence, Rollo. Can you identify the wall in this picture?' It was a whitewashed plank wall.

'It's the outhouse!' the farmer roared. 'The back of the outhouse! Let's go and dig it up!' He was out of his chair and halfway to the door.

'Not so fast!' Qwilleran said. 'We'd better clear it with the attorney.'

'Anyway, let's go down and have a look at it. Then I've got to go home and do chores.'

Qwilleran said, 'I'll ride with you, pick up my mail, and walk back.' Then, on the way down the lane, he asked, 'I wonder what happened to Mrs Coggin's dogs. She let them live in the shed.'

'Believe it or not,' said Rollo, 'when I started up here this afternoon, I saw this parade of broken-down mutts comin' down the highway, headed for our farm. The black one with the bad limp was in the lead, with the others hobblin' after him. I hollered to Culvert to come and take 'em in.'

There were two vehicles at the site of the fire: a sheriff's car and the pickup belonging to the fire department's watchman. The latter said to Rollo, 'I'm reporting it's safe to leave now.'

'How long will the yellow tape remain?' Qwilleran asked.

'Till the owners clean it up,' said the deputy. 'Till then, it's a danger spot. Kids could come pokin' around in the muck, lookin' for loot.'

'More than that, it's a health hazard,' Rollo said. 'When the outhouse burned down, it left an open latrine. It's gotta be treated with lime and filled up, or you'll wind up with a godawful swarm of flies, and the folks across the road'll have somethin' worse than mud to write to the paper about.'

The deputy said he'd report it to the board of health.

'Naw, they'll take a coon's age to fix it,' said the farmer. 'I got some lime in my barn. When I've done my chores, I'll run up here with a shovel and close it up. Best thing to do. Don't want to start an epidemic.'

Seven

Early Wednesday morning, when only farmers and Benjamin Franklin's disciples were abroad, Qwilleran received a phone call from Rollo McBee. 'Are you up?' he asked. 'Got somethin' to show you.'

'I'm never up at this ungodly hour. What have you got?'

'A two-pound coffee can. Found it accidentally when I was fillin' in the latrine.'

'I'm up!'

In less than ten minutes, the farmer's pickup came slowly up the lane. Qwilleran went out to meet him and was handed a plastic sack from Toodle's Market.

'Are you coming in?' he asked.

'No. Got chores to do. Thought your lawyer could put this in his safe, or somewhere.'

'How do you want me to explain it?'

'Well, I was treatin' the open latrine with lime and diggin' around to fill up the hole, and my shovel hit metal, and there was this coffee can. Didn't think I should leave it there for some looter to steal.'

'Well stated!' Qwilleran said. 'Did you look at the contents?'

'No. It's sealed with friction tape. Let the lawyers open it.'

'Suppose it's filled with rusty nails.'

'Shake it. Doesn't sound like nails.'

When Qwilleran carried the sack indoors and put the can on the snackbar, the Siamese had to investigate. They sensed it had been underground for a few weeks. As for Qwilleran, he was in no mood to go back to bed, and he astounded them by feeding them three hours ahead of schedule, although they made no objection.

With his coffee and a thawed Danish at the snackbar, he reread the newspaper account of the Coggin fire. Culvert had a twenty-four-point credit line for three photos, the largest of which showed Maude grinning at the wheel of her old truck. Did she imagine that she still drove it? The tires were rotting, and, according to Rollo, her license had been revoked five years before.

A sidebar to the story itself quoted the fire chief, Roy Gumboldt: 'Following a thorough investigation, it's evident that the fire was caused by an overheated kerosene stove in a room that was littered with flammable objects. The victim apparently fell asleep in her chair and was asphyxiated by smoke before the room burst into flames.' There followed the usual cautions about the prudent use of kerosene stoves and heaters – not that it would do any good. The volunteers were called to fight that kind of fire at least once a week, somewhere in the county.

As soon as the downtown offices opened, Qwilleran drove to Hasselrich Bennett & Barter to deliver the coffee can. In the municipal parking lot he was hailed by Wetherby Goode, who had been his neighbor in Indian Village the previous winter. The WPKX meteorologist was a husky, hearty glad-hander who entertained listeners with quips and quotes as well as weather predictions.

'What kind of weather are you giving us for the funeral tomorrow?' Qwilleran asked.

'The heavens smile! Did you know it's getting TV coverage? The network picked up the story from your paper and called us to confirm the time and check the weather. They're flying a crew up from the state capital.'

Qwilleran said, 'Another local-yokel story, I suppose, to entertain big-city viewers. How's everything in the Village?'

'Nothing new. Long time since we had dinner. How about Friday night?'

'How about Chet's palace of gastronomy in Kennebeck?'

'I thought you didn't like barbecue, Qwill.'

'I don't, but I feel the need to further my education.'

'Okay. Meet me there at seven-thirty? I'll have to go home and change. In the afternoon I'm speaking to a ladies' garden club, and that means a suit and tie. At Chet's anything dressier than a tank top looks pretentious. And be sure to wear a baseball cap. It's a hats-on dive.'

In the law office the coffee can was stripped of the black tape, and inside were five bundles of bills totaling a hundred thousand.

Qwilleran said, 'It should be four hundred thousand. They took advantage of a ninety-three-year-old woman.'

'How did you get involved?' Barter asked.

'She reminded me of the grandmother I never knew, and she was an interesting character. There aren't many Maude Coggins left, Bart. In fact, I'd like to stir up some well-deserved recognition. Okay if I use your phone to make a few calls?'

Given a phone and a cup of coffee, Qwilleran proceeded to call the offices of the mayor, city council, and county board of commissioners, leaking the news that the Coggin funeral was getting TV coverage and the *Something* was assigning a battery of reporters and photographers. He hinted that it might be a good idea to send flowers. Local reporters always looked at the name tags on such memorial tokens.

Next he called the Pickax police chief and said, 'Andy, do you realize there'll be a massive traffic snarl at the funeral tomorrow, unless you assign a special detail?'

The chief grunted. 'Dingleberry didn't apply for a permit.'

'That's because there's no church service and no procession. The obsequies will be at the graveside, and parking at the cemetery will be chaotic! Hundreds of mourners are expected, including the mayor and other officials.'

'How come it's so big?'

'The story in the *Something* touched a lot of hearts and even attracted the attention of the TV network. It would be appropriate if we had a piper.'

Andrew Brodie was a big Scot who looked ferocious in uniform but had a benign majesty when he wore his kilt and feather bonnet and played the bagpipe at funerals.

He was just waiting to be asked. 'I could play *Loch Lomond*, slow tempo, before the service,' he said, 'and *Amazing Grace* after.'

So far so good. Qwilleran knew he was gambling, but it seemed to be working. He called the newspaper and spoke with Junior Goodwinter. 'What kind of coverage are you giving the funeral?'

'We'll send someone to get a shot for the picture page, that's all. We've already done a banner-story.'

'Better think twice about that, Junior. I hear the mayor and all kinds of city and county officials are turning out, and Andy's assigning a special traffic detail. The network thinks it's important enough to send a TV crew up here.'

Testily the managing editor said, 'Why didn't we know about this?'

'Apparently it was a spontaneous reaction to your great story on page one. I just happened to hear about it.'

On the way back to his car, Qwilleran passed the florist shop and went in to check up on their funerary business. Besides, he always enjoyed talking with Claudine. She had long silky hair and a dreamy expression in her large blue eyes. Renoir would have painted her. The country music coming from her radio should have been Chopin.

'Getting many orders for the Coggin funeral?' he asked.

'Scads! I had to call for extra help,' she said. 'All kinds of important people have ordered. She must've been quite a lady!'

'I'd like to order another – a good-sized basket. I'll write the card.' He wrote: From Maude Coggin's best friends – Blackie, Spot, Dolly, Mabel, and Li'l Yaller. To Claudine he explained, 'They're the homeless old dogs she rescued.'

'Oh, Mr Q! You're making me cry!' she whimpered as tears flooded her eyes.

It was still too early for lunch, so Qwilleran drove out to Sandpit Road to order a tombstone. Next to the extensive H&H Sand and Gravel operation was a small fenced yard with polished granite slabs and tall Celtic crosses – the H&H Monument Works. As he walked toward the building in the rear, a strikingly white-haired man with gold-rimmed glasses came forward to greet him. He was the volunteer who had been on the stepladder at the Art Center, adjusting tracklights.

'You're Mr Q,' he said, eyeing the moustache. 'We almost met – but not quite – at the Art Center. I'm Thornton Haggis.'

Qwilleran concealed his surprise; the name was not an alias after all. There really was a Thornton Haggis. He said, 'You won Duff Campbell's watercolor! A nice piece of luck! . . . Are you the first H or the second H in the H&H enterprises?'

'I'm only the ampersand. My two sons own the business now. Come in and have a cup of coffee.' The office furniture in the anteroom of the shop was gray with age or granite dust. 'I'm more or less retired after joining the Zipper Club, although I feel great!'

'You, too? My friend Polly Duncan had bypass surgery, and she's like a new woman. With a name like Haggis, you must be Scottish.'

'That's a family joke. My great-grandfather, Eero Haakon, came from Finland to work in the quarries, but he was put on the payroll as Earl Haggis, and we've been Haggis for five generations, always in the tombstone business.'

'That's why I'm here,' Qwilleran said, 'to order a stone for the woman who lost her life in yesterday's fire.'

'Yes . . . yes . . . a real tragedy. It's a miracle that the Art Center didn't ignite. Beverly Forfar, instead of being thankful, feels guilty because she hated that farmhouse so much. She's very high-strung, Beverly is.'

'What is your function at the Art Center, Mr Haggis?'

'Call me Thornton. I'm a volunteer handyman and signwriter.' He kept running his hands through his white hair. 'I need a haircut, but my wife likes me to look like a floormop.'

Qwilleran said, 'If Beverly wants to ease her conscience, she could help to raise money for the tombstone. I happen to know the inscription Maude Coggin wanted.' He handed Thornton a card: 'Maude Coggin. Worked Hard. Loved Animals. Mound Her Own Business.'

'Mound?' the stonecutter questioned.

'That's it, verbatim. She spoke the Old Moose dialect, and you have to admit that "mound" makes sense as the past tense of "mind." You don't say, "I finded my watch and winded it," do you?'

Thornton laughed. 'You should write a column on that subject, Qwill. Mind if I call you Qwill? In fact, you should write one about old tombstones and how the old cemeteries reflect changes in our culture. History was my major in college Down Below, and I enjoy poking among old tombstones.'

'What do you find – besides poison ivy?'

'A lot of interesting things.'

'Okay if I tape this?'

'Sure. It started in pioneer days, when we had mostly hell-raising miners and lumberjacks. When one of them was killed in a brawl, his drinking buddies chipped in to buy him a tombstone. My great-grandfather recognized a business opportunity. For two bits a word he'd chisel anything they wanted on a thin slab of stone. There's one that says: STONE PAID FOR BY HIS PALS AT JEB'S SALOON. I have a photograph of it if you don't believe me. It's at Bloody Creek.'

'Where's that? I've never seen it on the map,' Qwilleran said.

'It was a thriving community in the old days. Now all that's left is a bridge and the burial ground – stones toppled over – some half-buried in sand . . . Then my grandfather went into the business. He chiseled his own tombstone. Stonecutters had a grim sense of humor, and his epitaph was: A CHISELER ALL HIS LIFE.'

Qwilleran said, 'It's a gag now, but was it funny in those days?'

'Absolutely! "Chiseling" was slang for "cheating" as far back as 1800. I looked it up. I found another kind of humor on an old stone near Dimsdale: HERE LIES A HAPPY MAN. NEVER MARRIED. Want to hear more? I've got a million of 'em. It's a hobby of mine, and when I get started . . .'

'Don't stop. I'd like to visit some of these graveyards.'

'I can tell you exactly where they are – and even go with you if you want a tour director. There's a curious one near Trawto that says: HE WAS A FAITHFUL HUSBAND. ONLY ONE I EVER HAD. Make your own interpretation.'

Qwilleran said abruptly, 'Let's drive to the Black Bear Café for a burger. My treat.'

They drove in his van, taking the backroads, while Thornton pointed out abandoned churchyards. He said, 'There was a period when inscriptions included the cause of death. I've seen DIED OF THE POX and HIS KIDNEYS DONE HIM IN. My favorite is ET BAD FISH. When prosperity came, affluent families ordered huge monuments with as many as a hundred words inscribed, listing the names of wives, kids, doctors, horses, and dogs – plus business successes.'

They were driving to the lakeside town of Brrr, so named because it was the coldest spot in the county. On the outskirts they stopped at a weed-choked plot to see what Thornton called the ultimate in his and hers. There were two stones. One said: SHOT BY HER DEAR HUSBAND. The other said: HANGED FOR KILLING HIS DEAR WIFE.

'Only in Moose County would you find something like that,' Qwilleran said.

A resort town, Brrr was noted for the historic Hotel Booze and its Black Bear Café. Guests were greeted at the entrance by an enormous mounted bear rearing on his hind legs. Splintery wooden chairs and wobbly wooden tables added to the primitive ambiance that attracted campers, fishermen, and boaters.

The two men sat in a booth and ordered the so-called bearburger, best chopped-beef sandwich in the county. 'Do you see what I see?' Qwilleran remarked. 'Gary Pratt has lost half a bushel of hair!'

The proprietor's shaggy beard and uncut hair, coupled with an ursine physique and lumbering gait, had always given him the personality of an amiable black bear. Now his beard was clipped and his hair tamed.

'Hey, you guys! Haven't seen you lately,' Gary said, shuffling to their booth with the coffee server. 'I thought you were both dead. I thought your cats were writing your column, Qwill. It seemed better than usual.'

'My ghostwriters appreciate the compliment,' Qwilleran said. 'But let's talk about you. What happened? Get caught in a food processor?'

'I'm getting married.'

'No!' the two customers said in unison.

'This is only for the wedding. Then I go back to normal.'

'Who's the unlucky girl?' Qwilleran asked.

'Nobody you know. She owns the Harborside Marina.'

'Don't let her redecorate this restaurant,' Thornton warned. 'It's the first thing she'll want to do.'

'Don't worry. It's written in our marriage contract. She doesn't tell me how to run the café, and I don't tell her how to run the marina . . . Say, that was some fire down your way the other night!'

The two men nodded solemnly as they bit into their burgers.

Gary went on. 'But it's an ill wind, as the saying goes. I hear the county's getting a piece of land for a new facility they've needed for years. Centrally located. On Trevelyan Road.'

'They didn't waste any time, did they?' Qwilleran said tartly, thinking of the promise made by Northern Land Improvement. 'Where did you hear this rumor?'

'A guy who comes in here. Engineer for the county.'

'What kind of facility?' Thornton asked with obvious apprehension.

'A parking lot for heavy road equipment: snow-blowers, plows, asphalt trucks, road-rollers – stuff like that. They've had it scattered all over. They want it together on one big lot.'

Thornton said, 'I don't know why. Wouldn't it make more sense to have several stations and deploy equipment to job sites as needed?'

Gary shrugged. 'Nobody ever said the county fathers had any sense. They also want to build a repair shop as big as a jet hangar.'

The two men exchanged glances.

'There goes the neighborhood,' Thornton said as Gary moved away. 'Beverly will burst a blood vessel if they put it across from the Art Center.'

'And Maude will turn over in her freshly dug grave, no matter where they put it on her beloved hundred acres. The purchaser agreed to use them for agriculture.'

'The rumor could be only a rumor – wishful thinking, along with the pickle factory they threatened to start in Pickax.'

They chewed in gloomy silence for a while. Then Thornton

said, 'I could tell you an interesting tale about the Coggin farm – not for publication.'

'That's okay. Let's hear it.'

'This was before I was born, but my dad told me after I started getting interested in local history. After World War One, he said, the stonecutting business wasn't doing too well. The mines had closed; the county had been lumbered over, and there was an economic bust and general exodus. Thousands were going Down Below to work in factories – and to die there, apparently. At any rate, they weren't coming north to be buried. He had a Model T truck and did some hauling jobs to make ends meet, but it was rough. People were living on oatmeal and turnips, and families were having to double up.

'Then, one day Bert Coggin came in to order a tombstone for his uncle, who'd been living with them. The old fellow had been struck down by lightning and was being buried on the farm. Dad chiseled a stone and delivered it in his truck – all Bert had was an oxcart – and the two of them set up the stone on a fresh grave by the river. Dad was glad to get the business; his family was in need of shoes, and Bert paid cash.

'In a week or so, Bert was back for another stone; his aunt had died of a broken heart. Dad cut the stone and, while delivering it, wondered about burying somebody on a riverbank. What if there was a flood? . . . Anyway, he and Bert set up the stone, and Bert asked to look at the truck; he was thinking of buying one. To Dad's embarrassment, it wouldn't start! He tinkered with the motor until the farmbell called Bert in to supper.

'As soon as Bert had left, Dad sneaked back to the graves. He'd only pretended the truck wouldn't start. Scraping the topsoil away, he found some loose planks, and under the planks he found cases of booze! Old Log Cabin whiskey from Canada.'

'That's the brand Al Capone drank during Prohibition,' Qwilleran said.

'Exactly! Rum-runners were bringing it across the lake and up the river, where it was stashed on Bert's farm until it could be delivered Down Below . . . Well! Dad had three options: report 'em, ignore 'em, or join 'em. Prohibition was bringing prosperity back to Moose County. People were flocking north by the trainload, and everybody was smuggling contraband in from Canada or out by train and Model T. Some of today's old families who claim to be descended from lumber barons or mining tycoons are really descended from bootleggers.'

'What course did your father take, Thornton?'

'He never told us. He merely explained that there was a lot of tombstone business during Prohibition. We lived in a nice house and always had shoes, and all of us kids went away to college.'

Qwilleran went home with a feeling of satisfaction after a productive morning and enjoyable afternoon. His housemates obviously felt neglected, however. Their motto was: when unhappy, tear something up. The interior of the barn had been given the confetti treatment, and the front page of yesterday's *Something* lay in shreds.

Moreover, Koko was bleating his new lament: *aaaa-aaaaaaaaaaaa.*To assuage their grievances and bolster their morale, Qwilleran brushed them, gave them an extra treat, and read to them; Koko's choice was *The Day of the Locust*. Then they all went to the gazebo for an adventure with the wildlife. While Yum Yum looked for insects, Koko made friends with the crows and mourning doves. He found the squabbling blue jays interesting, but the pileated woodpecker annoyed him with its ratchety cry. Whenever Koko heard the piercing *kek-kek-kek-kek-kek*, he talked back with a *kek-kek-kek-kek-kek* of his own.

Once, he turned away from the birds, listened sharply, and yowled. A moment later, the phone could be heard ringing indoors, and Qwilleran ran to the barn.

Dawn McBee was calling. 'Sorry to bother you, Mr Q.'

'That's all right. Everything checks out A-OK for the funeral. Is there anything I can do for you?'

'Well, Culvert has an idea. He wants to take Maude's dogs to the funeral. He thinks Maude would like it.'

Qwilleran did some swift thinking about propriety, public reaction, logistics. The media, he knew, would gobble it up. 'Could he control them?'

'He says he could rig a harness like the ones they use for dogsledding. And the dogs love him. They'd behave.'

Qwilleran okayed the idea, and when he discussed it with Polly later, she agreed. Pickax liked a good funeral. They still told how Ephraim Goodwinter's casket had been escorted to the grave by thirty-seven carriages and fifty-two buggies. The length of the procession was considered the measure of public respect for the deceased.

Qwilleran told her, 'There'll be no procession tomorrow – just services at the graveside – but there'll be a traffic jam at the cemetery requiring the help of police and state troopers. It'll be a memorable event, with lots of flowers and VIPs and a TV crew from the state capital and Brodie in his kilt and bonnet. He'll play *Loch Lomond* in slow tempo.'

'That's a lovely choice,' she said, 'although many won't realize its significance.'

'Of whom you may count me one – if you'll pardon the tangled syntax. I've never understood that song. There are two unidentified individuals; let's call them A and B. Apparently A takes the high road and B takes the low road, and B reaches Scotland before A, yet B never sees his true love again. How do you explain that?'

'As I understand it, Qwill, there are two Scottish soldiers who have been captured. One is to be shot; the other set free. The doomed man's song is based on an old belief that a Scot's soul always returned to Scotland by an underground route – the low road, in other words. The melody is especially poignant when played at a slow tempo.'

Koko was on the desk close to the mouthpiece. '*Aaaaaaaaaaaaa*,' he bleated.

'What's that awful noise?' Polly asked.

'Koko is grieving for Maude Coggin.'

Eight

At the corner of Trevelyan and Cemetery Roads, four parcels of land met: the cemetery on the northwest corner; catercornered from that, the former Coggin acreage; on the northeast, Boyd McBee's farm; on the southwest, a half-square mile of woodland placed in conservancy by the Klingenschoen Foundation – not to retard the growth of the city but to promote ecologically the well-being of the residents.

On Thursday morning the intersection was the scene of a well-ordered invasion. Cars, vans, and pickups lined both shoulders of both highways, and crowds streamed on foot toward the last remaining grave, where Maude Coggin would be laid to rest beside her husband. The cemetery, which had served Pickax for a century, was a dense forest of tombstones, all facing west. On a late afternoon it was a striking sight when the sun emblazoned the stones – an army of memories summed up in one breath-taking panorama. The need to extend its boundaries had concerned the city council for several years, the problem being to find land not too wet, not too rocky, not too far from the city limits, and not too expensive. Arguments in the council chamber and editorials in the newspaper had failed to find a solution.

Qwilleran chose to walk from the barn to the site of the funeral. The casket was in place, ready to be lowered, covered with floral sprays and surrounded by wreaths and flower baskets. Standing under a canvas canopy was a solemn man wearing a surplice and holding a prayer book; Qwilleran recognized him as the pastor of the Little Stone Church. Andrew Brodie, in his towering feather bonnet, looked eight feet tall, an impressive figure with his armful of pipes and shoulderful of swathed plaid. The Dingleberry brothers in their black suits were grouping the mourners: Art Center volunteers in their blue smocks; members of the Farmers' Collective in work denims and feed caps; Home Visitors from the church, each holding a single flower. Places were reserved for civic leaders and the McBee clan. Boyd was there with his wife and three children in Sunday garb, but Rollo and his family were late.

Just as the mayor arrived, chauffeured in the official limousine, a pickup with a camper top came up Trevelyan Road and stole the show from His Honor. The three tardy McBees tumbled out, and Rollo hurried to open the tailgate. Out hobbled a string of lame, battered, arthritic hound dogs, each with a makeshift collar of twisted red bandanna. As gasps, whimpers, and sobs came from the assembled mourners, the dogs, linked by a jute rope, followed Culvert and were glad to sit when tapped on the hindquarters.

Eyes that had remained dry at the advent of the dogs gave way to tears as the slow strains of *Loch Lomond* skirled around the cemetery. The service opened with a few words from the pastor concerning Maude Coggin's lifelong love of the soil and her concern for old, ailing, unwanted animals. She was lauded as the last traditional farmwife in Moose County – working shoulder-to-shoulder with her husband in the field, rearing a family, making garments out of feedbags, raising chickens, tending a kitchen garden, baking and canning, scrubbing clothes, and doing without. Qwilleran surmised that Boyd's wife had written it; she was a substitute teacher who wrote frequent letters to the editor.

At the end of the burial rites the bagpiper played *Amazing Grace*, and the Home Visitors dropped their flowers into the grave as the casket was lowered.

The mayor, council members, and commissioners were the first to depart, having spoken a few words into radio and TV mikes thrust in front of them. Other mourners were reluctant to leave, milling about, speaking in muffled voices, preserving the inspired melancholy of the moment. Qwilleran spoke with G. Allen Barter, the McBee families, and staffers from the *Something*. Then he walked back down Trevelyan Road, telling everyone who offered him a ride that he was walking for his health.

Actually he was walking to organize his thoughts, after the turmoil of the last few days. If rumors were true, the county was in a disrespectful hurry to grab a chunk of the former Coggin land for a county workyard. Would the City of Pickax want another chunk for a cemetery extension? And would XYZ Enterprises make a bid for the riverfront as a site for Indian Village Two? No doubt Northern Land Improvement would be only too happy to sell. Their stated intention of putting the land in 'taters and beans' had been a ruse to trick Maude into virtually giving away her cherished farm. And how about their promise that she could continue to live there rent-free? That proved to be a term of short duration.

'Hah!' he said aloud as he walked. 'All's fair in love and war – and business!' Pounding his moustache with his knuckles, he wondered if the fire caused by 'an over-heated kerosene stove' could indeed have had another cause. There had been no wind to carry sparks from the house to any other building – on either side of the highway – yet each of the farm's outbuildings had burned to the ground, leaving a precise rectangle of charred rubble.

Then there was Koko's curious behavior, before and after the fire. Trying to figure that one, Qwilleran decided, could drive one batty.

He had reached the Art Center, now opening for the regular afternoon hours. There were several cars in the parking lot. He recognized the H&H van, Beverly's small yellow convertible, and the Butterfly Girl's magenta coupe. Partway up the lane he saw the Doonescape truck; Kevin's crew were planting things in the meadow.

The foreman explained. 'There are shrubs that will attract butterflies. We're also putting in a puddle. Butterflies like to puddle.'

Qwilleran went on his way, thinking, At least they won't require feeding . . . and won't wake me up at five a.m. . . . and won't leave droppings on my car! Perhaps that was why butterflies were so popular. The community college was giving an evening course in lepidopterology, and Phoebe could hardly paint fast enough to meet the demand. The spirit of Mrs Fish-eye was telling him to jump on the bandwagon and write a thousand words about butterflies.

Arriving at the barn, Qwilleran first phoned the Art Center

and made an appointment with Phoebe for an afternoon interview. Then he went to the library on Park Circle and checked out a book on butterflies to mitigate his utter ignorance. By three o'clock he knew the difference between a larva and a pupa, and why butterflies puddle, and how many species there are: seventeen thousand! At four o'clock he walked back down the lane.

As the landscaper had promised, there was now a 'puddle' in the meadow – a large shallow saucer rimmed with flat rocks and filled with dry sand. According to the library book, it should be wet sand, but not too wet. Qwilleran huffed into his moustache. Was he supposed to carry pails of water down from the barn every day? And what if too many inches of rain fell and oversoaked the sand? The book also recommended splashing the stone rim with stale beer.

At the Art Center the collagist was conducting a hands-on workshop in the main room, but the gallery was vacant, and he took the opportunity to view the exhibit without an elbow-to-elbow crowd. He saw the totem pole he had bought, now marked with a red dot. He saw landscapes, still lifes, abstractions, portraits, and one brilliant painting signed 'P. Sloan.' In the perfectly beamed spotlight its colors virtually leaped from the frame, and two blue-winged butterflies seemed ready to take flight. The label read: 'Brazilian Morpho, acrylic, $150.' A red dot indicated it had been sold. There were not many red dots in the gallery.

Beverly Forfar rushed into the space; no one escaped her notice. 'Hello, Mr Q. I hear you're interviewing Phoebe. Please don't say anything about the parrot.'

'I believe we'll be concentrating on lepidoptera,' he assured her. 'I didn't see you at the funeral this morning.'

'I don't like funerals.' She tossed her helmet of hair, every strand of which remained perfectly aligned. 'Some of the volunteers went, though. They said the dogs were there. I'm surprised they were allowed.'

'They were close friends of the deceased. The mayor was there, and he didn't seem to object.' He waved an arm around the gallery. 'Good show! My compliments!'

He was less amiable than usual, being somewhat annoyed by the prospect of irrigating the butterfly puddle. If they could take care of themselves in the wilds of Brazil, he saw no reason to pamper them with stale beer in Pickax.

Phoebe Sloan was concentrating on mixing colors when he entered the studio, leaving it to Jasper to greet him in his raucous voice: '*Hi, knucklehead! Got any dirty pictures? Ha ha ha ha ha!*'

The artist jumped up and threw a blanket over the cage. 'Naughty boy! Go to sleep! . . . Isn't he gross? Come in, Mr Q, and sit down. Sorry they don't give us decent chairs. Do you mind a stool?'

'Do you mind a tape recorder?' he countered as he set it up between them.

'I'd rather not have it, if it's okay with you,' she said, beseeching him with her lustrous brown eyes.

'No problem.' It saved him the trouble of taking notes and insured accuracy, but . . .

'What do you want to talk about?' she asked.

'Your paintings. Why do you specialize in butterflies?'

'I guess because I'm thrilled with the variety of hues. I love bright colors.' She flicked the collar of her tangerine blouse. 'Beverly wants me to wear the Art Center smock, but it's too dull – and too warm.' Her blouses were always sleeveless,

Qwilleran had noted; they showed off her graceful arms. When she threw a blanket over the parrot's cage, it was like a dance movement.

He was asking standard warm-up questions. 'How did you become hooked on butterflies?'

'Well, I learned that collectors catch them in nets, chloroform them, and pin them in display trays, and I thought, How horrible! I'd rather preserve them in paint.'

'Did you study art?'

'I wanted to, but I'm an only child, and Dad expected me to attend a college of pharmacy for five years and then take over the drug store. Five years! I thought, No way! We had an awful battle, but my grandmother was on my side, and we won. She sent me a book on painting with acrylics, and here I am! What I do isn't great art, but it makes people happy, and it's more fun than counting pills.'

'Why acrylics?' he asked.

'They dry fast.'

'Tell me about the Brazilian Morpho.'

'Isn't it gorgeous? It's the male that has those unusual wings in metallic blue. Morphos used to be used in making butterfly jewelry . . .Ugh!'

'I concur. What is the butterfly's function in nature?'

'They pollinate wildflowers. Most people prefer lawns to meadows nowadays, and pretty soon butterflies will be extinct in America, if we don't do something about it. I raise them in a box and then set them free. My grandmother sends me the caterpillars from California.'

To test her knowledge he asked some questions gleaned from the book: What do they feed on? Why do they have spots on their wings? Why do they rest with their wings together? What is their life cycle? He was beginning to feel vaguely dissatisfied with the interview. He was asking the wrong questions. She was not giving quotable replies. The subject matter failed to grab him. The stool was uncomfortable.

Finally he said, 'Tell you what: Why not bring your butterfly box to the studio someday, and I'll come back and have a look at it?'

'That would be neat,' she said. 'I'm just starting a new hatch, but before you go, Mr Q, could I ask your advice?'

'There'll be a slight charge,' he said lightly.

'Don't you think I'm old enough to have an apartment of my own? I'm twenty-three, although I know I look younger. My boyfriend thinks I should have a place of my own where I can paint and raise butterflies and keep Jasper.'

'Are you saying your parents object to your moving out?' It was a common family problem in Moose County.

'Well, the main trouble is . . . they don't like Jake. He's only a bartender.'

'For what it's worth, I worked my way through college as a bartender,' Qwilleran said. 'Does he have long-range goals? What other skills does he have? Has he adequate education?'

She cast her eyes down. 'Not really, but he's going to be promoted to manager of the restaurant, and' – she giggled – 'he's one sexy guy!'

He groaned inwardly. Why were young women always asking his advice? Just because he wrote columns on everything from jazz to bee-keeping, they considered him a pundit. He cleared his throat. 'Some of us are grown-up at age twelve; some of us never mature. It's not a question of whether you're old enough to make your own decision; are you old enough to take responsibility for the outcome if it turns out to be a bad decision?'

'You sound just like my dad,' she said.

Qwilleran was glad to leave and return to his uncomplicated household where family members merely tore up newspapers and talked to crows.

He was having dinner that evening with Hixie Rice, promotion director of the *Something* and once a neighbor of his Down Below. She had won over the locals with her energy and personality, while retaining her big-city ideas. They were meeting at the Old Stone Mill, a picturesque restaurant converted from a historic grist mill. The ancient waterwheel, wrecked during the spring floods, had been replaced by an accurate reproduction, but it would never be the same. As the purists said, 'Old is old, and new is new.'

Taking guests out to dinner was one of Qwilleran's favorite pastimes. Tonight he was the guest, and Hixie was treating on her expense account, which meant she was about to ask a favor. For the Ice Festival she had talked him into being grand marshal of the torchlight parade in sub-zero weather, but he was saved by the freak thaw.

As soon as the two news staffers were seated in their favorite alcove, an exuberant and extremely tall waitperson bounced up to their table. 'Hi, you guys,' he hailed them with the flip disrespect he reserved for VIPs. 'I've been offered a new job.'

'Here?' Qwilleran asked. 'If they want to make you head chef, I'm taking by business elsewhere.'

Derek Cuttlebrink had the height (six feet eight) and the outgoing nature that gave him carte blanche around town, and he assumed that everyone was interested in his personal life. His customers enjoyed his breezy style; young women adored him; audiences at the theater club's productions were wild about

Derek's performances. Now, to his credit, he had enrolled in the restaurant management program at the Moose County Community College. At last he was being viewed by serious observers as a 'comer' and not just an engaging clown.

'So whaddaya think?' Derek persisted. 'It's the manager's job at Chet's Bar and Barbecue in Kennebeck. It's a good deal.'

'Can you handle it and still finish school?' Qwilleran asked with genuine concern, being one of those who thought the young man had potential.

'I'll have to cut back on classes, but it'll look good on my resumé – manager of a hundred-seat restaurant, you know.'

'It depends on the restaurant. This one has an upscale menu and a certain cachet. You work flexible hours. You get good tips . . . Meanwhile, I think the lady would like a glass of white wine, Derek.'

'We have an acceptable little sauvignon blanc by the glass.'

Hixie took his recommendation, and Qwilleran ordered his usual Squunk water with a lemon twist. 'Just the zest, not the pith,' he requested. To Hixie he said, as the waiter left the table, 'What do you know about that joint in Kennebeck? Barbecue is not my favorite food.'

'It's a dump. I've been there to get ad contracts signed, and Dwight and I had a meal there once. It's very popular, and on Saturday nights it's really rowdy, but the food is good: mountains of pork barbecue with baked beans and coleslaw, served on plastic plates with plastic forks. The office is upstairs – also an apartment, sort of a pied à terre for Chet. He has a girlfriend, you know.'

'No, I didn't know,' Qwilleran said.

'He invited me in for a drink. It's quite luxurious. He can be a charming host, but he's a hard-driving businessman. He wanted Dwight to do his public relations, but Dwight's agency doesn't handle politicians.'

'Why do you suppose they offered Derek the job?'

'He has a personal following,' she said. 'As manager he'll bring in customers they've never had before.'

Derek returned with the drinks. 'Are you interested in tonight's specials? The soup is a chilled gazpacho garnished with crème fraîche, and the entrées are quail stuffed with mushroom and prune duxelle, and roasted snapper with étouffée sauce and spinach.'

'Give us a moment to think about it,' Qwilleran said.

Instead, they thought about Derek's offer. How would his girlfriend react? She was a Chicago heiress who had breezed in the previous summer, discovered Derek, and decided to stay. It was she who had convinced him to enroll in MCCC and who, according to gossip, paid his tuition.

Qwilleran said, 'A girlfriend with a large trust fund has a strong power of veto . . . But never mind that. What's on your mind?'

'The adult spelling bee. What do you think of it?'

'Great idea! I won all the spelling bees when I was a kid. I taught myself to read by studying cereal boxes on the breakfast table. I could spell "ingredients" when my peers were struggling with c-a-t.'

'You must have been unbearably precocious,' Hixie said.

'Cute, too. I had curls.'

Hixie hooted with laughter. 'I'd love to see an early picture of you.'

'My family pictures were all lost in a fire,' he said ruefully. It was an innocent prevarication, invented on the spur of the moment. Actually, all mementos of his past had disappeared during the Black Period of his life. He had not even a picture of his mother.

He was silent long enough for Hixie to change the conversation from flip to businesslike. 'Want to hear the names of our sponsors? This restaurant, the bank, the funeral home, the drug store, Gippel's Garage, and XYZ Enterprises, plus four not-for-profit sponsors: the Art Center, Theatre Club, Pickax Boosters, and Farmers' Collective.'

'If there's something you want me to do, Hixie, don't keep me in suspense.'

'Well, we need four officials: a master of ceremonies, someone to pronounce the words, a judge, and a timekeeper.'

'I volunteer for timekeeper.'

'No no no! With your wonderful theater voice you'll make a perfect wordmaster.'

'Why not Wetherby Goode? He has a wonderful radio voice.'

'He's going to be emcee.'

Derek, overhearing their conversation, said, 'I'm going to be on the spelling team for the Theatre Club. The boss here wanted me to spell for the Mill, but I may be gone by then.'

'What does your girlfriend think of your job offer?' Qwilleran asked.

'She wants me to do whatever's best for *me*,' he said with a smile so smug that Qwilleran wished he had a cream pie handy.

Nine

There were times when Koko made Qwilleran's head ache. It happened in the process of thought transference. The cat stared at the man's forehead, and the latter suddenly remembered it was time to feed the cats or change the litter in their commode. If slow in remembering, he experienced a dull ache between the eyes as the staring intensified.

For example, one day Qwilleran was slumping on the sofa with his feet on the coffee table, trying to think of a topic for the 'Qwill Pen.' Writing more than a hundred original columns a year put a strain on his inventiveness. Suddenly he swung his feet to the floor. He had an idea! Why not write a thousand words in praise of 'the ample moustache'? There had been many moustaches of amplitude, made famous by Mark Twain, Teddy Roosevelt, Pancho Villa, A.G. Spalding, Einstein, Groucho Marx, Simon Legree, British airmen in World War II . . . and Qwilleran himself knew a thing or two about the advantages and disadvantages of an ample moustache. He could easily milk a thousand words out of this topic.

He touched his forehead; the dull ache between the eyes was subsiding. He glanced at Koko, who was sitting on a large book on the coffee table. It was Qwilleran's pleasure to have a few important books on display: new, large-format, and handsome. They were good for browsing, effective conversation starters when he had guests, and especially appreciated by the bibliocat. Koko liked to sit on a large book – 'keeping it warm,' as Qwilleran said.

At this moment there were three books on the table: one on baseball history, one on Andrew Wyeth. The book that Koko was keeping warm was *Mark Twain A to Z*, a reference work with a jacket photo of the great American writer and his great moustache! Qwilleran slapped his forehead as the truth struck him: Koko had done it again! It was happening more and more in recent months. Qwilleran thought, Mine not to question how – or why; just accept it and be grateful.

It happened again on the day after Maude Coggin's funeral. He was lolling in the library, listening to tapes, and the Siamese were on hand, enjoying the propinquity of a family threesome. Yum Yum had her back turned, but Koko was watching Qwilleran intently. Halfway through the recording, it occurred to him that he had never listened to the taped conversation with Maude Coggin. Without finishing the reel, he switched to the reedy, high-pitched voice of the ninety-three-year-old. The cats were silent as she talked about her life – silent until the remark about 'taters and beans.' It brought an unexpected yowl from Koko – imperative enough to make Qwilleran play the passage again:

> 'But how do you cultivate all this acreage, Mrs Coggin?'

'Some young lads been tillin' it since Bert passed on. Hunnerd acres, all-a-ways back to the river. With them big machines, it ain't like it were. Good lads, they be. Paid me rent, they did, for twenty year, 'thout missin' a month.'

'I think I know them – the McBee brothers.'

'Don't rent the land no more. Sold the whole caboodle! No more taxes to pay, an' I can live here 'thout payin' rent. This new feller loves the soil, he does, like Bert did. He's gonna plant food crops – taters an' beans—'

Koko yowled again. Something about the message was bothering him, and Qwilleran was feeling tremors on his upper lip. He turned off the machine and phoned Rollo McBee. The farmer was in the barnyard, but his wife was eager to talk.

'Did you see the six o'clock news?' she asked excitedly. 'They showed the dogs, and Culvert, and the flowers, and the farmers, but not His Royal Highness, the mayor! Isn't that a joke? Him and his limousine!'

'You can compliment Culvert on his handling of the dogs,' Qwilleran said. 'And thank the pastor for his appropriate remarks – also the Farmers' Collective for turning out in such numbers.'

'Yes, it was a nice mark of respect for the poor soul, wasn't it?'

'Are you going to keep the dogs?'

'It looks like it. Culvert has decided he wants to be a veterinarian, so I guess we're starting with a five-bed dog hospital.'

'Good for him! . . . By the way, I'm glad to hear the Collective is sponsoring a team in the spelling bee.'

'So am I. It's a good cause. My sister-in-law is going to spell for the farmers, and Culvert would love to be on the team, but I told him it's just for adults. I bet he could beat 'em all, though.'

'I believe it,' Qwilleran said. Then he edged into his reason for calling. 'The organizers of the spelling bee would like to line up some Lockmaster sponsors, and I thought about Northern Land Improvement. Do you have their address and/or phone number?'

'Wait till I get the rent file, Mr Q.' She returned with a phone number but no address – only a post office box.

As the conversation ended, Koko walked from the room with a resolute step and slightly lowered head. Qwilleran thought, There's something on his mind; he's going to do something rash . . . A moment later there was a crash, accompanied by a metallic, bell-like clatter.

Qwilleran rushed to the foyer and found the antique brass handbell on the stone floor. There was no damage to the bell – only a small chip out of the flagstone.

'Bad cat!' he scolded. 'Very bad cat!'

Koko was not there to hear the reprimand.

The phone number of Northern Land Improvement was indeed a Lockmaster exchange, and Qwilleran called several times without getting an answer, or even an answering machine. Koko only made matters more irritating by bleating in a pessimistic monotone. Qwilleran said, 'I wish you'd stop your eternal kvetching!' yet he himself felt dispirited. He pounded his moustache with his fist. He was getting a hunch that Northern Land Improvement was a sub rosa division of XYZ Enterprises. It was the developers' scheme to obtain prime land at a favorable price. Sellers always upped their asking price when XYZ showed an interest in buying. As it had happened, Maude Coggin was a pushover, and after fleecing the aged woman out of her property, the bogus company would dissolve. That was Qwilleran's train of thought.

The Coggin farm backed up to the east fork of the Ittibittiwassee River, where water rushed over giant boulders and willows grew on the banks. It would be ideal for another Indian Village, closer to town. As for the rumors about a possible cemetery and an unsightly facility for the road commission, they could be no more than that – rumors, planted by XYZ.

Qwilleran had no respect for the organization that had botched Breakfast Island. Their residential projects made a good show but cut corners on construction. The Indian Village development in Suffix Township, where Qwilleran had bought a condo for winter use, was a case in point. Yet it was a moneymaker for XYZ.

His reflections were interrupted by a phone call from Derek Cuttlebrink's girlfriend, Elizabeth Hart. She had used some of her inherited wealth to open a gift boutique in the resort town of Mooseville. It was a venture that only an heiress could afford; gift boutiques had never done well in this fishing, boating, camping mecca. Bait shacks and T-shirt shops were the best bet. Qwilleran could guess why she was calling, and he was right.

'Has Derek told you about his job offer?' she asked anxiously without polite preliminaries.

'Yes, and he seems quite flattered,' he replied.

'Flattered! Have you ever been to that place, Qwill? He took me there one night, and I refused to stay. Horrid food, cheap service, mindless noise, with everyone shouting and screaming, while two television channels blasted at each other! It would be a dreadful work environment for anyone with Derek's qualities. I wish you would dissuade him from accepting, Qwill. He respects your judgment.'

'It's not for me to interfere with his career choices,' Qwilleran said, 'especially since I've never been to Chet's, but I'll tell you what I'll do: although barbecue isn't my favorite food, I'll sacrifice my tastebuds for your sake and go there tonight.'

'Thank you, thank you, Qwill. I'm counting on your support.'

'How's the boutique business?'

'My shop has just opened. When are you coming to see it?'

'This weekend.'

'How are the kitties?'

'They're fine. Yum Yum is chief bug catcher, and Koko is taking singing lessons from the birds.'

Hanging up, Qwilleran turned to Koko, who was listening with ears pointed inquisitively. 'That was Elizabeth Hart. She asked about you.'

As Qwilleran prepared dinner for the Siamese, they had their feline Happy Hour, chasing up and down the ramp. On the way up, Koko was the chaser and Yum Yum the chasee. At the top she slammed on the brakes and chased him all the way down. Time: sixteen seconds.

Qwilleran, dressed in grubbies for his dinner date at Chet's Bar & Barbecue, watched them gobble their canned crabmeat garnished with goat cheese. He said to them, 'You guys are dining better than I am tonight.'

There were two restaurants in Kennebeck. He and his friends patronized Tipsy's Tavern, founded in the 1930s and named after the owner's cat. Famous for high-caliber steak and fish, it occupied a sprawling log cabin. Chet's, in a cinder block building down the street, advertised 'Plain, Clean, and Friendly.'

When Qwilleran entered Chet's for the first time, all the tables were filled, and the atmosphere was hazy with smoke. Wetherby Goode signaled him from the bar. Normally known as a snappy dresser, he looked suitably grungy for the occasion.

'It wasn't easy,' he explained. 'I threw everything out in the driveway and ran over it with the van a couple of times.'

'It's crowded,' Qwilleran observed.

'It's always crowded. Let's have a drink at the bar and grab the first table that is available.' He turned to the red-headed bartender. 'Give the gentleman a Squunk water with a twist.'

'Hi, Mr Q,' said the young man. 'First time I ever seen you here.'

'I hope it won't be the last,' Qwilleran replied with tactful ambiguity.

In the center of the backbar was a portrait of Chester Ramsbottom, the one that Paul Skumble had been painting at the Art Center. Surrounding it were ten framed watercolors of shafthouses, labeled with the names of the ten historic mines, now abandoned: Buckshot, Goodwinter, Moosejaw, Old Glory, Big B, Dimsdale, Black Creek, Honey Hill, Smith's Folly, and Three Pines.

As Qwilleran analyzed the variations in light, shadow, angle, coloration, and season of the year, the bartender said, 'My great-grandfather worked in the Buckshot.'

'It had a cave-in this year during the flood,' the weatherman said.

'Yeah . . . Say, you guys live in Indian Village, don't you? I'm thinkin' of buyin' a condo there.'

The two customers glanced at each other. The condos at

Indian Village, despite their questionable construction, were pricey and occupied by successful professionals or persons of independent means.

Qwilleran said, 'They look good, but they're poorly constructed. You might be sorry.'

'The windows rattle,' Wetherby said.

'The floors bounce when a cat walks across them.'

'You can hear your next-door neighbor stirring sugar in his coffee.'

'I don't care. I always wanted to live there,' said the bartender. Then he leaned across the bar and said in a confidential voice, 'I'm gettin' promoted. I'm gonna be manager. It's a good deal . . . Hey! There's an empty table!'

The men made a dash for it, and when they sat down, Wetherby remarked, 'Chet must pay his manager good money if he can afford to live in Indian Village.'

'Somebody's got his signals crossed,' Qwilleran said. 'Derek Cuttlebrink's been offered the job.'

An overworked waitress interrupted. 'Pork, beef, or turkey? Sandwich or platter? Hot-mild, hot-hot or call 911?' In a matter of two seconds she was back with plastic plates piled high, while two fluffy white rolls teetered on the summit. 'If you want seconds of anythin', wave your fork.'

Everyone in the restaurant had to shout in order to be heard above the general din, and that resulted in a privacy of sorts – the privacy of deafening noise. Loudly Qwilleran and Wetherby talked about the dogs at the funeral, the parrot at the Art Center, and the weatherman's cat, Jet Stream.

'I've built Jet-boy a screened porch outside the kitchen window,' Wetherby said. 'It's two-by-two-by-two feet, screened on three sides and carpeted wall-to-wall. The land slopes down to the river, so he has an aerial view.'

'Does he stare at you when he wants something?' Qwilleran asked.

'No, he stares at the refrigerator when he wants food and stares at the kitchen window when he wants out.'

'That makes sense . . . Koko and Yum Yum have developed an unnatural friendship with seven crows who hang around, strutting back and forth like a drill team, bouncing up and down and fluttering their wings. I don't know exactly what's going on.'

'I have a cousin in Virginia who's a corvidologist, and she says crows are among the smartest of birds. She believes they'll be the next big animal fad. We've had frogs, owls, monkeys, pigs, whales, and dinosaurs. Now she thinks we're due for crow posters, crow T-shirts, crow jewelry, and who knows what else. Let's face it, crows are neat!'

'Thoreau liked the sound of crows,' Qwilleran said.

'Teresa – that's my cousin – has an idea for an animated feature film about crows, but she needs someone to work up a scenario. Would you be interested?'

'It would be quite a challenge, quite an adventure.'

'She's coming up here to visit family this summer, and we'll get you two together. I think you'll like her.'

The waitress kept returning, urging them to have more of this or more of that.

Wetherby said to Qwilleran, 'Did you know that Chet's father was a bootlegger during Prohibition? He had a blind pig in one of the abandoned shafthouses. The rule was: if you fall down the mineshaft, you've had too many.'

'I keep looking at his portrait and wondering if his expression is one of intelligence or craftiness. Paul Skumble is said to have a talent for revealing two sides of a persona. I've commissioned him to paint Polly's portrait.'

'You'd better chaperon the sittings,' Wetherby said. 'He also has a talent for charming the socks off his female subjects.'

'Thanks for warning me, Joe.' Wetherby Goode was an alias; his real name was Joe Bunker.

There was a scream at the other end of the room, and everyone in the restaurant joined in singing 'Happy Birthday.'

'Let's get out of here,' Qwilleran said. 'I've had enough barbecue to last a lifetime.'

Outdoors, the silence of a small town fell on their ears like a blessing. As they were saying good night, Qwilleran asked Wetherby if he had ever heard of Northern Land Improvement in Lockmaster.

'No, but I'm not much into real estate,' the weatherman said.

'I have their phone number but don't get an answer. If I could get in touch with the principals, I could throw some business their way. They must have registered their assumed name with the county clerk. Do you have any contact at the county building?'

'No, but I can track 'em down easily enough . . . If you're selling some of your lake frontage, I'll make an offer.'

'You'll have first refusal, Joe. Enjoyed the evening. Give Jet Stream my regards.'

Ten

Qwilleran's dinner at Chet's Bar & Barbecue was not a total loss. He always enjoyed the company of the WPKX meteorologist, a colorful character about town. Wetherby gave lectures to clubs, played cocktail piano at parties, and might enliven his weather forecast with a few glissandi from *Rustle of Spring.* Qwilleran himself would have given anything to be a jazz pianist and regretted his boyhood choice of batting practice over piano practice. Who but Wetherby Goode would have a corvidologist for a cousin? That was another plus added to the evening: the prospect of writing a scenario for an animated film about crows.

Equally rewarding was Qwilleran's introduction to Duff Campbell's shafthouses, which he had previously considered local landmarks to be sold to vacationers as souvenirs, like the Cape Hatteras lighthouse and Eiffel Tower. In one watercolor, painted on a hazy day, one could virtually feel the humidity; in a bleak winter scene the shafthouse rose from monstrous snowdrifts, its many-angled rooftops blanketed with a foot of snow – the picture of cold and loneliness.

Qwilleran looked up the artist in the telephone directory – there was a whole page of Campbells – and found a Duffield Campbell on Purple Point. The man who answered, after several rings, was indeed the Shafthouse King, and he seemed surprised and pleased to be called. He suggested the next morning for an appointment.

Purple Point was a peninsula extending two miles into the lake. In the boom years it had been a shipbuilding center, but that was a century ago. The economic collapse and decades of high winds and surf had changed it completely. Now it was a ribbon of sandy beach and vacation homes on the west shore, while the east shore was a strip of rocks.

Duff Campbell lived alone on the rocky beach, in a small weathered building that resembled a boathouse more than a dwelling. The man who came out to meet Qwilleran looked more like an aged fisherman than an artist. Although probably not more than sixty, he was thin to the point of frailty and slightly stooped from bending over his drawing board. It was a pleasantly warm day, but he wore two sweaters, and a stocking cap on his long gray hair.

'I'll bet you see some extravagant sunrises,' Qwilleran said.

'No two alike,' he replied with pleasure.

'You have a picturesque cottage, I must say.'

'A derelict rescued from the waves,' the artist explained. 'Moved it to higher ground and fixed it up – did it all myself. I was a lot younger then. Come around front and sit on the porch, and I'll see if I can scare up a cup of coffee.'

The porch was a concrete slab overlooking the water, with two flimsy folding chairs woven with plastic webbing. Qwilleran lowered himself warily into one of them, which squeaked and shuddered as it adjusted to his height and weight. When the host returned, carefully carrying two plastic mugs filled to the brim, he set them on an upended crate between the chairs.

'Surely you don't stay here in the winter, Mr Campbell.'

'Call me Duff,' he said. 'No, I used to have a room in town during bad weather. Now that I'm retired, I stay with relatives in Florida and teach at a university there.'

Qwilleran gave him a searching look as he set up his tape recorder on the crate. 'How long have you been painting?'

'Can't remember when I started. When I was a kid, they didn't teach art in the school here, but I started drawing with a pencil. We lived near the Old Glory shafthouse in those days. It was a mysterious sight, with its towering height, old boards, and quirky shape. Must have sketched it a thousand times from different angles. Then I discovered some brushes and paints in a Sears Roebuck catalogue and asked my parents if I could have them. They let me send for them. I'll never forget the thrill when the box arrived. Father was a preacher and said the Lord worked in mysterious ways. Mother was proud of me and let me send away for a correspondence course in art. I learned a few things from it, made mistakes, read all the art books in the library, and painted every weekend for the next fifty years.'

'Did you have a job during the week?'

'Sure did! Forty years at Pickax Feed and Seed. Retired when my paintings started selling. A gallery in Lockmaster takes most of 'em.'

'I must tell you, Duff, that your work has opened my eyes. You see things in those old wrecks that I didn't know were there. Thank you for the experience.'

The artist smiled for the first time and nodded modestly.

'Well, I've spent a lot of time looking at shafthouses – in thunderstorms, snow, sleet, scorching sun, dirty tornado weather, fog, sunrise, sunset, clear sky, cloudy sky . . .'

'I assume you paint on location.'

'Sure do! One thing to avoid, though, is wind. Blows stuff into the paint.'

'Why watercolors instead of oils?' Qwilleran found himself speaking in Duff's telegraphic style.

'Fast . . . spontaneous . . . no fussing. Sometimes people watch me, and they say, "Hey, hardly anythin' to it. He don't even cover the whole paper!" You can't help laughing at the dumb things they say.'

Qwilleran said, 'I'd like to see you work. I promise not to make any dumb remarks.'

'Let's go! Take my van,' Duff said.

They drove to Smith's Folly, the minesite closest to Purple Point, and Duff set up his gear, including a golf umbrella with a long handle to stick in the ground. 'Prefer painting in shade,' he explained. 'Eliminates glare on the white paper. Paint doesn't dry too fast . . .' For a taboret he used the bottom of the wooden crate that had transported a jar of brushes, a supply of water, tubes of paint, and a white china palette. He himself sat on a low folding stool. In front of him, at a lower level, was a painting board with rough white paper clipped in place.

When he began to paint, after making a rough pencil sketch, his arm and shoulder and wrist moved swiftly with ease and grace, brushing the paper with water and then flowing the color over it.

'Have to make fast decisions before it dries,' he noted tersely. 'Have to know when to stop, too.'

Qwilleran saw orange, purple, and blue disappearing into

the boards of the building that took form on the paper. He saw a dribble of water turning the painted surface into a row of weeds.

'How do you describe your style?' he asked as they drove back to the rocky beach.

'Descriptive but not realistic. Makes viewers use a little imagination. That's good for 'em. Imagination's a muscle; needs exercise.'

At Duff's cottage Qwilleran was invited indoors to see paintings tacked to the walls, awaiting frames. One scene, under a blue sky with puffy white clouds, had a deer grazing at the base of the architectural relic. Another, under a gloomy sky, showed a ghostly tower behind a high fence with a red DANGER sign; a hawk wheeled overhead.

'Different people like different mood-images,' Duff said.

'Well, I don't mind telling you, I'm vastly impressed. The column will run Tuesday, and it'll be a privilege and a pleasure to write. I hope we meet again.' They walked together toward Qwilleran's van. 'You may be interested to know what brought me here for an interview. Last night I saw the collection of ten shafthouses at Chet's Barbecue.'

The artist's face flushed alarmingly. 'Didn't get 'em from me!' he exploded. 'Must've bought 'em in Lockmaster. Wouldn't sell one to that snake for a million dollars!'

Qwilleran was momentarily speechless before recovering enough to ask innocently, 'Do you have something against Mr Ramsbottom?'

'Only that he ruined my family.'

'What do you mean?'

'*He ruined my family!* That's all I'll say.'

It was an awkward way to end an enjoyable visit. Qwilleran

slid behind the wheel, mumbling something, and Duff Campbell turned away and trudged back to his meagre cottage on the rocks.

The violent outburst from the gentle-mannered artist prompted Qwilleran to question Derek's job offer that so concerned his girlfriend, especially since the bartender thought he was being promoted to manager. The county commissioner's name often came up in the coffee houses. There were rumors that he bought votes and accepted kickbacks, as well as hints of a suppressed scandal. No details were ever disclosed. The locals kept their secrets from outsiders, as a measure of loyalty to their hometown, and Qwilleran was still an outsider from Down Below.

Now he headed for Mooseville and Elizabeth Hart's boutique. The resort town was little more than a two-lane highway between the lake and a high sand dune. On the lakeside were the municipal docks, private marinas, and the Northern Lights Hotel. At the foot of the dune were the Shipwreck Tavern and other commercial buildings built of logs, or concrete cast and painted to resemble logs.

One of them was the Nasty Pasty, a café that served a superior version of the regional specialty: not too large, not too rich, with not too thick a crust and *no turnips*! The controversy about pasty ingredients was forever ongoing, and Qwilleran expected some local politician (probably Chet Ramsbottom) to promote an ordinance prohibiting suet and making turnips mandatory. His pasty platform would no doubt get him elected to state legislator, then governor.

The Nasty Pasty was a light, cheerful café decorated with fishing nets, boat lines, and plastic seagulls perched on old piling.

'Hi, Mr Q! Haven't seen you for a while,' said the waitress.

'Gonna have a pasty?' Assured that he was, she asked, 'Would you like Dijon mustard or horseradish?'

'*What!* Did I hear you correctly?' he replied in consternation.

'That's what some of the tourists ask for.'

He said, 'I like pasties to taste like pasties, hot dogs to taste like hot dogs, and lamb chops to taste like lamb chops. I'm a purist. If you put mustard and horseradish and ketchup and chopped onions and pickle relish on everything, it all tastes alike. No thanks!'

She served him a pasty neat and said, 'Everybody's sorry about the old lady. I would've liked to go to the funeral. It was on TV. Those old dogs broke my heart.'

Customers at nearby tables joined in. 'That woman was a saint. Why is it that abandoned animals always know what house to go to? . . . Something should be done about homeless dogs. All we have is a part-time dogcatcher, and then what does he do with the dogs he picks up?'

'You should write letters to the paper,' Qwilleran said. 'Lots of letters. That's what it takes to get the politicians' attention.'

The owner of the café came to his table with the coffee server. 'Now or later, Mr Q? What brings you to town?'

'Just looking around. What do you think of the new boutique?'

'It's different. A bit citified for Mooseville, but God knows we don't need any more T-shirt shops. Elizabeth's nice – very enthusiastic. She came to a C. of C. meeting and spoke right up. Got herself on the beautification committee.'

Qwilleran had first met her on Breakfast Island, where she was unhappy and unfocused after the death of her father. In moving to Moose County she had found her niche, and it was a pleasure to see her live up to her potential.

Her boutique, though invitingly rustic, was not truly in tune with the campers, boaters, and fishermen who vacationed in the area. It was Saturday afternoon, however, and several of them were browsing in the shop when Qwilleran entered. There were no souvenir mugs, plastic seagulls, or raunchy bumper stickers, but there was a 'rainy day corner' with paperback books, indoor games, toys, and jigsaw puzzles. Otherwise the stock represented Elizabeth's own taste: a case of antique jewelry and other curios; exotic hats, vests, caftans and tunics from other continents; and a table of tarot cards, horoscopes, booklets on numerology and handwriting analysis, rune stones, and aromatherapy oils.

Elizabeth was talking with animation to a trio of bemused hikers when she spotted Qwilleran. She excused herself and beckoned him to the rear of the shop. In a desperate whisper she said, 'It's too late, Qwill! He's taken the job!'

'Sorry to hear that,' he said, 'but bear in mind that he's intelligent and six feet eight and will be able to handle any situation that arises.'

'That's not what I worry about. He'll come home with his clothing reeking of cigarette smoke and stale beer!'

'Does anyone know why the previous manager left?'

'His wife got a job Down Below, closer to her parents, who are elderly.'

'I see.'

'Another thing that bothers me, Qwill: the bartender had been promised the manager's job, and Derek expects some hostility in that quarter.'

'I see.'

She said with a sigh, 'It's such a disappointment. I have some capital to invest, and I've dreamed of backing Derek in an upscale dining club as soon as he finishes school. But now he'll have to cut back on classes – and for what good reason? A barbecue is no background for running a fine restaurant.'

Qwilleran was genuinely sympathetic and searched for some comforting words. 'I applaud your ambition, Elizabeth. Don't give up; this detour could be shorter than you think. Sometimes a setback can lead to an unexpected leap ahead. Remember: if you hadn't been bitten by that snake at Breakfast Island, you wouldn't be here today. You're good for Derek, and everything will work out well, I'm convinced. Think positive thoughts.'

He said to himself, Here I go again with platitudes – playing kindly uncle to distressed youth. It was a role he avoided, yet his willingness to listen and the concerned look in his brooding eyes inevitably involved him.

To cheer her up he said, 'You have some unusually interesting things in your shop. How's business?'

'Weekends I draw mostly the browsers, but that's all right. Traffic is important. My best customers come during the week – Chicagoans vacationing at the Grand Island Club. They come over here in their yachts, have a drink at the Shipwreck Tavern, and lunch at the Nasty Pasty. They think it's all so *quaint*! Then they come in here and tell me about it and spend some money. I've sold quite a few pieces of jewelry that belonged to my paternal grandmother and great-grandmother. And I had two sterling silver cigarette cases that I sold to a collector of old silver . . . The checker set is unusual. The board is inlaid ebony and teak; the red men are cinnabar and the black men are jet. It's a conversation piece, even if you don't play. Does Koko play checkers? I remember he played dominoes on the island.'

'And he played a mean game of Scrabble Down Below . . . Let me think . . . I'm getting an idea. I have an eighteenth-century English tavern table that's just standing around with nothing on it. It's important enough to demand something of equal status on its surface. At least, that's what my designer says. I'll take it!'

'I'm happy to see it going to you, Qwill. I just want it to have a good home. It belonged to one of my ancestors, a railroad magnate, who saved it from the great Chicago fire in 1871.'

'Elizabeth, I don't question your veracity,' Qwilleran said, 'but you sound exactly like a hard-core antique dealer.'

'It's true! And it comes in its own leather case. I'll put it together for you.'

When the transaction was completed and Qwilleran was leaving the shop, he said, 'Seriously, Elizabeth, if Derek is going to sidetrack his career to work for Mr Ramsbottom, I think he should have some sort of agreement in writing. Who's your attorney?'

'He's in Chicago.'

'Do you know him well enough to phone him and ask for some informal advice?' He smoothed his moustache as he spoke.

'He's my godfather.'

'Then do it!'

She snatched a yo-yo from the toy display. 'Take this to the kitties – with my compliments.'

On the way home Qwilleran wondered about the viper – or was it a serpent? – who had ruined Duff Campbell's family and was now about to be Derek's employer. How this ruin had been accomplished was a tantalizing question, and unanswered questions bothered Qwilleran more than hunger, thirst, or deerflies. Any inquiry had to be handled with circumspection. In no way did he want to be associated with such a nosey search.

He was too prominent a figure in the community, and anything he did or said was bandied about with glee.

Amanda Goodwinter might know the answer. She was a politician herself and a foe of Chester Ramsbottom for some unexplained reason. She was city; he was county.

Or Fran Brodie, the police chief's daughter, could be approached in strict confidence . . . but she was still on vacation.

Or Brodie himself might talk if invited over for a nightcap.

Or Polly could sound out her assistant, who was an encyclopedia of local secrets.

Or Lisa Compton would definitely know. Her maiden name was Campbell, but would she talk? Celia Robinson could get her to talk. They both worked at the Senior Care Facility – Celia as a volunteer – and they were good friends. Furthermore, Celia liked undercover assignments. Celia was the solution.

Arriving at the barn, Qwilleran found Yum Yum rifling wastebaskets and Koko watching crows through the foyer window.

'Treat!' he announced, and the two responded at once, racing to the kitchen and colliding broadside.

After they had crunched their Kabibbles, he produced Elizabeth's yo-yo and bounced it up and down for their amusement, saying, 'A friend of yours sent this to you. Jump for it!' They followed the rise and fall of his hand with dreamy inattention, sitting side by side on their briskets. They were only mildly curious about this latest eccentricity of the person who provided their bed and board.

'Come on! Let's play! Jump! Oompah! Oompah!'

They looked at each other as if questioning his sanity.

'Cats!' he muttered and threw the yo-yo into the wastebasket.

It was Saturday; Polly would have had her first session with the portrait artist, wearing her blue silk dress, sitting in a highback Windsor in front of leather-bound books inherited from the family of her late husband, and holding a volume of *Hamlet*. Even before the picture was painted, Qwilleran could see it in his mind's eye, and he was eager to hear the details of its making.

Meanwhile, a phone call from Celia Robinson demanded his attention. 'Are you there?' she asked.

'No, I'm only a reasonable facsimile of the person you called.'

Her shrill laughter made him move the receiver away from his ear. 'I have some things for you, Chief. Okay if I bring them down there now?'

'Please do, and I hope you can stay for a glass of fruit juice.'

The Siamese knew she was driving through the evergreen woods long before the little red car appeared. Qwilleran went out to meet her.

'Look in the backseat,' she said. 'It's my brother-in-law's picture, and I've got some things for your freezer. Are you going to show me the picture? . . . Or is it something you think I shouldn't see,' she added slyly.

'It's strictly adult art, but I think you're old enough to view it without damage to your morals,' he said, bracing himself for another shriek of laughter. Then, while Celia put the chili cartons in the freezer and the potato salad in the refrigerator, he removed the staples from the crated art and presented *The Whiteness of White*.

'What is it?' she asked after a moment's hesitation.

'A snowflake, but it may have some erotic symbolism.'

'You're kidding me, Chief. Why is it . . . ? How is it . . . ?'

'It's an intaglio. The design is pressed into the paper. Don't ask me how. I merely bought a raffle ticket and won.'

'Where are you going to hang it?'

'Good question,' he said as he poured cranberry juice into stemmed wine glasses.

They took their drinks into the lounge area, and Celia rummaged in her oversize handbag until she found a business card. 'How do you like this, Chief?'

It read: 'Robin O'Dell Catering . . . Luncheons, Receptions.'

'Well! Congratulations!' he said. 'That's a pleasant-sounding name, sort of Sherwoodian.'

'If you say so,' she laughed.

'Does it mean Mr O'Dell is involved?'

She nodded happily. 'We're going to be partners. His house has a big kitchen.'

Qwilleran had suspected the two retirees were headed for some kind of partnership. They were well matched. 'I hope this won't interfere with the . . . undercover work you do for me.'

'Oh, no, no! Never! Is there anything I can do for you right now, Chief?'

'Yes, there is. Get out your notebook.' He waited while she dug into her handbag and finally found a pad and pencil. 'There is a tract of land between Trevelyan Road and the river, bounded on the north by Cemetery Road and on the south by Base Line. I don't want it known that I'm interested, but you might go to the county building and find out who owns it. If the owner is Northern Land Improvement, it's supposed to be registered as an assumed name – in which case, get the names of the principals.' He stroked his moustache; he'd be willing to wager they were Exbridge, Young and Zoller.

'That should be easy,' Celia said.

'And if you'd like an assignment that's challenging, try to

get Lisa Compton to tell you about a Campbell scandal that happened a few years back. Commissioner Ramsbottom was involved.'

Eleven

It was Saturday evening. The Siamese had dined royally on red salmon and had groomed themselves fastidiously when Qwilleran brought the checker set in from his van and set it up on the antique tavern table. Like hawks, the cats watched from an aerial vantage: she on the fireplace cube, he on the Pennsylvania German *Schrank.* As soon as the twelve red checkers and twelve black checkers were arranged on the squares, Koko came sailing down from the tall cupboard and landed on the checkerboard, sending the discs flying in all directions. Yum Yum came down too and hid one under a rug.

'Cats!' Qwilleran spluttered. He gathered up the set and put it in a safe place before dressing for dinner.

Polly lived in the rustic riverside development called Indian Village, as did many of their friends. Qwilleran himself owned a condominium for winter use when the barn was impractical.

From there it was a short drive to Tipsy's Tavern, where the menu was limited but the quality superb.

As soon as they were on the road, Polly said, 'I'm afraid I have to report growing unrest at the library.'

'Because of the electronic cataloguing? I'm not surprised.'

'We offered a series of workshops to acquaint subscribers with its use, and only two persons signed up. And they were young, I might add. Now three of our volunteers have resigned because they feel uncomfortable with the new system, and you know how much we depend on volunteers. Most of them are of retirement age, and they seem to like the status quo.'

Qwilleran said, 'If it's a matter of being shorthanded, why not hire some teens for the summer? By the time they go back to school, everyone will be getting adjusted to automation. Get the board to budget a few extra dollars for a summer youth program.'

Tipsy's Tavern was busy but not noisy; a happy rumble of voices set the tone. Qwilleran and Polly sat in the main dining room, under the oil portrait of Tipsy, the founder's black-and-white cat. The furnishings and table settings were countrified; the waitpersons were older women who mixed neighborliness with roadhouse efficiency. 'Steak or fish? How do you want it done? Anything from the bar?'

Qwilleran said to Polly, 'Did you have your first sitting today? I ran into Paul Skumble at the Art Center this week, and he said you'll be a joy to paint. He said one's features express one's thoughts, and you have a lively mind.'

'How nice of him to say that! He's a kind man . . . Speaking of portraits, did you read about Ramsbottom in the Newsbyte column?' Sandwiched between brief items about a runaway cow and a jack-knifed truck, it had read:

A portrait of Chester Ramsbottom honoring his 25 years of public service was unveiled yesterday at a dedication ceremony at Chet's Bar & Barbecue. City and county officials attended. The portrait was painted by Paul Skumble.

Polly said, 'I knew the man would find a way to charge his portrait to the taxpayers! I wonder if Paul was paid with a Moose County check. I'll ask him. He'll tell me. I'll be very sweet to him.'

'Not too sweet, please,' Qwilleran warned.

'I've discovered that he likes a sip of brandy while he's working.'

The salad was served: torn iceberg lettuce with French dressing, and she said, 'One has to admit that this wonderful restaurant serves a sad salad. I always fork through mine, hoping to find half a cherry tomato or a slice of radish.'

'Your complaint is falling on deaf ears,' said Qwilleran, who avoided salads of any kind. 'Tell me about your date with Skumble.'

'It was hardly a date, dear,' she said, reproving him with an arched eyebrow. 'It was a business appointment resulting from your insistence on having my portrait painted.'

He shrugged an apology. 'Okay, I retract that. Tell me about your business appointment.'

'Today he did the underpainting. I didn't see it afterward. He turned the easel to the wall.'

'Weren't you tempted to peek?'

'Paul's advice is: "no peek – no critique – until it's finished," and I concur.'

'What do you talk about during the sitting?'

'There's no real conversation. He concentrates on his painting, and I sit there reciting *Hamlet* to myself.'

Qwilleran chuckled. 'I can imagine his confusion as your expression changes from the melancholy prince of Denmark – to the passionate Gertrude – to pompous Polonius – to gentle Ophelia. I suppose he'll be back tomorrow afternoon.'

'He promised to show up at one o'clock, but he's not very punctual . . . And I don't know whether I should tell you this, Qwill, but he asked if he could stay overnight in the guestroom – to avoid the long commute. I told him, as politely as I could, that it wasn't available at weekends.'

Qwilleran patted his moustache. 'That was nervy, if you ask me! If he makes any more passes, let me know, and we'll get someone else to paint over his underpainting.'

The entrées were served, and they were silent for a while. Polly asked for another wedge of lemon; Qwilleran asked for horseradish and then said, 'Last night I took my life in my hands and went to Chet's Barbecue with Wetherby. Derek has accepted a job as manager, and I wanted to check it out.'

She was aghast. 'I can't believe it. Derek has more class than that!'

'Was there a scandal involving Chet's Bar a few years ago – before I came to town?'

'I vaguely remember. Ramsbottom was charged with something, but charges were dropped. That was before we had a real newspaper. The *Pickax Picayune*, with all due respect to Junior's late father, never printed anything that might embarrass anyone.'

'Koko did something strange when I came home. He bit me! He's never done that before.'

She gasped. 'Did he draw blood?'

'No, he just wanted to get my attention, but it was a forceful way of doing it. We were having our bedtime read, and he suddenly nipped the thumb holding the book. I assumed he was telling me to close the book, serve his nocturnal snack, and turn out the bleeping lights. He's been edgy lately.'

'What were you reading?'

'A Rebecca West that I picked up this week. *The Birds Fall Down.*'

'Today Brutus was sniffing Catta indiscreetly, and that little girl turned and hit him on the nose – hard! Was he surprised! It was laughable.'

Qwilleran said, 'She'll grow up to be a tough lady cat who knows her rights and doesn't take harassment from man or beast. I say we should groom her for the first feline vice president.'

'I say you're hallucinating, dear. How's your steak?'

'Perfect! How's your fish?'

'Delectable!'

'Any world-shaking news at Indian Village?'

'Yes! My lovely next-door neighbors are leaving, and who knows what noisy characters will move in? The walls are so thin, as you well know, and the Cavendish sisters are so quiet, I'm spoiled.'

'Where are they going?'

'To the new retirement village near Kennebeck. Ruth can't drive anymore, and Jennie has trouble with her knees. At Ittibittiwassee Estates they can have a one-story unit, and transportation is available. Also there's an infirmary on the grounds.'

'What about their cats?' Qwilleran asked.

'Small indoor pets are permitted. They wouldn't go anywhere without Pinky and Quinky.'

'Did you know that the Ittibittiwassee Estates development isn't on the Ittibittiwassee River? It's on Bloody Creek, but they thought Bloody Creek Estates would lack marketing appeal.'

Polly added, 'Especially since they have so many accidents at the Bloody Creek bridge. They should install some kind of safeguard.'

'They keep talking about it, but nothing is ever done. Perhaps Junior should write a hard-hitting editorial.'

'By the way, Qwill, did Hixie call you about the spelling bee?'

'She did, and she twisted my arm. She wants me to be the wordmaster. I wanted to be timekeeper.'

'Your talents would be wasted. Anyone can hold a stopwatch and ring a bell.'

'What's your assignment?'

'Chairing the wordlist committee. We have to compile a list of three hundred words, ranging from those commonly misspelled to the virtually unspellable. It's a practice list for the spellers to study in advance.'

'I'll give you two for your list,' he said. '*Believable* and *knowledgeable* have plagued me all my life. To E or not to E? That is the question. I've considered having my left forearm tattooed: *No E before the A in believable*.'

'I have a problem with *seize*, *siege*, and *sieve*,' she said. 'Why don't we go home and make some wordlists? We can have coffee and dessert there.'

On Sunday afternoon, while Polly was again sitting for the portrait painter, Qwilleran wrote a thousand words about Duff Campbell and his watercolors. Mrs Fish-eye's influence was in high gear, and the column virtually wrote itself, leaving him time to think about Polly's wordlist. Batting words around gave him as much pleasure as batting the horsehide had ever done.

He began jotting down words that had tripped up spellers in the days when he was winning bees. Confusion over single and double consonants was one stumbling block: *raccoon* and *vacuum*, *embarrass* and *harass*, *exaggerate* and *belligerent*, *lassitude* and *verisimilitude*, *confetti* and *graffiti*, *irrational* and *irascible*, *parrot* and *pirouette* . . .

His mind wandered to Jasper . . . and the Art Center . . . and the Click Club that was being dedicated. It was John Bushland's idea – a space on the lower level for photo exhibitions, slide showings, video-viewing, and talks on photography. 'Bushy,' as he was called, was the town's leading commercial photographer, who also freelanced for the *Moose County Something*. Qwilleran believed he should put in an appearance.

Beverly Forfar met him in the lobby of the Art Center. 'Are you coming to see the Click Club? It's a neat facility! And John Bushland is adorable. Is he married?'

'Not now,' Qwilleran said.

'And we have another reason to celebrate. Jasper has moved to another address! He's no longer insulting our visitors.'

'I hope he left voluntarily,' Qwilleran quipped. 'Otherwise we could be sued for violating animal rights.'

She lowered her voice a tone. 'I've also told Phoebe she can't have that butterfly contraption. This is an art center, and we have to have some standards. What do you think, Mr Q?'

'If you're the manager, you have to manage.'

'Well, Phoebe's miffed about it. See if you can talk some sense into her head.'

He went to the Butterfly Girl's studio instead of the Click

Club. 'Where's your buddy?' he asked.

The artist flinched, surprised out of her intense concentration on her work. 'Oh, it's you, Mr Q. I didn't know anyone was around. They're all downstairs.'

'Where's Jasper?'

'Jake took him,' Phoebe said, looking pleased.

'I thought Jake's roommate was allergic to feathers.'

'Oh, that's all changed now. Jake bought a condo in Indian Village.'

'Did he get his promotion?' Qwilleran inquired casually.

'No, he's going to continue doing what he likes best – tending bar and gabbing with customers. But he just got an inheritance from an old uncle in Montana. That's where Jake comes from. He says it's just like Moose County, only larger.'

'An apt description,' Qwilleran said. 'So that's a stroke of luck, isn't it? And what else is new in your glamorous young life? Are you going to be on the drug store spelling team?' He was making idle conversation as he contemplated the news about Jake.

'I don't think so. I'm not getting along with my parents right now. The trouble is . . .'

'The trouble is what?'

'I broke the news that I'm moving into Jake's condo.'

'I see.' He was unable to think of a better response.

'Another problem is that Jake doesn't want me to raise butterflies. He's squeamish about caterpillars, and I've just started a new hatch of Painted Ladies. Would you like to take them, Mr Q? They'll be ready to fly in a couple of weeks, and then you can set them free . . . See! They're over there on Jasper's table. They have to be kept out of direct sunlight.'

They occupied a cardboard box about the size of a small TV,

with viewing windows of clear plastic on the top and three sides. There were several of them, crawling around and munching on green leaves – not attractive insects, being spiny and wormlike.

'Well, I don't know,' Qwilleran said. 'Are you sure these ugly things are going to turn into butterflies?'

'I'll show you a picture of the Painted Lady,' Phoebe said. 'I love to paint them. They have a lacy pattern of orange and black with white spots.'

'Hmmm,' he mused, thinking he might salvage his uninspired interview with Phoebe and get a column out of it after all. 'Let me think about it for a while. I'm going down to the Click Club, and I'll get back to you.'

Going downstairs, he could hear the hubbub on the lower level; apparently there was a good turnout. He was halfway down when he saw a white head of hair coming up.

'Thornton Haggis!' he said.

'It's too crowded. You can't see a thing. Go back up,' said the man from the monument yard.

Qwilleran backed up and, at the top of the flight, said, 'Did you notice that Jasper's gone?'

Thornton nodded gravely. 'And now our friend Beverly wants Phoebe to get rid of her butterfly box.'

'I know. She offered it to me.'

'You, too? Already my wife thinks I'm on the brink and if I went home with a box of caterpillars, she'd know I'm over the edge. How about you?'

'In my case it might be ink for the "Qwill Pen." It would be something different, at any rate. But I need to ask some questions.'

They presented themselves in Phoebe's studio. 'You decided?' she asked eagerly.

'It all depends on what it entails,' Qwilleran said. 'I may not be qualified to be midwife to a flock of butterflies.'

'It's simple,' she said. 'First you keep the caterpillars supplied with food. There's a door at the back of the box for putting in green leaves and cleaning out the frass.'

'Frass? What's that?' he asked. 'I'm afraid to ask.'

'I'll give you an instruction booklet. If you watch, you can see them spinning silk. Then they turn into chrysalises, and nothing happens for a few days until suddenly the butterflies struggle to unfurl their wings and get out. It's magic, Mr Q! You see them pumping up their wings and then starting to flutter about. At that point you give them some flowers sprinkled with sugar-water. After a few days you take the box outside and open the door and they fly into the great outdoors, so happy to be free! It gives you a wonderful feeling of joy!'

'Do you guarantee that? I'll have to go and get my van. I walked down here.'

Thornton offered to drive him and the caterpillars home, and on the way to the barn he asked, 'Do you know if they ever found out who broke in and stole Daphne's nudes? My sons and I were having drinks at the Shipwreck Tavern the other night, and the bartender showed us a drawing he had bought from a customer, who'd bought it from another guy in another bar. It sure looked like Daphne's work, but the signature was blotted out.'

'Did he say how much he'd paid for it?'

'No, and we didn't ask.'

Thornton had never been to the barn before, and when he saw the ramps spiraling up the octagonal wall to the lofty roof, he said, 'Hey! This is the Guggenheim of Moose County! Was it your idea? Wait till my wife hears about this!'

'All the credit goes to a designer from Down Below. It was the last job he ever did.'

'Where are the famous Siamese?'

'Watching you. Don't make one false move!'

They put the butterfly box in the guestroom on the second balcony, away from direct sunlight and away from inquisitive cats. Then Qwilleran served refreshments in the gazebo.

Thornton said, 'I see you don't have any grass to cut. My wife likes a broad green lawn, but she doesn't have to cut it. No matter how easy they make power-mowing, it's still *something else to do*! My two sons used to do the grass-cutting, but now they have houses and lawns of their own. I don't think you've ever met Eric and Shane, have you? I'm proud of them – good family men, good businessmen. If you ever want to write a column on the sand and gravel business, call them; they have all the dirt.'

'It may come to that,' Qwilleran said.

'They sell to the county, you know, and one of the highway engineers tipped them off about a big paving job planned for Trevelyan Road, north of Base Line.'

'So that corroborates the rumor we heard from Gary at the Black Bear. It means that a few acres across from the Art Center will look like a slum. Who's selling the county the land?'

'They're not buying it; they're leasing it. The owner of the property doesn't want to sell, and you can understand why. The value of that tract is going to zoom sky-high in a few years. It backs on the river, and some smart developer like XYZ could build another Indian Village there.'

Qwilleran thought, It's already owned by XYZ Enterprises, a.k.a. Northern Land Improvement. No doubt the 'new feller' who charmed Maude Coggin into selling her land cheap, who 'loved the soil,' who was going to plant 'taters and beans' was Don Exbridge, the X of XYZ Enterprises. Qwilleran had never liked him.

Twelve

Paroxysm, arraign, zealot, catastrophe, aphid, privilege, concatenation, xenophobe. Qwilleran found the compilation of a wordlist irresistible, and he kept adding to it as he drank his breakfast coffee. *Octogenarian, nonagenarian, paradigm, heinous, mnemonics, etymology*, and yes, *irresistible.* To escape from this obsessive collecting of words, he took to his bicycle.

His Silverlight was stabled in one of the stalls of the carriage house, and his janitorial service kept it shining. The copy for his Tuesday column was in his pocket as he biked downtown on Monday morning, the sun shining on his yellow helmet and the gleaming spokes. At least once on every outing someone on the sidewalk would shout, 'Heigh-ho, Silver!'

He wheeled it into the lobby of the *Something* and hung his helmet on the handlebars, knowing there would be a group of fellow staffers around it when he finished his business.

After tossing his copy on Junior Goodwinter's desk and commenting on the outcome of Sunday's ballgame in

Minneapolis, he went to the business office to pick up his fan mail. The office manager, Sarah Plensdorf, was one of his avid fans; she felt it a privilege to hand him his mail personally. She was an older woman from a good family, well educated but rather prim. Qwilleran had believed her to be descended from a wealthy shipbuilder on Purple Point, but – no thanks to Thornton Haggis – he now suspected a less respectable heritage. He and Sarah had dined together one evening, under unusual circumstances, and had discovered a shared interest: baseball.

'What did you think of the game yesterday?' he asked.

'Wasn't it thrilling? If Father had been alive, he would have had a heart attack!'

Briefly he thought of flying Sarah to Minneapolis for a weekend game while Polly was busy with Paul Skumble, but it was only a whim. Everyone in the office would talk, and Polly would go into shock.

'Would you like me to slit the envelopes for you, Qwill?' she asked.

'I'd appreciate it,' he said, knowing that she liked to perform this small service. While waiting, he noticed a trio of butterfly paintings on the wall over her desk. No doubt they had been there right along, before lepidoptera had entered his consciousness. 'Those are Phoebe Sloan's,' he remarked.

'Aren't they beautiful? A California Dogface, Hungarian Jester, and Queen Alexandra Birdwing, which is an endangered species. I have them all over my apartment, too. They give my spirit a lift whenever I enter a room.'

'How many do you have?'

'Eighteen, and she's doing an Orange Albatross for me. I was the first to start collecting, and now everyone's doing it. We're thinking of starting a Phoebe Sloan fan club and getting together to help the conservation of rare butterflies.'

'Your enthusiasm is commendable,' he murmured.

'Well, I've known Phoebe since she was a baby, you see, and I'm terribly proud of her. Our families have known each other for generations. We belong to the same church. I was a bridesmaid at her parents' wedding.'

She spoke happily, and he wondered if she knew about the Sloans' current family problem. If so, she was too well bred to mention it. As for himself, he followed Shakespeare's advice: *Give every man thy ear but few thy voice.* Nevertheless, he said slyly, 'I suppose Phoebe will be spelling for the drug store team.'

'No doubt!' she said with the same cheerful conviction that all's right with the world.

'I'd like to write a column about Phoebe's specialty but haven't been able to get a handle on it. Perhaps I should interview collectors and get their individual viewpoints, especially if they organize a fan club with a constructive agenda.'

'Oh, please do, Qwill! You don't have to mention me. I just want Phoebe to have some nice publicity.'

He left the office carrying two dozen fan letters and reflecting that Sarah Plensdorf was a remarkably kind, selfless woman. She gave generously to good causes and spoke ill of no one. He would have to consult the county historian about the Plensdorf background: Was it shipbuilding, or what?

He was on the way to the lobby to retrieve his Silverlight from an admiring throng when footsteps came running down the hall behind him.

'Qwill! Qwill!' came a woman's anxious voice. It was Hixie Rice. 'Got a minute?' She beckoned him to follow her to the conference room. 'Sit down, Qwill.' She closed the door.

'I smell a sinister plot,' he said lightly, then noticed that she looked troubled. Uh-oh, he thought; has another good idea bombed? . . . She's jinxed!

'We have a problem,' she blurted. 'It's the spelling bee. I don't dare tell Arch – not after the Ice Festival fiasco.'

'That was an act of God, Hixie. No one could predict we'd get April weather in February . . . What's the hang-up now? I thought you had ten enthusiastic sponsors lined up.'

'We do! We do! And they've paid their entry fees up front. It's their employees who are dragging their feet. They don't want to stand up and spell in front of an audience. Relatives of employees are eligible, too, but we've still got only seven spellers. We need thirty to man ten teams.'

'Do they know they'll have a practice wordlist to study in advance?'

'They know that, and still we haven't been able to spark any interest. The *Lockmaster Ledger* is sponsoring a similar event – they always copy us – and they're finding the same lack of response. I don't understand it, Qwill! Adult spelling bees are highly successful Down Below.'

'They draw from a population of millions,' he reminded her. 'Also, what works for them doesn't necessarily work 400 miles north of everywhere.'

'Could you suggest a solution?' she asked without much show of hope.

'I'd need to think about it. Give me a few hours, and I'll get back to you. And cheer up, Hixie! There's a solution to every problem.'

Qwilleran returned to the lobby, answered questions about his bike, put on his yellow helmet, and pedaled home. Although he claimed to do his best thinking while biking or sitting in an easy chair with his feet up, he had not produced a single useful thought by the time he wheeled the Silverlight into the carriage house.

From there he trudged through the woods to the barn. The kitchen window was open, and he could hear the Siamese yowling through the screen long before he came in view. It was twelve noon and time for their treat. That was the reason for the clamor – not any eagerness for his agreeable presence. That was all right. He was used to playing second fiddle to a bowl of Kabibbles.

Having taken care of their needs, he prepared coffee and carried a mug to the lounge area where he could sit with his feet up and doodle ideas on a legal pad. The Siamese watched, sitting comfortably on their briskets – Yum Yum on the rug, Koko on the coffee table, keeping a book warm.

What the spelling bee needed, Qwilleran told himself, was a new approach entirely: a new name for the event . . . new terminology . . . a new format.

'Yow!' came a comment from the coffee table.

'Thank you for the encouragement,' Qwilleran said. 'In other words, what we need is a whole new ball game!'

Koko jumped down to the floor and ran around in circles.

'Ball game! That's it! Of course! Why not?'

Only then did he realize that the book Koko had been keeping warm was *Baseball, An Illustrated History.* Had Koko sensed the problem that was on his mind? The idea of a telepathic connection between man and animal was not unthinkable in today's science. But could a cat – even one with sixty whiskers – go so far as to convey a solution? Not likely. It was simply a coincidence that the baseball book had been on the coffee table at that time. Even so, stranger things had happened in that household.

As for the baseball theme, it was perfect for Moose County, where folks went berserk over a softball game between scrub teams. How about ten teams of all-star spellers competing in an orthographic pennant race, with the mayor of Pickax pitching out the first word? And how about a World Series in September between the pennant winners of Moose County and Lockmaster? And how about having the Pickax barbershop quartet sing 'Take me out to the spell game'?

Qwilleran looked for the issue of the *Something* that had first announced names of sponsors. The ten teams would need nicknames, and the spellers would need baseball caps in their team colors. And how about T-shirts with the team name on the front and the speller's number on the back? 'You can't tell the spellers without a scorecard!' Hawkers could sell peanuts and Cracker Jack. He poured another mug of coffee and went to work on the nicknames:

MONEYBAGS . . . Pickax People's National Bank
NAILHEADS . . . XYZ Enterprises
OILERS . . . Gippel's Garage
LADDERS . . . Pickax Boosters
CHOWHEADS . . . Old Stone Mill
DAUBERS . . . The Art Center
PILLS . . . Sloan's Drug Store
MUCKERS . . . Farmers' Collective
HAMS . . . Pickax Theatre Club
DIGGERS . . . Dingleberry Funeral Home

Qwilleran phoned the newspaper and read his notes to Hixie,

who greeted them with yelps of relief. 'We'll announce it on page one tomorrow!' she said, almost breathless with enthusiasm. 'Spellers will clamor to sign up! Everyone in town will be pumped up!'

'The trick will be to move fast while it's hot,' he advised.

'Next week. We can swing it in ten days.'

'What about uniforms for the spellers?'

'One of the T-shirt shops in Mooseville does custom imprinting. The baseball caps can be ordered air express. Polly will have to scrape up a wordlist in a hurry.'

'You'll have to sound out the *Lockmaster Ledger* about the World Series,' he reminded her.

'Oh, they'll go for it! I know those guys.'

'Another thing, Hixie: instead of emcee, wordmaster, and judge, the officials should be coach, pitcher, and umpire.'

'Qwill! What can I say?' she cried. 'You're a lifesaver!'

'Okay. You owe me a dinner at the Palomino Paddock.'

Qwilleran hung up with a sense of satisfaction. Next he would have to help Polly with her wordlist: *mayonnaise, reminiscence, sherbet, schizophrenia, raisin, complexion, lettuce, exacerbate, vichyssoise.* The preponderance of edibles reminded him that he had had no lunch. He made a sandwich and went on listing while he ate it: *charismatic, assassination, penicillin, physiological, chaperon, doggerel, precocious, illiteracy.*

It was an exciting week for the residents of Moose County. Tuesday's paper carried the front-page announcement with all the buzz words: All-Stars, Pennant Race, World Series. 'Take me out to the spell game' was the slogan on posters everywhere: in store windows, on the bulletin board at the library, in church fellowship rooms. On street corners and in coffee shops it was the chief topic of conversation. Tickets, run off overnight in the *Something* printing plant, went on sale at the bank, drug store, and Old Stone Mill. Sales were so brisk that the venue was changed from the community hall to the high-school auditorium, which had double the capacity.

As for the spellers, some important names were signing up: Dr Diane Lanspeak for the Pills, Whannell MacWhannell for the Moneybags, and Derek Cuttlebrink for the Hams. Then it was Hixie's idea to sign up a battery of pinch spellers – celebrities who would sit in the front row and add glamour to the event, although they would not be called upon to spell.

Meanwhile, Qwilleran had a relatively quiet week. He went for daily rides on the Silverlight. He took the Siamese on trips to the gazebo and visits to the caterpillars in the guestroom. The larvae were still wiggling and stuffing themselves with green leaves. Although Koko was unimpressed, Yum Yum trembled with catly ecstasy. Even when the door to the guestroom was closed, she knew something vital was happening within, and she sat outside for hours.

Qwilleran also wrote his long-promised tribute to Mrs Fish-eye. It was a preface to a 'Qwill Pen' on the common hen's-egg – that ovoid porcelain jewel with golden orb quivering in a puddle of transparent viscosity as it waited to be fried, scrambled, or poached. He quoted egg farmers, chefs, nursery rhymes, Shakespeare, and Cervantes, who advised against putting all one's eggs in one basket.

When Qwilleran handed in his copy to Junior, just in time for the Friday noon deadline, the managing editor scanned it rapidly and said, 'Up goes the price of eggs all over Moose County!'

Riding home on the Silverlight, Qwilleran was waved down

by a motorist. He pulled over to the curb, and the driver parked ahead of him. Elizabeth Hart jumped out of the car, wearing a long colorless tunic over a long full skirt, equally colorless.

'What brings you to town?' he asked, removing his helmet.

'I had business at the bank, so I bought some tickets for the spell game. Derek is spelling for the Hams.'

'Has he started his new job?'

'Yes, and I don't see very much of him. He works late and has morning classes.'

'What does he think of the restaurant?'

'Well, you know Derek, he's really cool. Being an actor, he can adjust to situations. He plays a role.'

'Does he like his boss?'

'Mr Ramsbottom rarely makes an appearance. Derek is in total charge. He says he takes a lot of phone messages from Mrs Ramsbottom and also from a woman named Bunny.'

'Is the bartender as hostile as Derek anticipated?'

'Well, his girlfriend comes to the bar every night and stays till closing, and she likes to talk with Derek. The bartender doesn't care for that greatly. Her name is Monkey.'

'I know her,' Qwilleran said. 'She's a successful artist.'

'Is she attractive?' Elizabeth asked, bristling slightly.

Tactfully he replied, 'Not really.'

A police car pulled alongside, and the officer pointed to the No Parking sign. Elizabeth ran back to her car, and Qwilleran said, 'Sorry, officer. We had a little problem here. Nothing serious.'

'Take care, Mr Q.'

He received two phone calls that afternoon – one conveying information he expected and one coming as an eye-opener.

First, Wetherby Goode called, as upbeat as ever, but brief

and to the point. 'My cousin is on cloud nine about collaborating with you, Qwill. She's sending you some info on crows to give you an idea of the possibilities.'

'Sounds good. How soon will she be visiting here?'

'Late July . . . What do you think of the spell game? Hixie comes up with some neat ideas, doesn't she?'

'That she does,' Qwilleran replied, aware that credit and discredit were always heaped on the hapless promotion director as her projects soared and crashed.

'But why I really called, Qwill . . . the county offices in Lockmaster don't have any record of a business firm by the name of Northern Land Improvement.'

'Thanks, Joe. That's all I wanted to know.'

The news merely confirmed his suspicions: the NLI was a front for XYZ Enterprises. Before he could give it a second thought, however, a call came from the owner of the department store.

'Qwill, will you be free and at liberty after five-thirty? Pender and I would like to have a few words with you.'

'Come on over! We'll have a TGIF drink in the gazebo.'

'Okay. Right after store-closing.'

Qwilleran could guess what they had in mind. Both men were charter members of the new gourmet club, and they would want to hold the July dinner in the barn or even in the gazebo. It would mean serving twelve persons at three small tables – no problem, as long as they didn't expect him to cook.

Larry Lanspeak was a successful merchant who lived with his wife, Carol, in the affluent suburb of West Middle Hummock, and they were spark plugs for the theater club as well as every new community project.

Pender Wilmot was an attorney without Moose County roots,

who had recently moved his young family to the Hummocks. He would be spelling for the Ladders; the Lanspeaks' daughter was the MD who would spell for the Pills.

When Larry's station wagon pulled into the yard, Qwilleran went out to meet the two men and usher them around to the gazebo. The Siamese and a bar tray were already waiting there, and Koko was mimicking the birds' evensong in spirit if not in the right key.

'I don't believe it! That cat's singing!' Pender said. 'Is this the one that broke up the cheese party last winter?'

'Same one! He has a wealth of interests,' Qwilleran said. He served drinks: one wine spritzer, one rum and cola, and a ginger ale on the rocks.

'Qwill doesn't have a lawn,' Larry remarked to Pender with a triumphant smile.

'I like everything natural,' their host explained.

'We came to the right place! . . . Qwill, as residents of West Middle Hummock and Planet Earth, we came here today with a humble suggestion for the "Qwill Pen" column.'

'You don't have to be humble. I'm always on the prowl for ideas.'

'Well, then . . . This is it: the whole thing about the Hummocks, as you know, is the natural landscape: rolling hills, meadows and pastures, winding dirt roads, quaint wooden bridges, patches of woods lining the streams, and wildflowers on the roadside.'

Larry was a man of moderate build with undistinguished facial features, but his great theater voice and the energy that infused him onstage were compelling whenever he expounded a cause.

'But something insidious has been happening in the last few

years,' he went on. 'New people are moving to the country and bringing their town ideas with them. They like broad green lawns that have to be fertilized and watered and weeded and mowed twice a week and – my God! – sprayed green!'

Pender said, 'I have a third-grader at home who knows more about ecology than I do, and he comes running indoors, yelling, "Daddy! They're spraying again!" He knows all about chemical run-off in the water and pollution of the atmosphere. And it's kids like Timmie who have a future that needs protecting.'

Qwilleran asked, 'How prevalent is this green blight that you describe?'

'About thirty percent, but they're very vocal at village meetings. They urge cutting down trees to straighten the roads, widening the bridges, mowing the roadsides once a month – all to make it safer! They tell how Mr Fetter died in a car crash on a twisting road. They don't mention that his son was driving seventy!' said Larry. 'The Hummocks weren't intended to be speedways or thoroughfares for eighteen-wheelers, but that's what they'll become if we don't fight it.'

'Let me add something bizarre,' said Pender. 'Natural landscaping is trendy Down Below, and backyard naturalists are challenging the so-called weed laws and winning their cases in court . . . But up here, 400 miles north of everywhere, a local politician wants to legislate against native grasses and wildflowers. He wants everyone to have a neat clipped lawn, sprayed green.'

Larry said, 'He bought the Trevelyan house near us. He also wants the dirt roads paved, and he has a lot of pull.'

Pender added, 'He'll get a kickback, of course.'

'This is getting dirty. I'm going home,' said Larry, standing up.

'Who wants the roads paved?' Qwilleran asked. 'Who bought the Trevelyan house?'

'Ramsbottom.'

'If he's as crooked as people say, why does he keep getting reelected?'

'He saves the taxpayers money by opposing education and cultural improvements. Then the K Fund steps in and underwrites the new facilities. He's got it made!'

Qwilleran walked with them to their car.

'Think about it,' Larry told him. 'Kevin Doone can tell you a lot about natural landscaping. He's a real pro. And people will listen to what you say, Qwill.'

Thirteen

A Saturday night dinner at the Palomino Paddock would be a special occasion on anyone's calendar, and Polly – for her date with Qwilleran – wore her pink silk suit and opal jewelry. She glowed with rosy happiness when he arrived at her condo.

'Pink looks remarkably good on you,' he said. He had disliked the insipid pink worn by the late Iris Cobb – when she was his landlady Down Below, then as his housekeeper in Pickax, and finally as manager of the Farmhouse Museum.

'It's really hot pink,' Polly told him. 'And I love your outfit!'

It was a summer suit in his favorite khaki, with a blue shirt and a daring tie (blue, pink, and white). Sartorially he had come a long way since his days Down Below.

Brutus and Catta came to see them off, looking vacantly at Qwilleran when he said, 'Pax vobiscum!' To Polly he said, 'Let's drive your car. It's more appropriate than a van with your pink suit and your opals.'

The route lay through quaint villages: Little Hope, early home of Maude Coggin; Wildcat, a community inhabited entirely by Cuttlebrinks; Black Creek Junction, with its lofty trestle bridge, site of many a train wreck. Across the county border the terrain was less craggy and more agreeably sloped. Then came Flapjack, formerly a lumber camp and now a public recreation park. Here the route signs pointed left to Horseradish, birthplace of Wetherby Goode, and right to Whinny Hills and the celebrated Palomino Paddock.

En route Qwilleran asked, 'How are you getting along with Skumble?'

'We're becoming accustomed to each other, and he's making progress.'

'On the canvas, I hope.'

'Of course, dear. It's amazing how Paul uses red, blue, yellow, and gray to model the contours of the face. He uses yellow, rose, and blue to give life and lustre to pearls. Today I was deeply touched when he brought me a gift – a handkerchief that had belonged to his grandmother. It's so delicate, I told him it must be woven of moonbeams and fairies' wings.'

Qwilleran thought, Does he give one to each of his female subjects? What did he give to Commissioner Ramsbottom? His grandfather's flask? . . . He huffed into his moustache; it sounded questionable . . . To Polly he said, 'I've never heard you wax so poetic. How did he react?'

'I think he was flattered. Actually, I was trying to cajole him into revealing who paid for the commissioner's portrait, but he wouldn't tell.'

'That means the county treasurer paid for it – with your tax dollars and mine. At least he didn't lie. How many more sittings will there be?'

'I haven't inquired. I don't want him to feel he's being rushed.

He says many *thin* coats of paint give transparency to the human skin, but they take time to dry. I'm getting to love the smell of turpentine.'

'How do Brutus and Catta react?'

'They simply disappear. He always says, "I thought you had cats." But they don't make an appearance until he leaves.'

'Maybe it isn't only the turpentine.'

'Oh, Qwill! You're so cynical.'

'Does he ever say anything about his forebears? Some of the good folk up here aren't always descended from the ancestors they claim. Did he say anything about this grandmother of his? Where do you suppose she got the handkerchief?'

'I'll ask him,' she said impudently. 'I'll tell him that Mr Qwilleran wants to know, badly.'

The Palomino looked like a working stable, and the interior was down-to-earth, with bales of hay standing around and tack hanging on the walls. Polly and Qwilleran were seated at a preferred table in a stall, and menus were presented by an enthusiastic young stable girl moonlighting as a server. There were no prices on Polly's menu, but they were known to be $$$$$ in the restaurant ratings, meaning extra-expensive. The evening's special was tenderloin of ostrich with smoked tomatoes, herbed polenta, and black currant coulis.

'Are you sure it's legal to eat ostrich?' Polly asked the server. 'It seems rather . . . rather *untoward*.' The birds, she was told, were raised on a farm especially for the better restaurants.

Not entirely convinced, she ordered a vegetarian curry. Qwilleran took a chance on the big bird, medium rare.

She asked, 'What have you been reading lately, dear?'

'Mark Twain, a writer after my own heart. That A-to-Z

reference book you gave me has fired my interest. Eddington is dredging up all the Mark Twain he can find. Right now I'm reading *Roughing It.* That's the one with the story about the big gray cat called Tom Quartz.'

'If you'll forgive the trivia,' she said, 'Theodore Roosevelt had a cat by that name.'

'Well, he got it from *Roughing It*, which was published in 1872. Tom Quartz hung around quartz mines. One day the miners were getting ready to blast and didn't know he was sleeping on a gunnysack in the shaft. The explosion blew him into the sky, tumbling end over end. He landed right-side-up, covered with soot, and walked away in disgust.'

His attention wavered as a man and woman were shown to a stall across the room. Then he asked, 'What were they gossiping about at the library this week?'

'The Pennant Race. Nothing else. My assistant's husband is spelling for the Oilers.'

'How about the workshop? Did it teach your patrons to love the electronic catalogue?'

Polly grinned. 'Only one attended, and there are rumblings of unrest among the volunteers. In fact, two of the oldest resigned. All the staff members, who are younger, love the computers, but . . .'

'As I told you, I prefer the old card catalogue myself, but since we all have to swing with the times, why not do something else to captivate the general public? You have to admit it's a grim old building, and the chairs are too hard! Modern libraries go in for color, comfort, and a friendly look. Fran Brodie could give you some ideas, when she gets back from vacation, if ever.'

The entrées were served, and they applied themselves to the

tastefully arranged plates of food. Qwilleran said the ostrich tasted exactly like filet of beef.

Polly said, 'Everyone loved your column on hen's-eggs and the tribute to Mrs Fish-eye. Do you have any other surprises lurking up your sleeve? I won't tell.'

'I'm raising a crop of butterflies in a box, hoping to write something intelligent on the subject. So far they don't show much promise, but Phoebe Sloan is moving and can't keep her incubator. So now I'm feeding caterpillars, which will metamorphose into chrysalises, which will metamorphose into Painted Ladies, which will be released to lay more eggs, which will produce more caterpillars . . . Would you excuse me a moment, Polly? I'm not in the habit of doing this, but I'd like to speak to someone with malice aforethought.'

He walked across the room to the stall where a large man with a bloated face was sitting across from an attractive young female companion.

'Excuse me, Mr Ramsbottom, it's hard to catch you in the course of a normal day. I'm Jim Qwilleran of the *Something*.'

'I know. I know,' the man said with political affability mixed with annoyance.

'I'd like to make an appointment with you for an in-depth interview covering your twenty-five years of public service – its ups and downs, so to speak. I hear there have been some interesting downs.'

The commissioner waved the intruder away with an impatient gesture. 'Don't bother me this year. See me in election year.'

Qwilleran returned to his table, thinking, At least, he knows he's being watched by the hungry press. 'Sorry,' he said to Polly. 'Shall we order dessert?'

* * *

On Sunday afternoon, while Polly sat for the portrait artist, Qwilleran sat with the Siamese and the *New York Times.* He always picked up the Sunday edition at Sloan's Drug Store, where they saved a copy for him under the counter. On this occasion Mrs Sloan was alone in the store and eager to talk. 'Where's your shiny bike, Mr Q?' she asked.

'Never on Sunday, Mrs Sloan,' he explained. 'The newspaper weighs more than the bike. It might damage the spokes.'

'We were supposed to get rain,' she said ruefully. 'My lawn needs it badly. I should really put in a sprinkler system.'

'Where do you live?'

'West Middle Hummock, and I have an acre of the most beautiful grass! Do you have a nice lawn, Mr Q?'

'I'm afraid not. I'm a nature boy. I let nature take its course.'

'Do you mean . . . you let it go to *weeds*?' she asked in mild horror.

'Frankly, I don't know what weeds are. The landscape gardener has put in native grasses and wildflowers . . . and forbs,' he added mischievously, enjoying her perplexed frown. 'Do you have any copies of the *New York Times* left?'

'I always save one for you, Mr Q. You know that!'

'Everyone's pleased to know you're sponsoring a team in the Pennant Race, and having Dr Diane spell for you is somewhat of a coup.'

'Well, I don't know about that, but she's a dear, sweet person, just like her parents. They're lucky to have her turn out so well. Our assistant pharmacist is spelling for us, too, and we hoped to have our daughter, but she decided to spell for the Art Center, which is understandable, except that it was a disappointment. They have such a large membership to recruit from, and we're so small.'

'Why not get the superintendent of schools?' Qwilleran suggested. 'He'd make a good Pill.'

She burst into laughter. Lyle Compton – always under attack by teachers, parents, and politicians – had adopted the persona of an old grouch, although he had an underlying sense of humor.

'Wouldn't that be funny? Do you think he would?' Mrs Sloan asked.

'I'll ask him. It'll be a crowd-pleaser, and he likes an audience.'

'We'll appreciate it no end, Mr Q.' She rang up his sale, which included mouthwash and shaving lotion, then said in a sadder voice, 'What do you think of our daughter's choice of career, Mr Q? We'd hoped to get her into health care – it's so secure – but all she can think about is painting.'

Once again Qwilleran was being expected to play the pundit. Why? Because he wrote a column? Because he had inherited money? He found it somewhat absurd. 'Well, Phoebe's doing something she enjoys enormously, and she does it well, and it makes people happy. I know one collector who has eighteen of her butterflies. What more could you want for your daughter?'

'I guess . . . I could wish . . . that she chose her friends more carefully. I know you don't have children, Mr Q, but can you understand the pain of a parent whose only child goes off with a man of dubious reputation? It's not just that he has no education or goals. We have other doubts about him. In a community like this, and with contacts like ours, we hear things, you know. What can I say? He's handsome, and Phoebe is vulnerable! This is presumptuous of me, I know, but I wish you could talk some sense into her head. She thinks highly of you, and she'd listen.'

Qwilleran said, 'You have my sympathy, I assure you, but

I've always believed that young people of her age have to make their own choices and take responsibility for their decisions—'

He was interrupted by the jangling bell on the front door, as two customers entered, chattering noisily. He and the storekeeper exchanged apologetic glances, and he muttered a vague promise as he moved away. Leaving the store, he was grateful that he had only two cats, who could be banished to their room if they created a problem.

When Qwilleran unlocked the kitchen door and let himself in, he was alarmed by a scraping sound elsewhere on the main floor. He dropped his packages and hurried to the foyer. Yum Yum was batting something about the stone floor. A yo-yo! A few days earlier he had tossed it into the wastebasket when the cats reacted with boredom. That little scamp had fished it out, hiding it under the sofa while awaiting an auspicious time to use it as a hockey puck.

She was smart in her way – inventive, mischievous. While Koko sensed the who, why, what, and where of crime and tried to communicate his suspicions, she hid the evidence under the sofa or the rug. Qwilleran picked her up and stroked her soft fur. 'When we run Catta for vice president,' he said, 'you can be campaign manager.'

After changing into casual clothes, he took the Siamese and his Sunday paper to the gazebo. He was reading and they were monitoring the airborne traffic when their fawn-colored necks stretched, brown ears swiveled, and black noses pointed due east.

Qwilleran thought, Sunday afternoon trespassers! . . . They had the nerve to unlatch the gate and drive past the PRIVATE sign . . . They were coming up for some unauthorized sightseeing. Frowning, he went out to confront them.

As soon as the vehicle came into view, he recognized it: the commercial van with discreet lettering on the side, 'Bushland Studio.'

'Bushy! What brings you in the back way?' he called out to the photographer.

'It's confusing, Qwill. The front way from Main Street leads to your back door, and the back way leads to your front door.'

'I'll have the barn turned around. Come on into the tiger cage and have a drink. What's your pleasure?'

'Do you have a gin and tonic?'

'I have everything. Talk to the cats while I'm bartending.'

John Bushland was a talented young photographer who was losing his hair early; hence his affectionate nickname. On several occasions he had tried to shoot the Siamese for an annual cat calendar, but they had been pointedly uncooperative. No matter how cautiously he raised his camera, they instantly rolled from a lyrical pose into a grotesque muddle of hind legs and nether parts. After every disappointed effort he said, 'I'm not licked yet!'

When the tray arrived with the drinks, he raised his glass in a toast. '*Oogly wa wa!* That's a Zulu blessing, or so I've been told.'

'Better get it confirmed in writing before you get into trouble,' Qwilleran advised. 'How's everything at the Art Center? Are the crowds breaking down the doors? Is Beverly making them take off their shoes?'

'That's why I came up here. Did you go to the opening of the Click Club?'

'I tried, but it was too crowded.'

'Well, there's been a break-in! Last night! No forced entry, just trespassing.'

'What did they take?'

'Nothing – not even a light bulb. But they used some of the equipment, and there was a smell of cigarette smoke.'

'Hmmm,' Qwilleran mused. 'Any theories? Does Beverly know about it?'

'Oh, God! Yes! She went through the roof! We decided not to notify the police. Publicity would only lead to more trespassing, and somehow we think this is an inside job.'

'Do individual members of the Click Club have keys to the building?'

'No. Mostly they attend group functions, but there's a "privilege key" available for members who want to use the equipment to screen their own film. They sign for it and return it to the office when the screening is over. No one had signed it out for last night, but someone might have borrowed the key during the week and had dupes made. Beverly is looking into that possibility. I feel sorry for her. She takes these things so hard.'

'Had they misused the equipment?'

'No, they just failed to put it back properly. They'd used the VCR and the slide projector, and they'd left beer cans and cigarette butts in the wastebasket, obviously ignoring the No Smoking signs.'

Qwilleran asked, 'What do you think they were viewing? Probably not *Gone with the Wind.*'

'Probably some kind of underground trash. The question is: Will they be back next weekend for another meeting of the Saturday Night After-Hours Art Film and Beer-drinking Society?' Bushy jumped up. 'Thanks for the drink. I've gotta get back to my dark room. Freelancers work an eight-day week.'

Qwilleran walked with him to his van, and the photographer said, 'Say! I may have found a way to shoot those ornery kids of yours! There was a camera lens patented a few decades ago – for use by photographers exploring primitive regions. Some cultures think they'll lose their souls if their picture is taken. This was a right-angle lens employing mirrors. If I could find one in a vintage collection of photo equipment, the cats wouldn't know I was shooting them.'

'Would it fit today's cameras?'

'I'd have to get an adapter.'

'If you can find such a lens, I'll buy it for you, Bushy. Full speed ahead!'

Later in the afternoon Qwilleran felt the need for exercise, and he walked down the lane to the Art Center, first taking the precaution of returning the Siamese to the barn.

It was nearly five o'clock, and there were few cars on the lot. Indoors he went to the gallery to look at the wood carving he had bought. To his indignation, it was gone. He went looking for Beverly Forfar.

'It's in my office,' she explained. 'Too many people wanted to buy it. They don't understand what the red dot means. One man got rather nasty, so I took it out of the show.'

'May I take it home now?' he asked.

'Not until the whole exhibit is dismantled. Everything has to be checked out in proper order.'

'How was the turnout today?'

'It's always good on Sundays. People come after church or after brunch, so they're decently dressed.'

One of her complaints was the sloppy attire of many visitors.

She herself always looked 'spiffy,' to use Qwilleran's word.

He asked, 'What's the public's reaction to the photo show downstairs?'

She groaned. 'Some unauthorized persons got in last night! We try so hard to give this town a fine facility, and someone has to abuse the privileges. But there's good news, too. Daphne's nudes have been returned!'

'All of them?' He recalled Thornton's experience in the Shipwreck Tavern.

'About half of them, and they were returned to the bin where they belong.'

'Don't let anyone touch them. It might be possible to get prints.'

'Would we all have to be fingerprinted? That would be embarrassing.'

The phone rang in her office, and Qwilleran went to see the Butterfly Girl. Phoebe was sitting alone, concentrating on her palette.

'Good afternoon,' he said quietly. 'I came to report on the caterpillars. They're stuffing themselves and getting fatter and sassier every day.'

'Oh, hello, Mr Q,' she said listlessly, glancing at him briefly and then back at her work.

He thought, She's tired; she goes to the bar nightly and stays till closing; and who knows what they do after-hours? He said, 'How's Jasper?'

She shrugged. 'He's happy anywhere, as long as he gets his peanuts.'

'I have a condo in the Village. I'm in the Willows. Which is your building?' The clusters had been named after indigenous trees.

'The Birches.'

The Birches had more luxuries than other clusters. The construction was no better, but the details were posh, like marble lavatories and walk-in closets.

'I hear you're spelling for the Daubers. Who else is on the team?'

'Thornton Haggis and Beverly.'

'You'll have a good time . . . Well, see you at the warm-up tomorrow night.'

Leaving the building and walking home, Qwilleran wondered about Phoebe's lacklustre spirit. She was not used to nightlife . . . She was feeling guilty about defying her parents . . . She was sulking. Beverly had succeeded in evicting Jasper and the caterpillars and may have pressured her into wearing the official smock: dull blue, long-sleeved, button-cuffed. It made Phoebe look drab. She probably felt drab, too.

At the barn Koko was jumping on and off the kitchen counter and looking out the window; it meant someone had left a delivery in the sea chest outside the kitchen door. Qwilleran investigated and found two meat pies, an envelope, and a 1966 book he had lent Celia Robinson: *The Birds Fall Down*, by Rebecca West. She would appreciate the spy story and perhaps the good writing. The note in the envelope read:

Dear Chief,

I catered a brunch in Black Creek today and made a couple of extra meat pies for you. Hope you like them. It's a new recipe. Thank you for letting me read the book. It was interesting. I never heard of her, but she's a very good writer. Sorry to be late with the stuff you wanted.

I've got a date with Lisa Compton tomorrow to find out about the Campbell case. The property you asked about isn't listed under Northern Land Improvement, they told me at the county building. The owner is Margaret Ramsbottom.

Agent 0013½

Qwilleran finished reading the note and made a dive for the Moose County telephone directory. He found only two Ramsbottom listings: one for Chester and Margaret, one for Craig and Kathy – all at the same address in West Middle Hummock. Ramsbottom probably had everything in his wife's name. The news meant, however, that Qwilleran had lost a bet with himself. It was not XYZ Enterprises who had purchased the Coggin property. It was really 'the commish' who had taken advantage of an old woman and had lost no time, after her death, in leasing twelve acres to the county. The board of commissioners would have to approve the deal, but no doubt the Barbecue King would arrange for them to vote right.

Qwilleran's first thought was to share the news with Rollo McBee, but when he phoned the farm on Base Line Road, there was only a noncommittal message on the answering machine. He phoned Boyd McBee and heard the same message. This was unusual for a Sunday afternoon. Qwilleran grabbed his car keys and drove down to Base Line.

Rollo's blue pickup was not in the barnyard, but another truck was there. Qwilleran parked and walked around behind the house, where a young man was feeding the raggle-taggle dogs who had come to live there.

'Hi, Mr Q,' he said. 'Lookin' for Rollo? I'm Randy. I work for him.'

'Where is he? There's no one at Boyd's house, either.'

'They all went to a funeral in Duluth. Their brother was in a bad accident – two trucks and a tanker! They'll be back Wednesday, maybe. Anythin' I can do for you?'

'No thanks. I just wanted to chew the rag.' That was what the farmers did at the coffee shops. 'I'll call later in the week. How are the poor mutts doing?'

'Look at 'em! Larky as a pack o' puppies!'

Qwilleran returned to the barn and phoned his attorney's home. The Ramsbottom connection was something Bart should be told, but his wife answered; her husband had flown to Chicago that morning for conferences with the K Fund.

To work off his frustration he read to the cats. Koko selected *The Birds Fall Down*. Qwilleran thought, Naturally! Wrigley's been sitting on it, keeping it warm while Celia had it.

Fourteen

So Phoebe and her red-headed boyfriend and disreputable parrot were living in Indian Village! It remained to be seen how they would synchronize with that quiet and eminently respectable neighborhood. They were young people who worked late and went on enjoying life after-hours, with Jasper's racy squawks adding to the racket. Condo owners, on the other hand, tended to have established professional careers with somewhat regulated hours. After the eleven o'clock news the entire village blacked out.

The newcomers were living in the Birches, Phoebe had said. That was the cluster of condos where the Rikers had a desirable end unit. Qwilleran's native curiosity and newshound instincts were prompting him to start asking questions. Perhaps, too, the unsettling sensation on his upper lip spurred him to action.

On Monday morning he drove downtown and handed in his copy for the Tuesday 'Qwill Pen.' He was twenty-four hours ahead of deadline.

'Wait till I pick myself up off the floor,' Junior said. 'What happened?'

'I had a little extra time on my hands.'

'Are you all set for the warm-up tonight?'

'I spent the weekend in the bullpen, perfecting my delivery. I'm ready to pitch fast words, slow words, curve words—'

'How about spit words?'

'They've been outlawed.'

Next he looked up Mildred Riker at the food desk and started with a cooking question. 'Did Iris Cobb's personal recipe for macaroni and cheese ever turn up in her papers? I'll never forget it. It had some secret ingredient.'

'I know. You've mentioned it before, but I haven't found it. Evidently she'd prepared it so often, she didn't need to write it down.'

He started to leave her office and then said, 'By the way, Mildred, do you happen to know if the vacant unit at the Birches is still on the market? I know someone who might be interested.'

'Apparently not,' she said. 'Someone moved in a few days ago. I don't know who they are.'

'Who else lives in the building?'

'Susan Exbridge in Two and Amanda Goodwinter in Four. Susan is a wonderful neighbor – never gives parties, never plays loud music. You know how thin the walls are!'

On the way out of the building he passed the publisher's office. Arch Riker called out, 'Looks as if we're home free! Only two days – till the spell game – and no calamities!'

'It's not over till it's over,' Qwilleran reminded him. 'The auditorium balcony could collapse. Wasn't it built by XYZ?'

Having acquired the information he needed, he headed for the central business district. Susan and Amanda! Two fussier neighbors could hardly be imagined for Phoebe and friends! He drove to Exbridge & Cobb Fine Antiques on Main Street.

The former wife of Don Exbridge was one of the most striking women in town, having alimony payments that she spent almost entirely on clothing from Down Below, and her interest in the theater club had given her a dramatic flair. 'Darling! Where have you been?' she cried when she saw Qwilleran.

'Working,' he said morosely to arouse her sympathy.

'You poor dear! And what you do looks so easy and so much fun! Are you here to hunt for ideas or spend money?'

'It all depends. Do you have any unusual items that are not too old and not too new?'

'Are you interested in early scientific instruments?'

'Not really.'

'You'll love the collection I bought from a little old billionaire in Dallas.' She unlocked a curio cabinet filled with objects of wood and brass.

'Who's going to buy this stuff in Pickax?' he demanded.

'Darling, I'd go broke if I depended on sheep ranchers and perch fishermen. I advertise in exclusive antique magazines and sell to serious collectors all over the country.'

'What's that round thing?' It looked like an attractive box, not too scientific. About three inches in diameter, the wood lid was fancifully inlaid with brass.

'A very old Italian compass with an interesting provenance.'

Skeptically he said, 'I suppose it came over on the *Nina*, the *Pinta*, or *Santa Maria* – or all three.'

'Wrong century, darling. It's circa 1650.' She removed the lid, revealing an ornamental dial under glass. Its boldest feature was an eight-pointed star. The dial quivered.

Susan said, 'It's described as a pivoted thirty-two-point

compass card, painted by hand. The north point is indicated by a star, the east by a cross.'

'How much?'

'You couldn't afford it, darling.'

'I'll take it!' he said and handed over his credit card. Then, while the transaction was being processed, he remarked in an offhand way, 'I hear you have a new neighbor. I hear the celebrated Butterfly Girl moved in next door.'

Susan stiffened with indignation. 'Is she the one who plays that godawful music at three in the morning? And has that screeching bird? I've complained to the manager three nights in a row. Last night someone called the sheriff!'

Goading her playfully, Qwilleran said, 'But they're young, Susan. Her boyfriend works late. They have to have some fun. Why don't you ask your stingy ex-husband to install soundproofing in the walls?'

'Go home, darling,' she scolded. 'Take your seventeenth-century compass and go home!'

He left the shop with a feeling of triumph. He had ruffled the aplomb of the unruffled Susan, and he had acquired a specimen of antiquity that would turn Arch Riker green with envy.

From there he visited Amanda's Studio of Interior Design, where Amanda herself sat scowling at the reception desk. Her usual bad temper was exacerbated by the long absence of her assistant. Feeling mischievous, he inquired if she had any paintings by the Butterfly Girl.

'You won't find any butterflies in this shop until they carry me out!' she fumed. 'I loathe butterflies in any form, and that includes that Sloan girl's stuff.'

'They sell well, and you could get a good markup,' he

persisted. 'And now that she's a neighbor of yours at the Birches . . .'

'What! Is that who's been disturbing the peace every night? I phoned the sheriff last night about the yelling and screaming and so-called music. I said, "Either you get over here in five minutes and muffle these ruffians, or I load my shotgun!" A deputy was there in less than five!'

'That's why you keep getting reelected, Amanda. You know how to get results. You and Chester Ramsbottom.'

'That reptile! Don't mention us in the same breath!'

'Is his wife a client of yours? I hear they bought the Trevelyan house in the Hummocks.'

'Margaret? She's a nice woman. I don't know how she lives with that man! I guess she doesn't – much. He has all kinds of outside interests . . . I'll say one thing for him, though. Doing over the Trevelyan house was a huge job, and I didn't have to wait for my money.'

After lunching at the Spoonery, a place specializing in soups, Qwilleran was driving home across the theater parking lot when he saw Celia Robinson getting into her car. He tooted the horn to alert her, and she hurried to meet him with her usual excess of smiles and happiness. 'I got your story, Chief. Are you going to fire me for taking so long?'

'No, but you'll be reassigned to New Zealand,' he said sternly.

This remark was greeted with gales of laughter. 'But I did something naughty. I didn't tell Lisa I was taping it. I used Clayton's little recorder.'

'Under the circumstances, that's not too naughty. Would you like to bring it to the barn later on – and have something wicked in the way of refreshments?'

After more merry laughter she declined, saying she was going to Mr O'Dell's to work on a catering job. 'But I'll give you the tape. It's upstairs. Wait here. I can get it in a jiffy.'

She ran to the carriage house, while Qwilleran marveled at the energy and youthful exuberance she brought to her many activities.

Returning, she said, 'I had to go to the Compton house to get the story. Lisa was afraid of being overheard at the office. So destroy it, Chief, after you've listened to it.'

'Is it okay if the cats hear it?'

Her laughter could still be heard as he drove away.

When Qwilleran arrived at the barn, he was greeted by two highly excited cats. They ran up the ramp and back down again to be sure he was following. He followed them. It was the guestroom on the second balcony that concerned them. They knew something was happening behind that door.

'Stand back! And don't rush in,' he warned. 'Let's not create any stress.'

He opened the door, and the cats rushed in. There were two butterflies flitting about the box, and three more were waiting to metamorphose. They looked like the Painted Ladies in the guidebook, all right. Now they would require fresh flowers sprinkled with sugar-water. He chased the Siamese out of the room, closed the door carefully, and drove into town to buy carnations.

'Only two?' the young florist asked.

'Well, make it three.'

'What color?'

The instruction manual had made no mention of desired color. 'Make it white,' he said.

Returning home, Qwilleran locked the cats in the broom

closet while he mixed sugar and water, sprinkled it on the petals, opened the door of the butterfly box carefully, thrust the flowers in quickly, closed the box, and stood back. The Painted Ladies showed no interest at all!

He went down the ramp, apologized to the Siamese for the ignominious incarceration, and applied himself to the answering machine. There were several messages, one of them from Dawn McBee.

'Were you looking for Rollo?' she asked when Qwilleran returned the call. 'We were in Duluth. Just got back. Rollo's in the barnyard right now.'

'I heard about the tragedy in your family. You have my deepest sympathy.'

'It was really sad. He was doing so well – building a new house – kids ready for college . . . You can never tell, can you?'

'Very true. Is there anything I can do for you?'

'Well, it's about the spell game. One of the Muckers has dropped out, and Culvert wants to know if he can substitute, seeing as how it's an emergency.'

'Well . . . it might be an amusing twist to have a nine-year-old among all the adults – especially if he spells better than they do . . . Okay, bring him to the warm-up tonight.'

'He's been studying his aunt's wordlist,' Dawn said.

'Good! I think the fans will love the idea, and all the kids will be rooting for him.'

'Thanks, Qwill. Culvert will be tickled pink, and Rollo will be so proud! Do you want him to phone when he's through with the chores?'

'Let's wait till tomorrow, Dawn. It's nothing urgent.'

The warm-up for the spell game was being held in the high-school auditorium to acquaint participants with the stage, the procedure, and the expected reaction from fifteen hundred fans. The overflow would have bleacher seats in the gym, watching the game on closed-circuit TV.

The auditorium played up the school colors: blue curtain, white walls, blue seats. The curtain was open when Qwilleran arrived, and on the stage were two rows of folding chairs, the second row elevated on a low platform. That was considered the dugout, where the teams would wait for their turn at the plate. A table for the coach and the pitcher was downstage left, with a second one downstage right for the umpire and the timekeeper. In the center, a floor-standing microphone was situated on a pentagonal mat like an oversized homeplate. What made the scene spectacular was the stageful of hanging banners in the team colors, each with a team name. There were ten of them: green for the Moneybags, pink for the Pills, black for the Diggers, as well as red, turquoise, orange, white, blue, yellow, and purple.

Qwilleran, who had a compulsion for counting everything and anything, observed an odd number of chairs: thirty-one instead of thirty. One of the stage managers explained that Scott Gippel, who weighed three hundred pounds, required two; Hixie had thought of everything!

Backstage a noisy horde of spellers was milling about in their baseball caps, which were also in the team color. The T-shirts being printed in Mooseville had not yet arrived, and Qwilleran sensed the kind of snafu that plagued Hixie's beautifully organized projects. He volunteered to camp out on the printer's doorstep and even assist with the printing if necessary. As a temporary measure, the spellers wore their team names on cards pinned to their shirts.

Assisting Hixie backstage were two efficient staffers from the *Something*: Sarah Plensdorf, office manager, and Wilfred Sugbury, Riker's secretary. They guided spellers and officials to their assigned seats onstage.

'There's one speller missing,' Hixie said.

'Phoebe Sloan,' her teammates called out.

'She's never very punctual,' Beverly Forfar added.

'I saw her yesterday at the Art Center,' Sarah shouted from the wings, 'and she was quite excited about coming tonight.'

'Okay, we'll start without her,' Hixie said, 'and you guys – Beverly and Thornton – will have to tell her what she missed . . . First of all, when the fans arrive on Wednesday night, the curtain will be closed, and preliminary entertainment will take place in front of it. *Spellers and officials will be offstage* . . . Got that? . . . At a given signal, you will jog onstage single file like professional athletes. You've all seen the players make their entrance on television. As each one appears, there'll be a burst of applause and cheers from the fans.'

'Can we rehearse the entrance?' someone asked.

'We sure can. Everyone offstage! Exit in orderly fashion. Stay in line. Then turn around and jog back onstage. Wilfred will start you off, one every five seconds.'

Wetherby whispered to Qwilleran, 'She's good, isn't she?'

'She directs plays for the theater club,' Qwilleran said, 'and she not only knows what she wants, she has a way of inspiring cooperation.' To himself he said, I hope – I hope – I hope nothing goes wrong.

Those taking directions from her were an attorney, the CEO of a large firm, an MD, and the superintendent of schools, as well as students, retirees, farmers, office workers, and one nine-year-old boy who would be ten in July.

'Here she comes!' someone yelled.

'Here's the late Phoebe Sloan!'

'Better late than never.'

'Sorry. I had to stop for gas,' Phoebe apologized as Sarah pushed her toward the one vacant chair.

'Okay, let's continue,' said Hixie. 'The teams have entered. They remain standing for the National Anthem. At a signal from the coach, you sit. I want thirty backsides to hit the chairseats simultaneously . . . Next, the coach calls a team to the plate. Three spellers jump to their feet and walk briskly to the mike. The pitcher throws out a word. The spellers go into a huddle and decide who'll spell. The designated speller steps to the mike and spells. The umpire rules thumbs-up for a hit, thumbs-down for a strike-out.'

'Are we supposed to remember all this?' Derek asked.

'Sarah has printouts. Ask for one as you leave.'

'What does the timekeeper do?' MacWhannell asked.

'After a word is pitched, the team has sixty seconds to respond, or the timekeeper rings a bell, and the team is sent back to the dugout.'

'What happens if a speller strikes out?' Pender Wilmot asked.

'The team gets a second chance in the next inning, but after two strike-outs, the team is sent to the showers; they leave the stage. As the field narrows down to fewer teams, it gets more exciting . . . Now we'll run through a whole inning once; every team gets a turn at the plate.'

Everyone was having a good time. Then Derek left, saying he had to go back to work. Phoebe slipped out soon afterward. No one else wanted to leave. They wanted to practice walking briskly to the plate, jogging onstage, hitting the chairseats simultaneously. They had to be chased out.

Hixie said to Qwilleran, 'It's great of you to ride herd on the T-shirts. The shop is called Tanks and Tees, right behind the Shipwreck Tavern. You might double-check the names and numbers before you accept them, and be sure they have one XXXL for Scott Gippel.'

'Don't worry. I proofread everything.'

Then Thornton said to him, 'Why is Phoebe wearing long sleeves all of a sudden? She has pretty arms. Something's rotten in Denmark.'

Qwilleran had asked himself the same question. 'She's not herself. What's going on?'

Thornton said, 'I've seen that boyfriend of hers, and he's not the type I'd want for my daughter, if I had one . . . How are the butterflies coming along?'

'Just before I left,' Qwilleran said, 'two of them hatched and were pumping up their wings, the way the manual said they would.'

Qwilleran was somewhat exhilarated when he returned from the warm-up. He would have phoned Polly, but she was out of town, attending a tri-county library conference in Lockmaster. He would have read aloud to the Siamese, but he was in no mood for *The Red Badge of Courage*, which was Koko's choice. What he was in the mood for was a dish of ice cream with chocolate sauce and a few peanuts. After that he was in the mood for playing Celia's tape:

LISA: Tell me again, Celia, why you want to hear this story.

CELIA: Well, I have a nephew Down Below who wants to invest some money in Moose County, and the deal involves a county official, but he heard a rumor of a scandal connected with this man. He's very careful about things like that. He asked me to look into it. In strict confidence, of course.

LISA: Is it Ramsbottom?

CELIA: That's the name.

LISA: We don't like to talk about it, but . . . I know you're not a gossip. It's like this . . . He owns a bar and was once charged with watering the liquor, which could cost him his license. He claimed to know nothing about it and put the blame on his bartender. His name was Broderick Campbell. He was a very upright young man. His father was a church deacon, and his uncle was the pastor. He had a wife and three small children and was working two jobs to support them. We were all furious about Chet's accusation, but we were stunned when Brod confessed!

CELIA: Oh, dear! I can imagine!

LISA: He was sentenced to a jail term, but Ramsbottom used his influence to get the sentence commuted, provided Brod left the county. He and his family left in disgrace – went somewhere Down Below. His parents were absolutely destroyed! His mother had a stroke and died, and his father went into a black depression. His uncle, the pastor, was distraught. As things went from bad to worse, Brod's father was persuaded to go and live with the pastor's family. Then one day he disappeared. The police hunted for two days before they found him hanging in the attic of the parsonage.

CELIA: Oh, Lisa! What a horrible story!

LISA: The pastor himself didn't live long after that.

CELIA: But why the bad feelings about Mr Ramsbottom? Didn't he save Broderick from a jail term?

LISA: Yes, but there's more to the story. One of the Campbell clan, traveling Down Below, found Brod in very successful circumstances. He was the owner of a large motel with swimming pool, restaurant, and everything. It was something he never could have afforded in a million years! Had Ramsbottom paid him to take the rap?

CELIA: If Brod was so honest, couldn't he have refused?

LISA: He was trapped, coming and going. To try to stand up against that powerful man would have been virtual suicide.

MAN'S VOICE: Hello! Hello! What goes on here? Why so gloomy?

LISA: Celia, this is my husband . . . Lyle, Celia Robinson is one of our most valued volunteers. Her nephew is contemplating a financial deal with Ramsbottom . . .

MAN'S VOICE: Hah! Tell him not to touch it with a ten-foot pole! The man's a crook! We all know he got a kickback from the new high-school building, and the cost overruns would have bankrupted the county if the K Fund hadn't stepped in.

CELIA: Well! I'm much obliged for the information. I'll tell my nephew to steer clear.

Click.

Qwilleran turned to Koko, who was sitting on the arm of the chair and listening. 'What do you think of that smelly mess?'

'*Aaaaaaaa*,' the cat bleated in his new all-purpose monotone.

Qwilleran looked at his watch. It was late, but not too late to call Celia and congratulate her on a job well done. He phoned the carriage house.

When she answered with a flat hello, he asked, 'Are you boiling potatoes for salad or putting a batch of brownies in the oven?'

'Oh, hello,' she said without any of her usual merriment.

'This tape,' he said, 'is one of the best things you've ever done. I'm destroying it, as you asked, but I predict the story will become another Moose County legend in fifty or a hundred years.'

'Glad you liked it,' she replied without adding any chatty comment of her own. He sensed a problem. This was not his secret agent 0013½. Was this why Koko had bleated his curious lament? Some news had deadened her spirit.

'Celia, are you feeling all right?' he demanded with the severity of a senior officer.

'Yes, I'm all right.'

'Is there something you want to tell me?' he asked more gently.

His neighborly concern touched a nerve, and she whimpered something indistinctly.

'I'll be right there, Celia! Pull yourself together!'

Taking a flashlight, he jogged the short distance through the woods. There was a predatory owl that lived among the dark branches, and Qwilleran had taken care to wear his yellow baseball cap. On the way he reviewed what he knew about her: a widow living with her grown son and his family on a farm in Illinois. She had moved to Pickax to start a new life: doing volunteer service, cheering the old and infirm, singing in the church choir, doing small catering jobs. Qwilleran himself had a vested interest in Celia's well-being. She not only supplied comfort food for his freezer and Kabibbles for the Siamese; she handled errands and inquiries for 'the Chief' when he required anonymity.

She also laughed uproariously at his mildest quips. What had happened? Bad news from the doctor? Death in the family?

At the carriage house he rang the doorbell, and a buzzer released the lock. The stairs were narrow and steep. At the top of the flight stood a husky cat named Wrigley, who challenged him to show his credentials.

'How's the good boy?' Qwilleran asked. Wrigley recognized the voice and trotted ahead into the living room.

Soberly and with downcast eyes Celia murmured, 'Would you like a glass of something?' Ordinarily she would have made a joking comment about his yellow baseball cap.

'No, thanks. Let's just sit down and talk for a few minutes. Something is worrying you, Celia, and it will do you good to unburden yourself.'

Obediently – she was used to taking orders from him – but in a hopeless tone of voice she said, 'I had a phone call from my son in Illinois. His wife has left him, and he wants me to go back to the farm and keep house for him.'

'Your grandson's stepmother, right? They didn't get along, right?'

She nodded. 'Clayton wanted to come and live with me, you know, but his dad put his foot down. My son is a very strict father.'

'And how do you feel about leaving Pickax?'

'I don't want to. I've been so happy here. But I feel an obligation to my family.'

'How old are you, Celia? I don't usually ask women their age, but this is important.'

'Seventy,' she said shyly.

'Then you've paid your dues. You've raised a family and worked on a farm for half a century. You're healthy. You have long years ahead of you. It's your turn to live your own life.'

'But he's my only son, and he needs me. My oldest was killed in the service.'

'Fate didn't send you to Pickax to wait for your son's wife to leave him. Fate sent you here to do good things for a large number of people. Your son's wife may return; he may marry again. Meanwhile he can hire a housekeeper. As for Clayton, he'll be going away to college soon. Your future is here! You've just started a business of your own – something you've always wanted. What does Mr O'Dell think of this turn of events?'

'I haven't told him,' she said softly. 'I just found out tonight.'

'How do you think he'll react?'

She shook her head, and tears came to her lowered eyes. 'We were . . . talking about . . . getting married.'

'Then for God's sake, Celia, live your own life! Your son's in his prime; let him live his own life. Clayton is about to start his own life. And your life is yours to live.' Qwilleran stood up. 'Do you understand?'

'Yes, Chief,' she said, smiling and weeping at the same time.

Fifteen

The shop called Tanks & Tees was a shabby establishment behind the Shipwreck Tavern. The work space looked like a collection of flotsam and jetsam, while the staff looked like shipwreck survivors. Nevertheless, the thirty shirts were ready when Qwilleran arrived, and the proprietors were proud to be filling such a large order for such an important event.

'I was told to inspect them,' Qwilleran said. 'The Pennant Race is a class act, and the promoters are fussy.'

The inspection revealed that the Daubers had their name misspelled; three shirts had to be redone. While waiting, Qwilleran had an early lunch at the Nasty Pasty and then wandered into Elizabeth's boutique. It was Tuesday, and there were no customers.

She came running toward him. 'Qwill, I saw Derek briefly this morning before his classes, and he had good news! The bartender was fired last night!'

'On what grounds?'

'I don't know. Derek wasn't told and didn't ask. He was simply glad to get rid of that man – not to mention the awkward situation with Monkey, his girlfriend. She's been there every night, wanting to talk to Derek.'

'Who'll be the replacement?'

'Derek could make some recommendations, but his policy is to do a good job and learn all he can without getting involved. He wants to give it one full year. Then, if he takes my advice, he'll put all his smelly clothes in a heap and have a bonfire.'

'Well, put a clothespin on your nose if necessary, but stick with Derek,' Qwilleran advised. 'He has potential. Those who know him have always been convinced of that, but it remained for you to come on the scene and be the good influence.'

'Oh, Qwill! That's so kind of you to say!'

When he delivered the T-shirts to Hixie, he picked up his fan mail from the office manager. She looked a trifle wan, as if the warm-up had been too strenuous for her.

He said, 'You and Wilfred did an efficient job backstage last night.'

'Thank you,' she said demurely. 'Would you like me to slit the envelopes for you?'

'I'd appreciate that.' Since she was not her usual talkative self, he left without pressing the conversation.

The Tuesday edition was newly off the press, and he picked up a copy in the lobby. There on the front page was an item that caused him to huff into his moustache:

**PICKAX TO GET
MEMORIAL PARK**

A much-needed expansion to the Pickax Cemetery has been made possible through the sudden availability of a suitable site – four acres in the southeast corner of the intersection of Trevelyan and Cemetery Roads. City Council voted last night to buy the land for $6,000 an acre.

A spokesperson for the city said, 'It meets the specific needs of a cemetery – high land without rocks. It's adjacent to the original burial grounds and away from city traffic, with plenty of roadside parking for funeral processions.'

Unlike the original cemetery with its assortment of monuments, the new extension will be a memorial park.

'This follows the trend to a broad expanse of lawn with grave markers recessed in the grass,' said the spokesperson. 'Bereaved families will find welcome serenity in the uninterrupted sweep of beautiful lawn. Also, it will facilitate mowing, providing better maintenance at lower cost.'

Qwilleran pounded his moustache in annoyance and drove directly to Amanda Goodwinter's design studio. He strode into the shop, waving the newspaper.

'I voted against it,' she said angrily, jumping up from the desk. 'Six thousand an acre! Can you guess what that rat paid for it? I bet he gave the poor woman not more than eleven hundred an acre!'

'Do you know his identity?'

'Of course I know! And I wouldn't trust that robber to hold my ice-cream cone!'

'The property was in his wife's name.'

'Naturally!'

'He'd promised Mrs Coggin he'd reserve the land for growing crops. It didn't take him long to change his mind.'

'And I wouldn't put it past him to burn down her house to speed matters!'

'That's an incendiary remark, Amanda.'

'Arrgh!'

'Is there any chance of an investigation?'

'Nah! He's got everybody in his pocket, including the mayor. Even Scott Gippel voted yes for the cemetery deal. D'you know why? He's got a bid in to sell the county a fleet of maintenance trucks!'

'I heard somewhere that what's-his-name was accused, at one time, of watering the liquor in his bar.'

'No comment!' she said, folding her arms across her chest and setting her jaw.

'But it turned out that the bartender was the culprit.'

'No comment!'

As Qwilleran started to leave the studio he asked, in a lighter vein, 'Are you looking forward to the big bash tomorrow night?'

'In a word, no! But somebody has to do it,' she said grouchily. Amanda was one of the celebrities who would 'add glamour' to the spell game. It was conventional wisdom in Pickax that she would go anywhere and do anything to get votes and/or publicity for her studio.

Before driving home, Qwilleran bought three more carnations. The florist was brimming with curiosity, although she knew not to ask questions. He returned to his van in time to see police and fire vehicles speeding down Main Street with sirens wailing. They were ahead of him as he drove toward Park Circle. Then he saw smoke – a thin column of it arising on the left – and the emergency vehicles were stopping. Northbound traffic was halted. He parked in a merchant's driveway, leaving his press card under the windshield wiper, and ran toward a scene of general commotion.

The focus of the disturbance was the front of the library, where a dozen protesters were marching with picket signs. They seemed to be having a good time. Onlookers were laughing, and police and firemen had to struggle to control their grins. The signs read: 'Pull the Plug.' 'Down with Computers.' 'We Want the Old Catalogue.' The smoke was coming from a backyard barbecue where patrons were burning their library cards.

Qwilleran himself felt sentimental about the old card catalogue and sympathized with the demonstrators, knowing their protest to be futile. Polly's assistant stood on the top step, uncertain how to react. Obviously the media had been notified. Roger MacGillivray was there with his camera, and a WPKX news reporter was thrusting a mike in front of rebellious volunteers and patrons.

Hurrying back to his van, Qwilleran apologized to the shopkeeper for parking in the drive and was immediately forgiven; no one ever begrudged the Klingenschoen heir a small favor. To avoid the traffic snarl around Park Circle, he then turned around and drove home the back way, via Trevelyan Road.

At the Art Center he saw Thornton's van in the parking lot and went into the building, where he found the white-haired volunteer at the reception desk in the foyer.

'What are you doing here?' Qwilleran asked.

'Making visitors wipe their feet, answering questions and trying to sell memberships. And what are you doing here, if I may ask?'

'I'm on my way home after witnessing a remarkable incident: library volunteers picketing to protest automation, and patrons burning their library cards.'

'That's no great shake; we're all getting new plastic cards anyway . . . Did you see the cemetery news on page one?'

'I certainly did! Why not come to the barn when you're through here, and we'll talk about it.'

When Thornton finally appeared, they settled in the library area with coffee, and the stonecutter began his harangue: 'So the city fathers are giving bereaved families a memorial park! I've been working with bereaved families for three decades, and I don't see they're going to derive much comfort from four acres of well-clipped grass! What they want is a ten-foot Celtic cross or a slab of granite with some words of solace chipped into the polished face – a visible memorial they can visit and talk to and point out to their grandchildren – plus, maybe, a memorial bench where they can sit and meditate.'

Qwilleran said, 'Did you ever see a traditional cemetery in the late afternoon, with all the stones facing west and the sun hitting them? It's a sight to stir the emotions. Is it a thing of the past?'

'Looks like it. We're phasing out our stonework and concentrating on sand and gravel. Do you know who sold the land to the city? There was no name in the paper.'

'Chester Ramsbottom, although the property was in his wife's name.'

'That old sharpie! No doubt he bought it for practically nothing.' Thornton peered across the room. 'Is that a checker set? I wouldn't figure you for a checker player. Chess, maybe, but not checkers.'

'It's just an interesting relic,' Qwilleran said. 'I pick up old things that appeal to me. Would you like to see a seventeenth-century compass?'

The treasure was safely stored in a desk drawer, away from inquisitive paws. He put it on the desktop. 'Come and look at it under the lamp. It has some very fine detail.'

Koko thought he was included in the invitation, and the three of them watched the compass card quivering and rotating under the glass.

'When it settles down, it'll be pointing to the dining room, which is north.'

Thornton was impressed. 'Can you imagine anything so delicate lasting all those years? I have a plastic compass that's brand new and not worth a tinker's dam. They don't make things as good as they used to.'

Stealthily, Koko was moving his nose closer to the strange object. Qwilleran was watching him. The nose twitched; the whiskers curved forward; the card started to quiver and move. In a few moments the north star was pointing toward the kitchen.

'That's west!' Thornton exclaimed. 'Is that what you call animal magnetism? How do you explain it?'

'What cats do can never be explained,' said Qwilleran lightly, at the same time wishing he could confide in someone about Koko's uncanny talents. He picked up the squirming, protesting cat, and the star returned to the north.

'Try it with the female,' Thornton suggested. Yum Yum was lifted to the desktop and showed interest in the shiny brass inlay of the lid but ignored the instrument itself. 'Try it once more with the male!'

Again Koko's nose sent the card slowly moving until the star pointed west.

'I'm going home,' he said. 'This is getting spooky! Will you sign an affidavit, Qwill? My wife will never believe me.'

'Before you go, you must see Phoebe's butterflies. They're on the second balcony.'

They walked up the ramp, followed by the Siamese, waving tails like flags. In the guestroom, two Painted Ladies were flitting about their enclosure, while three future ladies remained in the chrysalis stage, clinging to the ceiling of the box. Yum Yum was the most excited of the four observers; she knew they were insects, and insects of all kinds were her specialty. Koko was bored. With all the birds of the forest attending his gazebo parties, why should he flicker a whisker over a butterfly? Thornton was impressed and declared he would buy some caterpillars for his grandchildren.

As the two men walked toward Thornton's van, Qwilleran asked, 'Was Phoebe in her studio today?'

'Not a sign of her. I hope she's not getting cold feet about the spell game. She strikes me as being a little flighty.'

'Papilionaceous,' Qwilleran said.

'If you say so.'

When his visitor had gone, Qwilleran could think of many things to discuss with Rollo McBee: the Northern Land Improvement hoax; Ramsbottom, not XYZ, as purchaser of the Coggin land; the sale to the city at six thousand an acre; and increasing doubts about the commissioner's integrity. This was not an auspicious hour to go looking for a farmer, however. The trick was to catch him between supper and evening chores.

Meanwhile, he sat down to deal with his fan mail. There

was one businesslike envelope with a California postmark and the address in large print. The name in the lefthand corner was Martha V. Snyder. He read that one first:

Dear Jim,

I remember you when your name was Merlin and your ambition was to play with the Chicago Cubs. I know you remember me, although by another name. I am your Mrs Fish-eye, and I have been following your column in the *Moose County Something*. I have a granddaughter who trains race horses in Lockmaster, and she sends me everything you write. Not only do I applaud your writing skills but I am enormously flattered to know that I was a good influence.

When I was teaching you and your unpromising classmates in Chicago, it was no secret that the entire student body called me by a descriptive but uncomplimentary nickname. Fortunately, I had a sense of humor. Unfortunately, the prominent feature that inspired the sobriquet failed me in later life, and I am now a VIP – visually impaired person. This letter is being dictated to a talking computer, and since electronic spell-checks are less reliable than retired teachers of English, someone will proofread this letter.

I'm sure you know the story, possibly apocryphal, about a newspaper item concerning the beautiful paramour of a famous man. A semiliterate computer produced a memorable gaffe referring to his beautiful power-mower.

Your recent column expressing your gratitude to Mrs Fish-eye was doubly appreciated, coming forty years after the fact. Keep up the good work. Your columns are read aloud by gracious volunteers at the residence where I am comfortably ensconced, and they enjoy them too. Give my regards to Koko and Yum Yum.

Gratefully,
Martha V. Snyder

At the bottom of the letter there was a handwritten note by the volunteer proofreader, saying, 'The computer spelled your cat's name Coco. Mrs Snyder says it knows more about Chanel than about Gilbert and Sullivan.'

After the shock and pleasure of hearing from Mrs Fish-eye, he made himself a cup of coffee and lounged in his favorite chair, thinking. He thought about schooldays, his early success in journalism, his foolishness in throwing it all away, his struggle to regain his career, and his present good fortune. Whimsically he thought of Mrs Fish-eye and Aunt Fanny Klingenschoen as a pair of bookends supporting the volumes of his adult life. In this mood of reverie he completely forgot Rollo McBee until Koko climbed on the back of his chair and yowled in his ear.

When he phoned the farm, a young voice answered, and he said, 'This is Jim Qwilleran. Is your father there?'

'Yep, he's here.'

There was a pause.

'May I speak to him?'

'Okay . . . DAD!'

The farmer came on the phone, and Qwilleran said, 'First I want to tell you how sorry I am about the tragedy in your family.'

'It was hard to take,' Rollo said. 'The family was planning a cruise to Alaska. Had their tickets and everything. It happened just like *that*!' Rollo snapped his fingers. 'How're things with you?'

'I have some information to share. How busy are you?'

'Just finished supper.'

'If I walk down to my mailbox, would you care to meet me there?'

'Sure. Say when.'

'Give me fifteen minutes, Rollo.'

Before starting out, Qwilleran fed the cats, realizing that Koko's yowl had been about food and not about Rollo.

The farmer was waiting on the shoulder of the road. He kicked the post supporting Maude's dilapidated mailbox. 'How long does this baby have to stay there? I could use the post on the farm.'

'It would improve the neighborhood if you disposed of that eyesore – and the newspaper sleeve, too.'

'She never got much mail,' Rollo said. 'I used to check it every day and take her newspaper to her. She got it free. Who knows if she read it? She rolled the papers up tight, tied 'em with twine, and soaked 'em in water. When they dried out, she used 'em for firewood.'

'Speaking of newspapers, did you see today's front page?'

'Haven't had time to look at it yet.'

'Well, four acres of Maude's land, up at the intersection of Cemetery and Trevelyan, has been sold to the city for six thousand an acre.'

Rollo banged the old mailbox with his fist. 'I knew that Northern Land Improvement bunch was out to gyp her!'

'There's no such firm. The purchaser was Chester Ramsbottom.'

'It figgers! Any time you smell a dunghill, you know he's gone in the dairy business.'

Qwilleran said, 'There's a rumor that Ramsbottom is also going to lease twelve acres to the county for a workyard.'

'Nobody ever said a word to Boyd and me about any of this, and we'd paid rent for the second quarter. That really burns me!'

'I'm seeing the attorney as soon as he gets back from Chicago. I'll ask him what recourse you have.'

The farmer had turned away and was gazing across the burned field, now smothered in weeds. Finally he said, 'Do you know the fire chief?'

'I knew Bruce Scott, but I've never met the new one.'

'When someone's killed in a fire, you know, the chief has to report it to the state fire marshal, whether it's arson or not. We're pretty sure, Boyd and me, that the new guy didn't report the Coggin fire. At least there wasn't any follow-up, as far as we know. We thought it was off-base, but we didn't challenge his decision – didn't want to get in bad with the new chief.'

Qwilleran said, 'I know what you're getting at. Coming right after the vandalism, it looked to me as if it might be arson. That's another bug I'll put in the attorney's ear. What's the name of the new chief?'

'Gumboldt. Roy Gumboldt.'

'Do you think he could be in cahoots with Ramsbottom?'

'Hell! He's Chet's brother-in-law!' Then, before Qwilleran could react, he said calmly, 'I'll go get some tools and dig up these two babies. The mailbox is set in concrete. I planted it for Maude twenty years ago.'

Sixteen

Wednesday was the day of the big game, and an electric charge jolted the placid community 400 miles north of everywhere. Banners were strung between the light poles on Main Street. Pennant Race posters plastered the central business district, and the department store displayed the silver pennant that would be the winners' trophy. Betting was going on all over: private bets on street corners and office pools in every place of business. Even Qwilleran's Siamese sensed something momentous in the offing and prowled restlessly.

He himself, having a journalist's compulsion to be in the middle of the excitement, went early to breakfast at Lois's Luncheonette. The place was crowded. Two cooks were whirling around the kitchen, and Lois herself was taking orders, serving the ham and eggs, pouring coffee, and making change at the cash register. She was one of the celebrities being given pinch-speller status; the mayor had recently proclaimed a Lois Inchpot

Day in recognition of her thirty years of feeding hungry Pickaxians.

The other pinch-spellers, besides Amanda Goodwinter, would be Dr Prelligate, president of MCCC; Foxy Fred, the popular auctioneer; Grandma Toodle, matriarch of the grocery dominion; and Mr O'Dell, high-school custodian for forty years before his retirement.

Qwilleran asked Lois, 'Are you prepared to go up and spell in a pinch?'

'No! No sir! No way! Nothin' could get me up on that stage to spell! Do you know my boy Lenny is spellin' for the Nailheads?'

'If the Nailheads win, do we all get free coffee?'

'Absolutely!'

Next, Qwilleran went to the newspaper to watch them making up the front page with a banner story on the spell game and a photo strip on the pickets and card-burners at the library. The headline read: 'A Hot Time at the Library.'

After picking up groceries for Polly and transferring them to her car, he went into the building to see if she had returned from the conference. The august premises were unnaturally quiet.

'She's back,' said one of the clerks, gesturing toward the glass-enclosed office on the mezzanine.

'You missed the excitement' were his first words to Polly. 'What was your reaction when you heard about it?'

'My assistant phoned me in Lockmaster, and I confess I was rather amused. Apparently it turned into somewhat of a farce. But there's a serious side to it. Half of our volunteers have now resigned, and that's a great loss. They contribute thousands of work-hours every year.'

'Did you mention the situation at the conference?'

'Yes, and their attitude was: What do you expect of Moose County? The other libraries adjusted to automation without any trouble . . . Well, I'm not going to worry about it until tomorrow, after the spell game frenzy has simmered down.'

'Are you going to the game?'

'Of course! Indian Village has chartered a bus for the event. So many of our residents are spelling or otherwise involved!'

'By the way, two of Phoebe's butterflies have made their debut and are trying their wings.'

'Don't free them till I've seen them, Qwill.'

Driving home through the evergreen woods, he had a brief surge of euphoria that mystified him, and he stroked his moustache. It was a hunch that something was about to turn out well. The Siamese were jumping around in the kitchen window in boisterous fashion as he approached the barn. Before unlocking the door, he automatically checked the sea chest for deliveries. Strangely, the lid was ajar, propped open by a small stone. When he raised it, he quickly lowered it again and backed away. Everyone in Pickax was bomb-conscious following the hotel incident of the previous year. Were the cats warning him?

On second thought he had another cautious look at the contents of the chest. He saw a sizable cardboard carton tied with rope, and there were crayoned words on one flap. As he tried to decipher the message, he heard a faint murmur from inside the box. It sounded like a mewing cat! It sounded, in fact, like two cats! The message on the box flap, he figured out, read: *Please find us a good home.*

When he unknotted the rope and opened the carton, two pairs of imploring eyes gazed up at him. They were domestics with luxuriant fur – one orange, one tabby – curled together for mutual protection. He closed the chest and went indoors. Away from their ingratiating presence he could think intelligently. Who had dropped them off? It would be someone who knew he was an ailurophile . . . someone who knew where he lived . . . someone who knew he was away from home on that particular morning. Celia Robinson fitted the profile, but she would be more forthright. Yet . . . she had a large acquaintance, one of whom might have two waifs to give away.

He phoned her. 'Celia, did you leave anything in my sea chest this morning?'

'No, Chief, but I'll have some berry tarts later in the day.'

'Did you see a vehicle entering or leaving the woods?'

'Is this another investigation?' she asked enthusiastically.

'Not exactly. Someone left two cats in the sea chest with a note saying they need a good home.'

'Oh, my! Kittens or full-grown? Most people want kittens.'

'Full-grown, with nice fur, soulful eyes, appealing personalities.'

'Ohh! I wish I could take them, but Wrigley wouldn't like it. I'll ask around, if anyone wants to adopt them.'

'Are you going to the game tonight?'

'Oh, yes! Mr O'Dell is taking me. He's one of the pinch spellers. I'm going to root for the Diggers.'

Qwilleran hung up and said aloud, 'How do I get mixed up in these animal-adoption cases? Last winter, it was a schnauzer!'

'Yow!' came a voice from the coffee table. Koko was keeping one of the large books warm. He stirred, raised his hindquarters, and lowered his forequarters, pawing the book jacket.

'No, no! That's a library book!' Qwilleran scolded . . . and then he had an inspiration. He grabbed the book and his car keys and hurried to his van, stopping only to pick up the box of cats. Five minutes later he was at the library, heading for the stairs to the mezzanine. He barged into Polly's office and deposited the box on her desk.

She rolled her chair back in dismay. 'What's this?'

'The answer to your problem,' he said as he opened the box. 'Books and cats belong together. These two need a home, and the library needs a homey touch. Abracadabra!'

As he spoke, the two cats rose and stretched, then turned their large, wondering eyes on the librarian and mewed delicately.

Qwilleran said, 'They even have the right kind of voice for a library cat.'

'Honestly, Qwill, I don't know what to say!'

'Don't say anything. Just let them loose among the stacks, and they'll win over your alienated volunteers and patrons.'

'How shall I explain them?'

'Just say the Klingenschoen think tank in Chicago heard about the problem and prescribed them as a catalyst for change. I'll go to the pet shop for a commode, dishes, and food.' He started to leave.

'Wait a minute! What are their names?'

'No one knows. Have a contest to name them.'

'Don't forget litter for the commode!' she called after him.

Long before game time, hundreds of fans started assembling on the high-school parking lot. They came in cars, vans, pickups, recreation vehicles, and school buses. Eighteen followers of the Diggers piled out of three limousines usually used for more solemn occasions. Several bank employees arrived in an armored truck, carrying picket signs that supported the Moneybags. Placards on long sticks declared allegiance to favorite teams: 'Eat 'Em Up, Chowheads' and 'Muckers Don't Muck Up!' Photographers from the Lockmaster and Moose County papers and the TV crew from Down Below were kept busy.

When the doors opened, the crowd surged into the auditorium and gym. Backstage the spellers in T-shirts and baseball caps grouped in teams of three. Officials wore black T-shirts with white letters designating their function: coach, pitcher, umpire, and timekeeper. Pinch spellers were herded into the Green Room. Two stage managers checked and double-checked.

About ten minutes before game time, Sarah Plensdorf reported to Hixie Rice that Phoebe Sloan had not arrived and could not be reached by phone – anywhere.

Hixie said firmly, 'Well, the entertainment begins in ten minutes, and if she isn't here by that time, we'll call in a pinch speller . . . Wetherby, would you go to the Green Room and see who's willing to pinch-spell?'

Since the Butterfly Girl's T-shirt was extra-small, a DAUBER card was lettered – just in case – to hang around the neck of the substitute. Hixie, who saw the bright side of every cloud, stated that an emergency substitution would only add to the excitement. Already the uproar on the other side of the blue curtain was deafening. It fused the jabbering of fans, the shouts of hysterical partisans, and the cries of hawkers selling peanuts, Cracker Jack, and scorecards. Wetherby remarked that half the town would be hoarse as bullfrogs for a week! Dr Diane predicted an epidemic of hearing-impairment.

At seven-thirty it was announced on the loudspeakers that Dr Prelligate of Moose County Community College would pinch-spell for No. 79 on the scorecard. There was a roar of approval, but Qwilleran wondered how Phoebe's parents would feel, sitting in the auditorium and questioning her absence. Then the Pickax barbershop quartet – in striped blazers and straw boaters – marched smartly from the wings and lined up in front of the blue curtain to sing a tongue-twisting parody of a campfire favorite:

> Old MacDonald had a farm, A E I O U,
> And on that farm he learned to spell, A E I O U,
> With an E-I here and an I-E there,
> Here an A, there an O, everywhere a U-U.
> Old MacDonald had a farm, A E I O U,
> With a double-B here and a double-C there,
> Here a D, there a T, everywhere a G-G.
> With a double-M here and a double-N there,
> Here an L, there an F, everywhere an X-X.
> Old MacDonald had a farm . . .

It went on and on until the blue curtain parted, revealing the ten colorful banners and thirty-one empty chairs, while the quartet sang *Take me out to the spell game*. Then the spellers jogged onstage, each greeted by cheers and whistles. As a curtain-raiser it was, Qwilleran had to admit, impressive!

'Ladies and gentlemen, the National Anthem!' Wetherby Goode announced. Everyone rose. Everyone sang.

When the last notes faded and the fans reseated themselves, the mayor stepped into the spotlight and pitched a word to the audience: *literacy*. He thanked them for supporting a program that would teach adults to read and write, ending with 'Play ball!'

In the first inning, Qwilleran pitched the first word to the Daubers: *cat*. There was a hush in the auditorium and a pause onstage. Then Dr Prelligate stepped briskly to the mike and spelled it – correctly, according to the umpire's thumb. There were murmurs of bewilderment among the fans.

One by one the teams were called upon to spell three-letter words, until the Muckers took their turn at the plate. Qwilleran pitched the word: *antidisestablishmentarianism.* Two adults and one nine-year-old went into a huddle, and Culvert stepped to the mike and rattled off the twenty-eight letters. There was laughter, then applause, and the fans relaxed for the serious spelling: *ambidextrous, kaleidoscope, peripatetic.*

In the third inning the Oilers were sent to the showers. The Ladders were the next to go, then the Nailheads. At the seventh-inning stretch, only the Diggers, Pills, and Hams were left on the spelling field, and the Diggers struck out with *xenophobia* and *onomatopoeia.*

The two remaining teams were scrappy. The fans screamed and pumped their placards. The Pills' last chance was *vicissitude*, and they missed, but the Hams got it right.

The blue curtain closed, and all ten teams marched across the apron for their final acclamation, with the mayor presenting the silver pennant to the theater club's Hams.

Behind the curtain a corps of helpers was hurriedly removing the chairs.

'What's the rush?' Qwilleran asked. 'What's going on?'

Wetherby Goode grabbed his arm and said, 'Hixie wants to see you,' as he shoved Qwilleran into the spotlight out front.

Hixie was saying to the audience, 'Tonight we want to honor someone whose words entertain and inform us . . . who supports every local endeavor even if it means being a judge at a cat contest . . . who rides a bicycle while others pollute the air with automotive emissions . . . whose creative brain dreamed up the Pennant Race: James Mackintosh Qwilleran!'

The fans gave him a standing ovation, and Qwilleran bowed

graciously while maintaining his usual melancholy facade. The curtain behind him was parting.

Hixie went on. 'With appreciation and affection we present the ubiquitous and peripatetic Mr Q with a token of our esteem.' She gestured upstage, where the spotlight was on a peculiar contraption.

'What is it?' he asked, although he knew.

Hixie explained: 'A recumbent bicycle – the latest thing on two wheels! You claim to do your best thinking while you're biking or sitting with your feet up. Now you can do both at the same time.'

In his mellifluous stage voice he said, 'Words fail me! For the first time in my life I'm speechless! I'm completely overwhelmed! When you see me wheeling down Main Street in a reclining position, please remember that I'm not asleep. I'm thinking!'

Half a dozen spellers helped Qwilleran load the 'bent, as it was familiarly called, into his van. Many spellers were reluctant to leave, exhilarated by the show they had just presented. Sarah Plensdorf was one who lingered, and Qwilleran complimented her on her backstage efficiency.

In a low voice she said, 'There's something I didn't tell you, Qwill. About Phoebe. Monday night, after the warm-up, she came to my place in the middle of the night and asked to sleep in my guestroom. She'd locked herself out, she said, and didn't know when . . . *Jake* would be home. I have an instinctive dislike for that fellow, and I didn't believe her, especially since her right eye seemed to be swollen. I didn't know what to say. One doesn't like to pry . . . or meddle.'

'What did she say the next morning? Anything enlightening?'

'She was still sleeping when I left for work, and I went right from the office to a dinner meeting of my button club. When I came home, she was gone. Didn't even leave a note. And when she didn't show up tonight, I first thought she was embarrassed about her eye, but then I thought, She's gone to California! She's gone to her grandmother! Phoebe's quite impulsive, you know.'

Qwilleran said, 'One would think she'd leave you a note, though.'

Sarah dismissed the remark with a wave of the hand. 'Young people don't stop and think.'

'Well, thanks for telling me, Sarah. I'm sure she'll phone you from California. Keep me informed.'

Qwilleran drove home via the back road, not having picked up his mail or newspaper. For a moment he wondered if Phoebe might be in her studio, but the parking lot was empty, and the only light in the building was the night-light in the foyer.

As the van moved slowly up the lane, he could see the illuminated windows of the barn. At dusk a timer switched on all interior lights, transforming the four-story octagon into a giant lantern. He drove around the building and backed up to the kitchen door. He would park the odd bicycle in the lounge area, where there was room enough for it to lean against the stone wall. It would look arty there, he decided. Even if he never rode it, the recumbent would be a conversation piece, like the checker set he never used.

Before maneuvering the bike through the kitchen door, he went in to prepare the Siamese for something mystifying. What he saw was a floor covered with small dark objects, and what he heard was a guilty silence. Both cats were on the fireplace cube, arranged in compact bundles and looking somber.

Qwilleran turned on two lamps in the lounge area and

examined the clutter on the floor. They were checkers!

'You devils!' he said over his shoulder. 'What possessed you?'

A rumble came from Koko's chest, as if he was claiming credit for the chaos. Qwilleran gathered up the discs. Strangely, they were all red; the black checkers were still in place on the squares. To add insult to injury, Koko jumped down from his perch and landed on the telephone desk, scattering the envelopes that Qwilleran had brought from the mailbox. The cat was obviously in one of his destructive moods, and it seemed wise to leave the recumbent in the van until morning.

He leafed through the mail. Several pieces were commercial flyers addressed to 'Occupant,' and they went directly into the wastebasket. But one envelope had a butterfly sketched in the upper left-hand corner. He could hardly rip it open fast enough. It was hand-written, in a style he associated with artists. It was a long letter, and he read it twice before phoning the attorney's home.

Bart's wife answered. 'He's on his way home from Chicago, and I don't expect him until midnight. Is there anything I can do for you?' She was a law clerk at Hasselrich Bennett & Barter.

Qwilleran said, 'You could tell him I need to see him first thing in the morning. Tell him it's important. Tell him it's about fraud, bribery, arson and the murder of an elderly woman.'

Seventeen

In the days following the Pennant Race, Pickax could talk of nothing else – in the coffee shops, on street corners, at the supermarket:

'Tell you why the Hams won. They're young, and they've got good memories, and they're used to learnin' lines.'

'Nah! They're used to the bright lights, and they didn't have stage fright.'

'You'd think the head of the college would've done better.'

'He never saw the wordlist. Everybody else knew the words on the list.'

'Who said college presidents have to know how to spell those big words? He just runs things.'

'He was subbin' for the Butterfly Girl. Wonder why she didn't show?'

''Cause she's the type that dances to her own music, ever since she went to that school in Lockmaster.'

'How d'you like that crazy bike they gave Mr Q? I'll tell ya, I wouldn't ride it!'

'My wife won the office pool at Toodle's – ten bucks.'

'I was bettin' on the Chowheads! My cousin was spellin' for 'em.'

'Think we'll be able to beat Lockmaster in the World Series?'

'If it's fair and square. I don't trust that bunch down there.'

The morning after the spell game Qwilleran had an early appointment with G. Allen Barter. He was showering and shaving when the eight o'clock news was broadcast:

'Last night's Pennant Race spell-off raised an estimated ten thousand dollars for the Moose County literacy effort, according to backers. Winners of the silver pennant were the Hams, a team sponsored by the Pickax Theatre Club. Along with four runner-up teams the Hams will compete in the World Series in September, facing champion spellers from Lockmaster.'

Qwilleran made note of the fact that WPKX referred to 'backers.' They never gave the *Something* credit for anything – at least, not since the controversy over radio listings in the paper. The next item gave him a chuckle:

'A truckload of sheep escaped on Main Street late yesterday afternoon when the transport vehicle stopped for a red light and the tailgate popped open. According to a witness, one animal jumped out, and the rest followed – like sheep. Main Street traffic was rerouted for two hours while Pickax police and state troopers rounded up the flock. One animal is still at large. The driver of the truck was ticketed. Baaaaaaaaad trip!'

So that was the reason for the downtown detour! It had happened once before, only the last time it was pigs. Other newsbites mentioned a fire in a trailer home that resulted in one death . . . another single-car accident at the Bloody Creek bridge, in which the driver was killed . . . resumption of talks concerning a ring road for Pickax, routing heavy traffic north on Trevelyan and south on Sandpit Road. Qwilleran could picture Beverly Forfar's reaction to eighteen-wheelers, tankers, and dump trucks roaring past the Art Center all day.

Promptly at nine o'clock he reported to the offices of Hasselrich Bennett & Barter. Bart was waiting for him with mugs of coffee and some sweet rolls. He knew his client.

'How was the trip?' Qwilleran asked.

'I covered all the bases, and they took me to some great restaurants. Fran Brodie had been there, presenting her design theme for the hotel renovation.' The hotel, as well as the Limburger mansion, had been purchased by the K Fund, and Amanda's studio had the commission. 'It appears that Fran made a big hit, professionally and personally. I'd venture to say we're in danger of losing her.'

'I hope not.' Qwilleran smoothed his moustache. Fran, as daughter of the police chief, had occasionally leaked privileged information. 'We need her talent in this town – in the theater club as well as the design business. If Amanda retires—'

'She'll never retire.'

'But if Amanda should be struck by lightning, Fran would be the logical one to take over.'

'Does she have any personal attachment up here?' the attorney asked.

'She's been seen frequently with Dr Prelligate.'

'Not a bad duo,' Bart said. 'What did you think of the show last night? I hear you raised ten thousand. The K Fund will match it, of course. My wife took the boys, and now they both want to be champion spellers instead of champion gymnasts.

They change their life goals once a week . . . So what's on your mind, Qwill? Your message was provocative, to say the least.'

'While you were away, I did some thinking. At first I thought there were grounds for a civil suit; now it looks like a criminal case . . . You remember the farmhouse fire that killed the ninety-three-year-old Maude Coggin. It was blamed on a kerosene heater. Well . . . earlier in the year she had sold her hundred acres to Northern Land Improvement—'

'Never heard of them.'

'They told her they were a Lockmaster company. The selling price was a thousand an acre, about one-sixth of the going rate, with the understanding that it would be used for agricultural purposes. Now four acres of that purchase have been sold to the City of Pickax for a cemetery – at six thousand an acre! Furthermore, the company is about to lease twelve acres to the county for a workyard, according to my sources. What's your reaction?'

'That it's morally wrong to cheat such a woman, but it's actually only a sharp business practice, with no laws broken. She agreed to sell. She was apparently satisfied with that bundle in the coffee can.'

'Be that as it may, this nosey journalist had to investigate the Lockmaster profiteers. I was curious about who they really were. And guess what! There's no such company! The purchaser was one of our esteemed county commissioners, operating under an assumed name that was not registered in either county.'

'Which commissioner?'

'Ramsbottom.'

Bart wagged his head. 'Might have guessed!'

'Okay, forget the profiteering. Let's talk about the Coggin

fire. There are four interesting points: the fire occurred very soon after the land changed hands; it looked like arson to a couple of experienced firefighters; the new fire chief failed to report the fatality to the state fire marshal as required by law; and . . . he happens to be Chet Ramsbottom's brother-in-law.'

Calmly Bart said, 'You know, of course, that there's a certain amount of coincidence, hearsay and guesswork in your story.'

'Wait a minute. There's more. I have a letter from an informant indicating the farmhouse was torched.'

'Well, I'd say you're getting warmer. Who's the informant?'

'The torcher's girlfriend.'

'Would she come forward?'

'I'm afraid she's in California by now. She wrote this letter Tuesday.'

'Was she an accomplice?'

'No, a battered woman, running away. Actually she's a successful artist from a good family: the Sloans of West Middle Hummock.'

'Then what the devil was she doing with an abusive bum and alleged arsonist?'

'Bart, you've just asked an age-old question that's never been adequately answered. Read this letter.' Qwilleran reached in his pocket.

'One more question, if it isn't too personal. What was your connection with her? Why was she confiding in you?'

'That's another one that's hard to answer. People have a tendency to confide in writers. A French author attributed it to a writer's willingness to listen, a trait that he describes as half-tenderness and half-cannibalism . . . Whatever, read the letter, Bart.' Phoebe had written:

Tuesday

Hi!

Thank you so much for taking my butterfly box. I'm going away for a while. I'll call you to find out how the Painted Ladies turn out. Maybe I'll send you some Emperor caterpillars.

The attorney interrupted his reading to say, 'What's this about you and butterflies?'

'Nothing important. Just research I'm doing for a column . . . Read on.'

I'm going to my grandmother in California. No one understands me around here. They all try to tell me what to do. I admit I made one bad mistake, but it was my own decision, and I'd never do it again. I'm ten years older than I was a week ago. But Jake was so good-looking and so exciting, and that red hair really turned me on. I thought life was going to be thrilling.

One thing he promised me was a special room for painting and raising butterflies. Also there was some yellow spray paint in the garage, and I was going to paint the inside of it with huge Cleopatras and Sulphurs. But then he saw the caterpillars and freaked! He has a phobia about worms, so . . . no more butterfly-farming. I felt the same way about his buddies who came after-hours and partied till daylight. So things weren't as nice as I expected.

One night when he was at work, I was poking around his video collection, looking for a movie, and I found a stack of Daphne's figure drawings. When I asked about them, he said he bought them to give to the guys for Christmas. Suddenly I realized I hadn't lost my key to the Art Center. He took it from my handbag! Then he got in the building after dark and helped himself to Daphne's work – and got bitten by Jasper. He didn't cut it on a broken bottle, the way he said.

So I took them back to the Art Center, and when he found them missing, he blew up! That was the first time he got really rough. Then afterwards he'd be very sweet.

Then there was the trouble at the Click Club, and I knew it was Jake's gang who broke in to watch sex videos. Once he wanted to make a vulgar video of me, and I refused. He threw another fit, and it frightened me. My arms were already bruised, and I was wearing those ugly smocks to cover them up. I wanted to get away, but where would I go? I'd be too ashamed to go home. I thought of my grandmother in California. I had to figure something out. Why am I telling you all this? I guess it's because you've been so kind.

Well, anyway, last night after the rehearsal I went to the bar as usual and heard Jake asking Chet for more money. They were in the office upstairs, and I went up to use the phone – too noisy downstairs. I thought I'd call my grandmother collect. The office door was closed, but I could hear them talking. They were both angry.

Chet said – You've had your payoff. What is this? Blackmail?

And Jake said – You're getting a million-plus from XYZ for the river frontage. I want my cut, Chet, or you'll be in trouble.

And Chet said – Who'll be in trouble? You lit the match. That's arson and murder.

Then Jake said – You told me to torch the place, and I got it all on tape.

Suddenly I felt dizzy and sick, and I rushed out to my car. I didn't know what to do. Should I go to the police? Chet is an important man. I just couldn't believe it. So I decided to go home to the condo and play it cool. When Jake came home, he said – What happened to you, Monkey?

I said – I don't feel well.

He grabbed me and said – I've got a good cure for that. I pulled away from him and said – Get away from me, and don't call me Monkey. I was furious. I lost my cool and shouted something I shouldn't have. I said – I know where you got the money for this condo! It wasn't from your uncle in Montana. I know where you got it, and why!

As soon as I said it, I knew it was a stupid thing to do. He hit me with his fist, and I ran out of the house and drove to Sarah's apartment. That's where I am now. She's at work. My eye is black. I couldn't possibly be in the spelling bee tomorrow night.

I called my grandmother, and she told me to catch the morning shuttle plane. She's making the reservation for me. I'll stay here until tonight, when he's at work, and then I'll go over and pick up my clothes and things. I'm not even telling Sarah. You can tell her if you want to, and she'll tell my parents. I don't know about the police. What do you think? Is it better just to forget I ever heard them talking? Chet's such an important man, you know.

I'll leave it up to you. Thank you again for taking my butterflies.

Phoebe

When the attorney finished reading, he said. 'This can of worms has to be approached with circumspection. He is indeed a prominent citizen who's just been honored for twenty-five years of public service. And as I said before, there's hearsay involved. Could she possibly be a little wacky from being punched? How much of the story can be proved? I want to discuss it with my partners.'

Qwilleran stroked his moustache. 'I'd like to do a little discreet snooping myself. Do you remember the Campbell scandal? Or did that happen before you came to Moose County? Ramsbottom paid his way out of a misdemeanor, and he could pay his way out of a felony. I'll call you, or you call me.'

On the way home Qwilleran stopped at the florist shop for two more carnations.

'Again?' asked the young woman with the limpid gaze. She turned down the volume on the radio that was twanging country music. 'What color this time?'

'Red. And you'd better make it three.'

'Gee!' she said with a 'big spender' inflection.

Qwilleran decided to stop tormenting her. He explained, 'I'm doing research for a column, raising a crop of butterflies in captivity. They have to be fed sugar-water sprinkled on fresh flowers. So far, only two have hatched, but I'm expecting more . . . *What's that?*'

A radio announcer had interrupted the music with a news bulletin. Claudine turned up the volume:

'The name of the motorist killed in the Bloody Creek gorge has just been released. The victim is a twenty-three-year-old woman, Phoebe Sloan, a local artist known as the Butterfly Girl and daughter of Mary and Orville Sloan of West Middle Hummock. The single-car accident was reported by a truck driver who noticed skid marks on the pavement early this morning and stopped to look into the gorge. The bridge over the creek at that point has been the scene of several accidents, but petitions to have the hazardous crossing improved have resulted only in cautionary road signs.'

Qwilleran threw down some money, grabbed his carnations, and hurried back to Hasselrich Bennett & Barter.

The receptionist said, 'Mr Barter isn't seeing anyone this morning. He's just returned from several days out of town.'

'He'll see me! Send in my card.'

In a matter of seconds the attorney appeared and ushered Qwilleran into his office. 'I didn't expect you back so soon. Another cup of coffee?'

Qwilleran dropped into a chair. 'Skip the coffee this time. My informant – who was supposed to be in the spelling competition last night *and wasn't* and who was supposed to leave for California this morning *and didn't* – is Phoebe Sloan. It was her body that was found in Bloody Creek this morning, victim of a single-car accident.'

'Do you suppose she was speeding to catch the shuttle?'

'The airport is southwest of Indian Village, where she's been staying; the Bloody Creek bridge is northeast. What was she doing up there in the woods? As of this minute it's my contention that the medical examiner will find evidence of violent death prior to the car crash. I say she was murdered elsewhere and her body driven to the bridge. The obvious suspect: the guy she was living with – the bartender. You read her letter. I could reconstruct a scenario.'

'Go ahead. What's his name?'

'Jake Westrup. After he blackens her eye and she flees to a friend's house, she calls her grandmother and makes arrangements to fly to California. All she has to do it wait until he's at work and then go over and pick up her clothes and other belongings. She doesn't know he's been fired and will be there!'

'How do you know?'

'I get around. I hear things . . . So there they are, face to face. She knows too much, and he knows that she knows. There's only one thing to do, and he does it. He has to make it look like a car accident, and he has to wait till the following night. Who knows why? I can think of several reasons . . . Whatever, he drives the body to the Bloody Creek bridge, straps it into the driver's seat, then rolls the car into the gorge. From there he can easily cut through the woods and get home before daylight . . . I could tell you more, but the police should pick him up before he heads back to Montana. I'll leave it up to you and the prosecutor and the medical examiner. You can take Phoebe's letter, but leave me out of it.'

Walking away from the law office, Qwilleran experienced a singular reaction: suddenly he wanted nothing more to do with butterflies. He would set them free immediately, ready or not. There would be no celebration, no excited audience, no dissertation in the 'Qwill Pen' column. He was still clutching the three carnations wrapped in green tissue, and his impulse was to toss them in the nearest trash receptacle. On second thought he drove home and left them on Celia Robinson's doorstep; she would spend the rest of her life wondering who left them.

The Siamese were awaiting their noon treat impatiently, but he ignored them and ran up the ramp to the guestroom. All five Painted Ladies were now flying deliriously around their enclosure. He carried the box outdoors and opened it without ceremony. One of them could hardly wait to test the great outdoor world. The others followed cautiously, one by one, until all were joyously on the wing.

Qwilleran was neither glad nor sorry to see them go. He had a sense of desperation that he could not explain. The box he threw into the trash in the toolshed. Indoors he consigned all butterfly notes to the wastebasket and would have tossed the butterfly guidebook after them, but it had been borrowed from the library.

Was it anger? Or was it grief? The so-called Butterfly Girl had been just another interview subject, another newsworthy character, yet she had told him more about herself than he wanted to know. With an artist's instincts she had wanted to carve her own career and design her own lifestyle. One of her major decisions had been wrong, only to be followed up by impulses of equal mischance. One recollection that infuriated Qwilleran was that jackass's rude way of calling her Monkey. And she liked it!

Eighteen

The Siamese always had a calming effect on Qwilleran when he was perturbed by outside circumstances. With apologies for the delay he gave them their noontime treat and watched as they devoured the Kabibbles with serious crunching and rapturously waving tails. When the last morsel was gone, and no more could be found on the floor surrounding their plates, the two epicures washed up in unison: four licks of the paw, four swipes over the mask, four passes over the ear – all repeated with the other paw. The choreography was remarkable.

When the ritual was finished, Qwilleran announced 'Gazebo!' They rushed to the coat hooks and looked up at the tote bag. Then, while they communed with the birds and bees, he settled down to write another thousand-word opus for the 'Qwill Pen.' Equipped with a legal pad, some pencils, and a little dog-eared book, he intended to start another Pasty War among readers of the *Something*.

The meat-and-potato turnover was a regional specialty 400

miles north of everywhere. Whether or not it should contain turnip was a hotly debated issue – and had been for more than a century. Now a historical recipe had turned up in a tattered book that Eddington Smith discovered among memorabilia from an old farmhouse. Excitedly he had phoned the barn, saying, 'Qwill! Come quickly! I've found something!'

It proved to be a 1905 hardcover – thin as a slice of bread and brown with age and grease spots – and it contained a pasty recipe calling for 'pig's liver.' Qwilleran knew his readers would rise up in consternation. It would result in the biggest fracas since the controversy over Tipsy's feet in her portrait at the tavern. Now that the spell game was over, the public needed another electrifying topic to roil their passions.

The little book had been published, apparently, for families who raised hogs and did their own butchering. At one time in Moose County history that would include almost everyone. These folk would need ideas for using leftover ears, tails, entrails, and blood – from cattle and sheep as well as hogs. There were recipes for blood sausage, hog's pudding, cow heels, and Scottish haggis. Qwilleran had eaten haggis at the annual Scottish night in Pickax, always curious about the ingredients. Now he knew and wished he had remained ignorant.

There were instructions for stuffing a boar's head: 'About the snout, you have to sew it to keep it shut. About the ears, you can stick a parsnip or carrot in them to keep their shape. And be sure that the head has a large collar.'

While concentrating on these esoteric details, Qwilleran became aware of a rumbling in Koko's innards. Then the ears of both cats pointed east as the crunch of footsteps was heard in the lane. Peevishly he set aside his writing pad and went out to confront the intruder. It was Culvert.

'Hi!' the boy said. 'My mom sent you some cookies.' He handed Qwilleran a foil-wrapped package. 'Peanut butter and raisin. My favorite.'

'Well, thank you. Thank you very much!' said Qwilleran, whose list of favorites excluded peanut butter and raisin. 'Tell your mother I appreciate her thoughtfulness.'

'Here's a note.'

It was signed 'Dawn McBee,' and it read: 'Rollo and I would like to say thank-you for everything you've done. You made Maude's funeral important in ways no one else could do. And her tombstone! – it's so perfect, it makes me cry! Culvert was thrilled to see his pictures in the paper, and they actually sent him money, and when he was up on the stage with the Muckers, Rollo and I almost burst with pride. He spells that 28-letter word for everybody he meets. The Muckers are going to the World Series in September. Until then it'll be kind of hard living with a ten-year-old who's suddenly nine feet tall. He's nine now, but he'll be ten next month.'

Qwilleran said, 'Congratulations on your spelling last night.'

'Do you want me to spell that word for you?'

'Not right now. I have work to do. Some other time . . . Would you like a cookie to eat while you're walking home? Take two!'

On the way to the newspaper office to hand in his Friday copy, Qwilleran stopped at the library to drop off the butterfly guidebook. The parking lot was fairly well filled, and he assumed the patrons were gathering to commiserate over the death of the Butterfly Girl. At that time, the public assumed it was another accident at a dangerous bridge. They would be saying that something should be done about it; people should write letters to the paper; people should complain to the county commissioners; her parents must feel terrible; she was their only child; she painted those beautiful pictures.

That was what Qwilleran expected to hear, but such was not the case. There was an atmosphere of jollity in the library. Patrons were all smiles. Two volunteers who had been on the picket line were wheeling bookcarts and replenishing shelves. They waved and said, 'Hi, Mr Q!' Just then he stepped on a toy mouse.

He looked around and saw an orange cat lounging on the circulation desk with plumed tail drooping languidly over the edge. His fur was fluffy, and his large, gold, almond-shaped eyes brimmed with catly bliss. As Qwilleran approached the desk, a woman lifted a small boy up to drop pennies in a bowl already half filled with nickels, dimes, and quarters. She looked at Qwilleran and said, 'He took these pennies out of his own bank to help feed the kitties.'

Other patrons were scribbling on small slips of paper and dropping them in a pair of gift boxes with slots cut in the lids. One of the clerks behind the desk said, 'Would you like to help name he-cat and she-cat, Mr Q? They're our new mascots. That's her up on the stairs. She likes to supervise.'

Polly, coming down the stairs, stopped to stroke the brown-and-black fluffy fur with tortoiseshell markings. She said to Qwilleran, 'This is the best thing that's happened since the Dewey decimal system! One of the local veterinarians is going to give them a health check without charge. They seem completely happy here. When I came in today, they were playing tag among the stacks. The female is such a flirt! She flops down and looks at people upside down, and they're absolutely smitten. One man is going to construct an eight-foot carpeted cat-perch.'

'Did you call the paper?' Qwilleran asked.

'First thing! And Roger was here to take pictures.'

'I'll call Bushy. He might be able to get them on a cat calendar.'

'Be sure to drop some names for them in the boxes,' Polly reminded him. 'Have you found out who left them on your doorstep?'

'Not a thing! I predict it will go down in Moose County history as an unsolved mystery, like the fate of the lighthouse keepers on Breakfast Island.'

Qwilleran left the library without telling her that the Bloody Creek 'accident' was really murder. She would hear the shocking news soon enough.

It was aired by WPKX on the six o'clock news:

'The body found in a wrecked car in Bloody Creek early this morning was a victim of homicide, according to the medical examiner. He stated that Phoebe Sloan was killed about twenty-four hours before the car went into the gorge. A suspect has been arrested and will face arraignment tomorrow.'

In the late evening Qwilleran phoned the police chief at home and said, 'Andy, if you haven't gone on the wagon, how about putting on your shoes and coming over for a nightcap?'

Brodie lived conveniently close by, and in five minutes the headlights of his car came bouncing through the evergreen wood, monitored by Koko, standing on his hind legs in the kitchen window. The chief strode into the barn with the swagger of a bagpiper and the roaming eye of a law enforcement professional. The first thing he saw was the recumbent bicycle, leaning against the stone wall in the lounge area. 'What do you expect to do with that weird contraption?' he demanded. 'If you ride it on

Main Street, motorists will be running up on the sidewalk and killing pedestrians!' He took a seat at the snackbar, where his glass of Scotch and a wedge of cheese were waiting. He raised his glass and said, 'Cheers!'

Qwilleran raised his glass of Squunk water. 'Same to you . . . Okay, Andy, what happened today after the prosecutor was alerted?'

'The medical examiner had already ruled it death by a blow on the head some twenty-four hours before the car went into the gorge. When Barter came up with the name of a suspect, the investigators hotfooted it to Indian Village, but the suspect's van had already left. Roadblocks had already been set up in three counties. They stopped him in Lockmaster, south of Flapjack. He'll be charged tomorrow with arson and two counts of homicide. Amanda Goodwinter heard screams Tuesday night, followed by sudden silence. Mandy doesn't miss a thing!'

'How about the Ramsbottom connection?'

'It's a safe bet the suspect will implicate him in the Coggin incident. He'd be crazy not to.'

'*Aaaaaaaaaaaa*' came a comment from Koko.

'What kind of noise is that? Sounds like a dirty old ram!'

Qwilleran asked, 'Would you say Chet's glory trip is over?'

'You watch and see: besides the criminal charge, there'll be a civil suit filed by the Campbell clan. I wouldn't want to be in that guy's shoes, one way or another. It wouldn't surprise me if they got him on income tax evasion, too. He's been playing all the angles.'

'When Broderick Campbell confessed to watering the liquor, did the general public believe him? He had a reputation as an upstanding young man.'

'I'll tell you, Qwill: this town is always knee-deep in rumors and gossip and opinions, and people will believe what fits their own interests.'

'Let me freshen your drink,' Qwilleran offered. 'Have some more cheese.'

'How much did you have to do with this case, Qwill? Don't try to hide behind G. Allen Barter. How much did old Noseynose have to do with it?'

'Koko takes the Fifth.'

'I ran into Lieutenant Hames when I was Down Below last week. He asked about Koko. He told me some amazing things about that cat. I didn't know whether to believe him or not.'

Brodie and Hames were the only individuals Qwilleran had ever taken into his confidence on that score. The detective was an absolute believer; the police chief was still fifty percent skeptical.

'Well . . . as I've told you before, all cats have senses above and beyond those of humans,' Qwilleran began. 'You hear about house cats foiling a burglary, warning about a fire, predicting an earthquake. Koko goes a step further. When he senses something wrong – something of a criminal nature – he lets his suspicions be known in subtle ways. I'd like to demonstrate something, Andy.'

Qwilleran knew he was taking a chance. Koko, with his natural feline perversity, might not feel like cooperating. Or perhaps the previous feat was a fluke. Nevertheless, it was worth a try. Qwilleran brought the antique compass from its drawer and placed it with exaggerated reverence on the bar. 'Here's something I acquired from a rare source – a seventeenth-century Italian compass.'

'Does it still work?'

'Of course it works! They made things better in the old days, didn't they?' He removed the decorative lid, and the compass card quivered delicately before settling down with the star pointing toward the dining area.

'That's north, all right,' Brodie said.

Qwilleran was relieved to hear Koko jump down from the fireplace cube with a grunt. A second later he had jumped to the snackbar. Qwilleran moved the cheese away and said, 'Koko is fascinated by the earth's magnetic field. Watch what happens.'

The two men watched. Koko looked at the compass and then at the cheese. Qwilleran thought anxiously, Suppose nothing happens! How do I explain?

The brown tail bristled. The black nose twitched. The bold whiskers swept back as the cat approached the instrument in stealthy slow motion.

Qwilleran thought, What a ham!

The twitching nose hovered a half inch over the circle of glass. Underneath the glass the compass card shuddered and started to move – slowly, almost reluctantly, until the star pointed to the kitchen.

'Well, I'll be damned!' Brodie said. 'Does it mean he's hungry?'

'Not exactly,' Qwilleran said, enjoying a private moment of triumph. He returned the compass to its drawer and brought two books from the library area. 'If the dining room is north, the kitchen is west – right? Now examine these two books. I read aloud to the cats daily – actually because it's good for my lungs – and Koko is allowed to choose the title for each reading. It's a game we play. He sniffs the bindings and knocks a book off the shelf. Recently he's been hipped on *The Day of the Locust* and *The Birds Fall Down.* Why? What is your reaction to them?'

Brodie handled them gingerly, as if they might be booby-trapped. 'They're kind of old. Never heard of either of 'em. They smell old, too, like they've been in somebody's basement. Must've come from Eddington's.'

'Who are the authors? Look at the names on the title pages, Andy.'

Reluctantly he did as he was told. 'Nathanael West . . . and Rebecca West. Any relation?'

'Only in Koko's mind. He has a "west" fixation. What's the name of the guy in the county jail?'

'Jake Westrup.'

'So . . . ?' Qwilleran smoothed his moustache.

'Don't tell me you think there's a connection. It's just a coincidence.'

'Sure. A three-ply coincidence . . . Another splash of Scotch, Andy?'

Brodie held out his glass and had another look at the recumbent leaning against the stone wall. 'What does Koko think about that thing?'

'He won't go within ten feet of it.'

'The cat's smarter than I thought!'

At that moment Brodie's beeper sounded. He tossed off the last of his drink and bolted for the door, saying, 'Thanks! See ya!'

Qwilleran followed him to the parking lot and heard his radio squawking as he prepared to drive away.

The moon was bright, the temperature mild, the breeze playful. On such a night Qwilleran was in no hurry to go back indoors. He walked around the barn, thinking about the compass and the two books by authors named West. Brodie had a case; it was too absurd for a rational mind to accept, and yet . . . who could know anything about the circuitry in Koko's fantastic little brain? Only a Korzybski could comprehend the cat's connections between Things and Meanings and Messages.

As he took a second turn around the building he could hear an imperious baritone yowling. Thinking it a protest about the bedtime snack that was behind schedule, Qwilleran went indoors to dish up Kabibbles. There he found Koko alternately jumping at the door handle of the broom closet and running to the window in the foyer. This was no request for food.

It was a subtle hint that he, too, wanted a moonlight excursion, and he wanted it immediately. The cat's body was trembling with excitement as he was buckled into his gear. Yum Yum, who had an aversion to leather straps, was hiding in one of her many secret places.

The terrain was eerily illuminated by the full moon as the two adventurers set out down the lane, Koko riding on Qwilleran's shoulder and Qwilleran keeping a firm hand on the leash. The cat could see invisible movement in the underbrush, and he could hear inaudible sounds in the night air. Once a rabbit crossed their path; another time, a waddling raccoon. Once there had been a great horned owl in the woods who hooted in Morse code, but he had moved to wilder habitat after the Art Center was built. Koko liked to give the building a security check, tugging at the leash, walking about the studios, sniffing the aromas of the artists' turpentine, ink, and tuna sandwiches.

On this occasion Koko's body vibrated excessively as they neared the gate, and when they reached the Art Center he did his imitation of a pileated woodpecker: a rapid-fire *kek-kek-kek-kek-kek-kek-kek* like an automatic weapon in the still night. There was no traffic on Trevelyan Road. The empty parking lot looked blue in the moonlight.

When Qwilleran unlocked the front door, he felt a draft of

air, as if a window were open. He could see through the main room to the sliding glass doors and the moonlit landscape beyond. One door had been left half open; Beverly would have a fit if she knew, no matter how warm the weather. With Koko still on his shoulder, he closed it. There was no need to turn on lights. The interior had an enchanting chiaroscuro effect. Rectangles of moonlight made a checkerboard out of floor, walls, and furnishings.

At that point Koko struggled to get down and landed on the floor with a thump, where he stood like a statue with legs splayed and ears pricked. Then he pulled toward the studios. The darkness of the long hall was punctuated by pools of moonlight filtering through the studio doors. The floor squeaked under their feet, and Qwilleran thought, New building – squeaking floors – bad construction.

Suddenly the hush was broken by pounding footsteps coming up the basement stairs at the end of the hall, and a tall figure charged toward them in the half-light. Qwilleran stepped back into the manager's office, and at the same time Koko flew through the opposite door. Without intent, they had stretched the leash between them, and the fleeing intruder tripped and fell headlong.

Instantly Koko was on the man's back, digging in with his claws and rattling a menacing *kek-kek-kek-kek-kek-kek-kek.* At the same time Qwilleran reached back into the office to flip the wall switch, hoping to find a weapon . . . there it was! The totem pole.

As the prone figure struggled to rise, Qwilleran tapped him on the back of the head with the wood carving. 'Hands behind your head! Don't move! We have an attack animal here, and he doesn't fool around!'

The head went down and the hands came up. It was a head as red as the cap on a pileated woodpecker!

With the leash in his left hand and the totem pole under his left arm, Qwilleran reached back into the office for the phone and called 911: 'We're holding an escaped prisoner from the county jail . . . holding him at the Art Center . . . on Trevelyan Road.'

The prisoner was quiet. Every time he attempted to move, Koko threatened him with another *kek-kek-kek-kek-kek-kek-kek* and kneaded his back with his claws. In a matter of minutes the sirens and flashing lights converged on the building. As soon as possible Qwilleran and Koko made an unobtrusive exit. They weren't needed. The officers had their fugitive.

The next morning the WPKX newscast reported, 'A police prisoner who escaped from the county jail last evening was quickly apprehended by city and county officers in a hiding place at the Art Center on Trevelyan Road. As a suspect facing charges of arson and homicide, he will be arraigned today.'

Nineteen

On Friday afternoon when Qwilleran walked down the lane to pick up his newspaper and mail, he knew the Art Center would be closed, as a gesture of respect for one of their valued artists – closed for three days, in fact. Yet, there was a car in the parking lot: a yellow convertible backed up to the side door. Beverly Forfar was loading boxes into it.

'What are you doing?' Qwilleran called out to her. 'Burglarizing the collection?'

'I've resigned,' she said soberly. 'It's too much for me! I'm going back Down Below where I can get a quiet job in a museum.'

'Well, we're certainly sorry to see you go,' he said, 'but if you think you'll be more comfortable down there, that's the thing to do, and I wish you well . . . but we'll never find a manager quite like you.'

'Thank you, Mr Q. Mr Haggis has promised to keep an eye on the place until a manager is found.'

Then Qwilleran had a brilliant idea. He said, 'Do you remember that man who won the *Whiteness of White* intaglio in the raffle? His sister-in-law had picked it up and was supposed to ship it to him in San Francisco, but there's been an unexpected development. Professor Frobnitz has taken a chair at a university in Japan. He wants the intaglio given to someone who'll appreciate an artwork of that quality and sophistication. Would you like to have it? I understand it's quite valuable.'

'Oh, I'd love it!' she cried. 'How nice of you to think of me! And what a beautiful going-away present! I'll always think of you when I look at it, Mr Q.'

'How soon are you leaving?' he asked. 'I can pick it up from his sister-in-law and deliver it here.'

After retrieving it from his broom closet and delivering it, Qwilleran thought about the events that had driven Beverly Forfar from her post: first, the farm mud that tracked into the Art Center . . . the ugly farmhouse and rusty truck across the road . . . the dogs and chickens running onto the highway . . . then the fire that sprinkled the Art Center with soot, while the firefighters' hoses created more mud . . . followed by the break-in and theft of Daphne's drawings . . . and the bane of her life: Jasper! . . . the trespassers in the Click Club . . . the threat of a ring road funneling heavy trucks past the Art Center . . . and finally the murder of an artist! If anyone deserved a thousand-dollar intaglio, it was Beverly Forfar.

Qwilleran had been caught up in a rush of events and problems in recent weeks, and now that it was all over and his participation no longer needed, he felt restless. It was Saturday afternoon, and Polly was having her final sitting for Paul Skumble. He himself was scheduled to officiate at a small ceremony at the library. Meanwhile he took off in his van for destinations unplanned.

His first stop was Amanda Goodwinter's studio. 'Has everything simmered down in Indian Village?' he asked.

'Arrgh!' she growled. 'When they locked up that dunderhead, they left his parrot there without food, and the blasted bird has squawked non-stop for thirty-six hours! Not only was he noisy; he had a filthy mouth! At three-thirty this morning I phoned the sheriff at home – got him out of bed – and said, "You get over here and pick up that neighborhood nuisance in the next ten minutes, or I'll personally see that you never get reelected! Put him in a foster home . . . send him to Parrot Rehab . . . do anything! But get him out of here, and bring some peanuts with you, or he'll chew your arm off up to the elbow!" . . . Well, a deputy showed up in five minutes, and I haven't heard so much as a floor squeak ever since.'

From there Qwilleran drove to Mooseville, having invented an excuse for visiting Elizabeth's boutique. He found the proprietor fluttering around the shop in gauzy garments and a state of elation.

'Isn't it wonderful?' she gloated. 'The Barbecue is closed, and Derek's back at a full schedule at MCCC! I'm really sorry about the Butterfly Girl, though. Derek said she was a decent person who didn't belong in that place. I would have handled her paintings, but they were too pricey for tourists and too representational for the yachting crowd . . . What can I do for you, Qwill?'

'I'd like a gift for Polly. We have something to celebrate.'

'How wonderful! Why not a lounge outfit?' Elizabeth suggested. 'She likes caftans, and I have a lovely hand-woven cotton in saffron, with a hundred tiny tucks running vertically from neck to hem. Very simple! Very elegant!'

'I'll take it,' he said.

On the way back to Pickax, Qwilleran stopped at the stoneyard to see Thornton Haggis. In spite of his buoyant mop of white hair and friendly gold-rimmed glasses, he looked mournful. 'A sad day for the art community,' he said. 'How did she let herself get into such a mess?'

'Too late for questions,' Qwilleran said. 'She's gone, and so are her Painted Ladies.'

'Why didn't you call me? I wanted to see them take off.'

'Frankly, I didn't have the heart.'

'Ramsbottom will be paying the piper at long last, if that's any consolation. My sons were talking to the county engineer. It looks like the twelve acres of paving will be ditched. The hundred acres he bought from Maude Coggin will be going up for sale – to help cover legal fees, I suppose.'

Qwilleran asked, 'Have you heard anything about the cemetery expansion? That was part of the hundred acres.'

'I think that deal hadn't really gone through. The news must have been leaked prematurely, for some nefarious reason . . . Do you have time for lunch?'

'Not today, thanks. I have another appointment.'

His appointment was at the public library, where he was to draw the winning names for the two mascots.

At the library a crowd of a hundred or more waited for the drawing. Qwilleran took his place behind the circulation desk, on which were two boxes of names and one nonchalant he-cat.

'Tradition requires,' he announced, 'that we draw three names, and the third is the winner. All in favor?'

'Yea!' they shouted. It was the loudest clamor that had ever shaken the walls of that cathedral of information.

He stirred the contents of the she-cat box and withdrew the first non-winner: Bertha. There was a disappointed 'Aw!' from one person in the crowd.

The next non-winner was Minnie K, bringing a number of regretful wails. Minnie K was a prominent figure in Moose County history, but that was a long, indelicate story; the K stood for Klingenschoen.

Qwilleran shook the box vigorously before drawing the winning ticket. 'And she-cat will hereinafter be known as . . . Katie!'

There was a scream of delight, followed by applause from the others.

'Where is she? Katie, come and take a bow!'

Someone found her and he held her up for all to see. She was soft and fluffy, quite different from the sleek Siamese he brushed daily. He would be in the doghouse when he returned home; Yum Yum would resent his being chummy with another female.

The audience waited expectantly for the next drawing. To prolong the suspense Qwilleran recited a limerick he had composed for the occasion:

An amorous tomcat named Jet
Loved every she-cat he met,
But one day he got ill
And they gave him a pill,
And now he's suing the vet.

The limerick was received with laughter and screaming – another affront to the staid old building. Qwilleran went on: 'Okay, friends, are you ready to name this handsome fellow who is said to be a retired gentleman cat?'

'Yea!'

The first ticket drawn was . . . Moose. The second was . . . Dickens. 'And the winning name is' – Qwilleran blinked at the ticket – 'the winning name is Mackintosh!' It was his own middle name.

A young woman was squealing and jumping up and down. 'That's my ticket!' she shouted.

'Good choice! What gave you the idea?'

'My family has an apple orchard. I thought we could call him Mac.'

'And so,' Qwilleran concluded, 'let us welcome as official library mascots, *Mac and Katie*, who will do their purr-sonal best to make this a friendly place to browse or borrow books!'

In the days that followed, Moose County had more on its collective mind than Mac and Katie, or the spelling champs, or even the tragedy at Bloody Creek. In coffee shops and on street corners they talked about nothing but 'the commish.' All who had voted for him, praised his barbecue, winked at his kickbacks, and accepted his small bribes began circulating unsavory stories. They all knew what had really happened in the Campbell scandal. They all knew about Bunny. They said his wife was a saint; she'd stand by him, in spite of everything. They speculated that the house in the Hummocks would be sold, and Mrs Ramsbottom would go to live in Ittibittiwassee Estates . . . Even so, some were confident that 'the commish' would wiggle out of the charges.

Qwilleran and his attorney moved fast to arrange for the purchase of the Coggin land by the K Fund, which would put it in conservation for agricultural use. A search for Coggin heirs, as required by law, had so far produced no claimants for the contents of the coffee can.

Then there was an interesting political side effect: the sudden death of the proposed 'weed laws' and 'road improvements' in West Middle Hummock. Since their promoter was awaiting trial on criminal charges, the legislation was unpopular with both the lawn faction and the naturalists in that picturesque community.

One afternoon Paul Skumble delivered Polly's portrait to the barn and helped to hang it in the suite on the first balcony.

'I like it,' Qwilleran said as he wrote the check. 'Do you like it?'

'Yes, I'm quite proud of it,' the artist admitted. 'I think I captured her innate intelligence and compassion. She was a charming subject – cooperative and never bored or nervous.'

'I wonder what will happen to your portrait of Ramsbottom. The restaurant is closed.'

'I know one thing: it will appreciate in market value because of the notoriety. Meanwhile, it would be an honor to do your portrait without charge.'

'Are you still adamant about not painting cats?'

'I'm afraid so,' Skumble said.

In Polly's portrait she sat in a high-backed Windsor against a wall of leather-bound books, wearing a blue dress and pearls and holding a copy of *Hamlet*. When the Rikers saw it, Mildred said, 'It's one of the loveliest contemporary portraits I've ever seen. It depicts gentleness and strength.'

'Humor and dignity,' her husband said. 'Let's have your portrait done, Millie.'

'Not until I lose twenty pounds.'

'Perhaps he could paint you thinner.'

Polly said, 'I'm sure I lost a few pounds on canvas.'

The three of them had come to the barn directly from their offices for the unveiling and a brief celebratory drink. While the Siamese observed from the top of the fireplace cube, the foursome sat around the lounge area and exchanged news and views.

Arch said to Qwilleran, 'Are you going to leave that bike in the living room? It looks a little eccentric, if you don't mind my saying so.'

'I consider it a high-tech art object,' Qwilleran said.

'The cats will knock it over when they go racing around – the way they scuttled a few other things I could name.'

'They never go near it.'

Then Mildred announced that they were moving into their beach house for the summer, even though it meant a longer commute to the office. 'It will be a good summer for UFO sightings,' she said. 'They return every seven years.'

Arch and Qwilleran, who scoffed at visitors from outer space, exchanged dour glances, and Arch said, 'My sole reason for summering at the beach is to enjoy the revitalizing lake air in the company of my dear but wacky wife.' And he added that the *Moose County Something* would publish *no photographs* of mysterious lights in the night sky.

The guests were looking at their wristwatches. It was time to leave – Polly for her bird club and the Rikers for a dinner party. Qwilleran accompanied them to the parking area, where the farewells were prolonged as everyone thought of something else to say: The library was planning a reception to introduce their new mascots, Polly said. Mildred suggested inviting Derek to bring his guitar. Qwilleran ventured that Derek might compose a folk ballad about Mac and Katie.

The two cars finally pulled away, with tooting and waving, and Qwilleran went indoors to feed the cats. They were not waiting at the door. They were not on the fireplace cube. He stood still and did an eye-search of their usual haunts: the top of the refrigerator, the softest furniture, the balcony railings. No cats!

'Treat!' he shouted, and two furry bodies rose from the basketseat of the recumbent bike. 'You jokers! You think that's funny!' he said. 'You like to make a fool of anyone with only two legs!'

All three of them had their treat: roast beef from the deli. Some of it was diced and placed on two plates in the feeding station; some of it was sliced and placed on rye bread with tomatoes and horseradish. Then they all went to the gazebo.

Qwilleran stretched out on a lounge chair overlooking the bird garden, and Yum Yum landed weightlessly on his lap. Koko sat at his feet with an alert eye for movement in the bushes and an alert ear for birdsong. Soon he was chattering an obbligato or mewling a melodic phrase of his own.

Amazing! Qwilleran thought. More and more Koko's behavior convinced him that this was no normal feline. Koko was a natural predator who was never predatory. He had never been interested in catching mice, although Yum Yum had one or two to her credit. He made buddies of crows and sang for the wrens and robins. He was a house cat who knew when the telephone was about to ring and when something bad was happening half a mile away. He put ideas in one's head when there were problems to solve and secrets to uncover.

Furthermore, Koko had devised uncatly ways of communicating information. Long before 'the commish' was implicated in the Coggin case, Koko was bleating like 'a dirty old ram,' although Qwilleran had failed to read the message. Long before Phoebe's murder, he had taken a dislike to the woodpecker with a red topknot. And now that the case was in the hands of the prosecutor, he had suddenly lost interest in red checkers, the bell with a serpent for a handle, the antique compass, and Nathanael and Rebecca.

Such musings said more about Qwilleran's imagination than the cat's communication skills. But where could one draw the line between coincidence and a supercat's intelligence? Somewhere there was an answer. Qwilleran combed his moustache with his fingertips.

There was a noisy flapping of wings as seven crows landed outside the screen and Koko jumped down to greet them – in syllables not too different from their own language.

Qwilleran said to him, 'Koko, you are a remarkable, enigmatic, unpredictable, and sometimes exasperating cat!'

Koko turned away from the crows and gave the man a long look before opening his jaws in a wide, unlovely yawn.

The Cat Who Played Brahms

Lilian Jackson Braun

Is it just a case of summertime blues or a full-blown career crisis? Newspaper reporter Jim Qwilleran isn't sure, but he's hoping a few days in the country will help him sort out his life.

With cats Koko and Yum Yum for company, Qwilleran heads for a cabin owned by a long-time family friend, 'Aunt Fanny'. But from the moment he arrives, things turn strange. Eerie footsteps cross the roof at midnight. Local townsfolk become oddly secretive. And then, while fishing, Qwilleran hooks on to a murder mystery. Soon Qwilleran enters into a game of cat and mouse with the killer, while Koko develops a sudden and uncanny fondness for classical music . . .

Qwilleran – a prize-winning reporter with a nose for crime. Koko – a Siamese cat with extraordinary talents and a flair for mystery. Yum Yum – a loveable Siamese adored by her two male companions. The most unlikely, most unusual, most delightful team in detective fiction!

0 7472 5036 7

Jane and the Unpleasantness at Scargrave Manor

Stephanie Barron

To Jane Austen's surprise, her visit to the estate of young and beautiful Isobel Payne, Countess of Scargrave, is far from dull. She has scarcely arrived when the Earl is felled by a mysterious and agonizing ailment. His death seems a cruel blow of fate for the newly married Isobel. Yet the widow soon finds that it's only the beginning of her misfortune . . . as she receives a sinister missive accusing her and the Earl's nephew of adultery – and murder.

Afraid that the letter will expose her to the worst sort of scandal, Isobel begs her friend Jane for help. Which is how Jane finds herself embroiled in an investigation that will have her questioning the motives of Scargrave Manor's guests, stumbling upon the scene of a bloody murder, and following a trail of clues that leads all the way to Newgate Prison and the House of Lords.

'Succeeds on all levels. A robust tale of manners and mayhem that faithfully reproduces the Austen Style – and engrosses to the finish' *Kirkus Reviews*

0 7472 5375 7

HEADLINE